THE
RESIDENCE

THE
RESIDENCE

A Novel

Andrew Pyper

Published by Simon & Schuster
New York   London   Toronto   Sydney   New Delhi

Simon & Schuster Canada
A Division of Simon & Schuster, Inc.
166 King Street East, Suite 300
Toronto, Ontario M5A 1J3

This Simon & Schuster Canada edition September 2020

SIMON & SCHUSTER CANADA and colophon are trademarks
of Simon & Schuster, Inc.

For information about special discounts for bulk purchases,
please contact Simon & Schuster Special Sales at 1-800-268-3216
or CustomerService@simonandschuster.ca.

Interior design by Davina Mock-Maniscalco

Manufactured in the United States of America

10 9 8 7 6 5 4 3 2 1

Library and Archives Canada Cataloguing in Publication

Title: The residence / Andrew Pyper.
Names: Pyper, Andrew, author.
Description: Simon & Schuster Canada edition.
Identifiers: Canadiana 20200165941 | ISBN 9781982147365 (softcover)
Classification: LCC PS8581.Y64 R47 2020 | DDC C813/.54—dc23

ISBN 978-1-9821-4736-5
ISBN 978-1-9821-4737-2 (ebook)

To Heidi

THE
RESIDENCE

"Something occurred to me last night."

Jane Pierce looked up at her husband, her bluish lips tight in what was, for her, a signal of playfulness.

"In a dream?"

"The opposite of a dream," she said.

"Tell me."

"I must appreciate you before the nation swallows you up for the next four years."

"Possibly eight, Jeannie."

"Eight years?" She laughed, and the sound of it startled Franklin. It was on account of its rarity, but also its alien depth and volume, as if a man resided in her chest for this purpose alone. "I won't have it! One term only will I let the people take my husband on loan."

"Four years, then," he said. "After that, we will run away from the White House together."

She touched his hand. His skin dry as the mourning lace she wore on her sleeves.

For weeks Jane had been angry with him. It wasn't the submerged ire that resulted from his drinking, or the long hours he was not at home. This was out in the open between them, as was its source: the way he broke his promise to her.

Two months earlier, days before his birthday, Franklin took the electoral college in a landslide, 254 to 42. He was forty-seven years old. The youngest man the country had made president.

He'd told her it wasn't possible. He'd given her his word.

Yet now here she was, with her arm linked through his, the two of them standing so close she could smell the tallow of his shaving soap.

Forgive him.

The voice lewd and throaty as a rakehell's, but empty of passion. A being heard by Jane alone as she lay awake in the paleness of their room that morning.

Soon you will ask to be forgiven too.

"Good morning, Mr. President," she'd said to her husband over the breakfast table.

She hadn't spoken to him much over the preceding weeks, her anger at him too great. It's why she knew this small warmth would be all it required for him to take her back.

Within the hour, they were waiting for the train back to Concord. The Pierces were in Andover, where they had lingered following the funeral of Jane's beloved uncle Amos in Boston. Now the three of them—Jane, Franklin, and young Bennie—watched the snow click hard as tossed rice against the station windows. It was an inconsequential station that looked out on the rails and, beyond them, a line of hemlock standing in competition for a greater piece of sky. Yet the morning had the quality of the sublime about it. A common beauty that, as Jane admired it, showed to her a glimpse of its inner menace.

"Mama?"

Her boy turned from the glass. A face so guileless and untroubled it required effort for Jane not to break into emotion that would be considered inappropriate for the First Lady to display in a train station.

"Yes?"

"Is it cold in Washington?"

"Frigid in winter. Tropical in summer. A world unto itself."

"There is spring too? And autumn?"

"For one day each. Congress has outlawed all but the most extreme seasons, I'm afraid."

The boy weighed this. Nodded his acceptance of it.

"Summer and winter are enough," he declared, and stepped close, holding her and Franklin both, the boy's cheek warming Jane's side even through her long coat.

She had never been embraced by her husband and child at the same time before. It almost took the legs out from under her.

The newspapers invariably spoke of her in the most glum hues. Fragile, sickly, brittle. Heartbroken. What they didn't acknowledge was how enduring discomfort and the carrying of grief were Jane's primary talents. They afforded her a privilege too: the avoidance of expectations. She had the choice among a number of symptoms. Headaches that, judging from where she clutched her hands, existed in her stomach as often as her skull. Daily touches of fever. The pains she described to Franklin as "womanly concerns." All of it—the injustice of her condition—lit a candle of rage inside of her, burning so low as to be unseen but never going out.

Illness was a prison for the innocent. This was how Jane saw it. It's why even as a child she had wished for children, and then, once born, loved her children as fiercely as she did. She hoped that motherhood would release her from the confinements of her suffering. Her first boy was lost three days after delivery. The second succumbed to typhus at age four. Now she hoped only to hold close to the one life that remained, preserve the light in him, her Bennie.

"There's the whistle," a man said from behind them, and then Jane heard it too. The woebegone query—*who-who-whooo?*—of the steam engine pulling a single passenger car to the platform.

The Pierces untangled themselves to go outside and join the line. Nobody proceeded into the car. One by one the passengers looked back at them and stepped aside.

"Hur-*rah*!"

A single, jubilant shout before the small group broke into applause.

As Jane went ahead to board she took Bennie's hand. She knew even this modest celebration would sustain Franklin for the journey. It calmed his doubt that he didn't have a good reason for seeking the office aside from keeping things as they were. But then he'd catch himself in a mirror when he gave a speech, or see how others saw him, purposeful and steady, and held on to this image the same way believers grip the crosses at their necks.

Franklin sat next to Jane, Bennie asking to be on the wooden bench behind them. Having Bennie sit on his own gave her the slightest tug of concern, but the boy reminded her he was "eleven years going on twelve" and she said "Fine, *fine*, manly fellow," as the other passengers streamed up the aisle, staring at them with curiosity and—in the case of a couple of the women—critical assessment of her appearance.

As the engine started away she stared out at the dull New Hampshire forests and hardened fields. It was as familiar a landscape to her as there was in the world, yet she was alert to the distortions that lurked in it. Ever since she was twelve, and over the years that followed the day when everything changed, she felt that if she looked hard enough she could always find something hidden in the ordinary.

They weren't a mile out from the station when they felt it.

A shuddering through the car's frame that popped them up from the benches, hats and purses suspended. A woman's exclamation of astonishment—*Oh!*—followed by the shriek of metal.

They were flying.

Jane threw her hand back for Bennie. Her fingers grazed the collar of his coat before the boy was flung away from her, limbs swinging like the hands of a compass. His body passing other passengers, some of them aflight also but none as swiftly as her son, his spiraling interrupted only by the contact of his head with a varnished post before he met the far wall of the car.

The train rolled twice down a culvert and came to rest, upside down, next to a frozen creek bed.

There was a gap of time between the car settling and the passengers landing on the backs of its upturned benches, the metal-ribbed ceiling, each other's bodies. Franklin was the first to regain his footing. He saw Jane moving—a tendril of blood finding its way out from her ear—and carried on to where Bennie had been thrown.

Even through their shock, the passengers recognized the president and crawled aside to let him pass. Franklin noted in their expressions how it wasn't respect for his office that made them do it but hope. The wish for him to magically right the train, heal the wounded, bring back the dead.

Bennie was on his back. Hands over his heart, face up. It was how the boy slept. Franklin knelt next to him, and the hesitation to touch him was, at first, a courtesy not to waken him. He was a man who believed in believing things.

His son's eyes were open. Held that way, unseeing. The smooth cheeks, chorister's mouth, the nose that Franklin had often willed himself not to smile at on the occasions the boy's nostrils flared when setting himself to a difficult task. All of it unharmed. This was his sweet boy's body, free of twisting or laceration. But some internal absence left it a body only.

He was expecting the skin to be cool as it had been on the other bodies he had been a party to lifting onto wagons in the Mexican War, or his own father's corpse he'd insisted on helping into the casket. But the boy's throat—where Franklin laid his hand—was still warm. It allowed him to believe a second longer in the power of pretending. Franklin slipped both his hands under Bennie's shoulders and pulled him up, but moving the body revealed the wound to the back of the head. A cutaway of the skull from its meeting with the post.

He lay the boy down again. Arranged his hands over the quiet heart. Closed the eyes with his fingertips. He felt an anguished howl pushing up from inside of him, but he forced it down. It left him outside himself, capable of action but lifeless in all other respects.

When he stood his wife was there.

"No, Jeannie. It's not for you."

Jane pushed him away. Some of the passengers who were now getting to their knees paused to watch the First Lady's stick of a frame lowering to her child as if a bird settling to tend its nest.

A man's cry for help—his legs crushed under one of the benches— tore Franklin's attention away. It left Jane alone with Bennie. She gazed down at him, prepared for something to happen.

The boy opened his eyes.

His mouth too. His entire face collapsing bloodlessly inward, be- coming a passage, tunneling down through the back of his skull, the car- riage's ceiling, into the cold earth below. A darkness into which she felt herself being pulled.

All the boys will die. And all the women broken.

Jane heard her dead son speak. Not with his voice but the one that was always with her.

You will let me in.

She knew the thing inside her son's body was not her son. It was a thing outside the world. Louder than it had ever been before.

You will open the door.

Jane reared back.

To anyone watching—to Franklin, who turned from where he'd managed to tug the trapped man's legs free—it would appear as the revulsion of a parent recognizing the violence visited on her child. The truth is Jane pulled away from the boy's body because it opened its mouth to laugh at her. Because it was no longer Bennie but something else. Something wrong.

"Come away!"

Her husband was tugging at her arm, and Jane wondered if he meant away from having to move to Washington and play the part of president's wife.

"Come *away* now."

She let his hand half guide, half drag her from the car. There was smoke coming from its windows and new kinds of noise outside as men pressed handkerchiefs to their faces and went back through the door to rescue the injured still inside.

Later, they would learn that Bennie was the single fatality.

For now though, Franklin Pierce was the incoming president. He had only his wife left for a family. Even in this instant where he saw all he knew of connection and comfort deserting him, he wouldn't allow others to see him fall.

He bent his knees. He walked.

First to Jane, where he touched her face and asked if she could stand on her own in the drifted snow at the bottom of the culvert. And then he climbed back up into the train to pull the last survivors from the wreckage.

Jane's eyes drifted to a woman coming down the slope. One side of her face burned, her dress smoldering as she stumbled through the reeds.

Thank ye—thank ye, Jesus!

Jane saw the child. An infant perhaps two or three months of age held to the woman, its feet wriggling. Alive.

My beautiful boy! O thank ye, God!

The woman looked at Jane and saw it. The loss curdling into something else. It made the woman turn her back on her and veer away through the ice-cracking reeds.

Praise be for saving my little one!

Only Jane heard a second voice under the prayers the woman was casting skyward. A whisper seeping up through the snow, rising like a lover to place cold lips to her ear. A whisper that showed her things.

Bennie staring at her through the bars of his crib.

The thing she brought out of the cellar shadows when she was a girl.

A room in a mansion of white where God himself could not enter.

PART ONE

CAMPAIGN

1

For the weeks that followed the accident, Jane stayed in her bed, refusing food, weighing how to free herself from her life. She would lose herself in clouds of paregoric. She would slit her wrists with Franklin's straight razor. She would suffer, as she deserved to. Moving into the White House was not among the options she considered.

She knew her husband was trying, in his helpless way, to reach her. He wrote her the most gentle letters from Washington. He told her how much he missed her. How he grieved too, but that together they may provide some comfort to each other. It was lovely. It made no difference.

Go to him.

She covered her head in pillows. It didn't stop the voice from finding her.

There is one more step on the path. Only you can let me in.

Even her screams couldn't muffle its words.

Open the door for me. And I can open the door for you.

There was no way.

It was the only way.

She started out. When she reached Baltimore she took a suite in the Exchange Hotel and sent word to Franklin asking if he would come.

It was the day before the inauguration. He left the capital immediately.

She opened the door before he could knock. He hadn't seen her in a number of days and was reminded she was at her most beautiful when she had time to perfect her anguish.

"I feel I ought to ask if I can come in," he said.

"You are my husband. I cannot hold you."

It was a reply in which he tried to detect a trace of affection—the *hold you*, the possessive *my husband*—but no. Her tone as flat as a solicitor advising a client as to the extent of his property rights.

The room was overdecorated. Too small for the gold-painted Charles X chairs and the chandelier hung so low Franklin had to duck to pass under. It put Jane at an advantage, as she found her place on the scratchy-looking sofa with an ease he could never equal.

"I will not come," she said.

In the minutes before his arrival she had changed her mind. She would resist him. Not Franklin. The voice. It was what her father would have wanted, what he asked her to promise at his deathbed. She would make an effort in her father's memory at the expense of her husband's understanding.

"Do you mean you will not come now, with me? Or tomorrow, for the inauguration?"

She looked up at him. Smoothed her dress over her legs. "I will not come."

"It's an important occasion. You are important to me."

"Those are two arguments. Which do you wish to make?"

He went to the window. The street undulated three floors below, a dizziness within him that made all of Baltimore slither and writhe.

"You're all I have, Jeannie. I'm embarking on a journey, and I don't know the way."

"You have Nate Hawthorne and your senators for that."

"I'm not speaking of politics. I'm speaking of the direction we must take together."

"You don't require me for direction, Franklin."

It was hopeless. She would win at a contest of blame because he was the only one deserving of it. His one way out was through her mercy, and she wasn't ready to show him any of that, if she ever would again.

"I thought perhaps—" he said, turning, but stopped short at the sight of her crying.

"Something is happening," she said. "Can I tell you?"

"Of course."

"There are voices inside me."

She hesitated, as if to go any further would be to provoke some third presence in the room only she could see.

"Are they yours?"

"They are the voices of the world," she said. "The people on the train. My little brother John. My father. So loud you can't make out one from another, so their agony sounds as one. But then it *stops*."

"And you find relief?"

"There is no relief in realizing its cause."

"Which is what?"

"One voice that is apart from the others."

Franklin had heard this kind of talk before. Campaigning in small towns where he would come across a tent or barn where a preacher would be quoting fire from the Bible. He dreaded entering those places. What unsettled him most was when one of the assembled would stiffen or start to shake, spellbound, and speak to the congregation with a message of salvation or destruction. They called it the touch of the Holy Spirit. To Franklin it seemed less a touch than an invasion.

"If you won't come to Washington, will you please give me the locket?"

Her fingers went up to it. Rubbed the silver where it lay in the hollow at the base of her throat. The locket contained the hair of her two dead sons. A brown curl of Franky's and dark strands from Bennie tied with ribbon cut thin as thread.

"Why do you ask for this?"

"Bennie wished to be at my side for the swearing-in," he said. "I'd like to keep my promise to him."

"And what of your promises to me?"

He reached out to her and she slid to the end of the sofa as if against attack.

"You can punish me—you have grounds for it," he said, kneeling. "All I'm asking is to have my son with me tomorrow."

Her fingers gripped the locket tighter but didn't move to unclip it, the back of her fist turning white.

"He will stay with me."

"I was his *father*, Jeannie. If you won't stand with me, it will leave me to stand alone when—"

"He will *stay* with *ME*!"

She tugged. The locket's chain snapped with a sound like a coin dropped in a pool.

Franklin held out his open hand. But she only gripped the locket tighter against her ribs.

"You think you hold sole ownership over pain. Perhaps you believe you invented it," he said. "I have my arrogance. But this, Jeannie—this is yours."

He stood. It made her look even smaller to him. Something a stage magician would introduce in his act as the Shrinking Woman.

"Those suffering voices in your head?" he said. "Has it occurred to you that the only suffering you could ever hear is your own?"

She didn't relent. The locket stayed buried at her side, and her body withered more and more, transforming her from delicate woman to wrinkled child. When his back came up against the door he realized the illusion of her shrinking was the result of his retreat.

"If I could, I would stop it," she whimpered.

"Stop what?"

"All that is to come."

"We are both quite powerless against that."

It was only when he was out of the room and escaping down the stairwell that he heard it as an odd thing for the president to say.

★ ★ ★

The day of the inauguration was blurred with wet snow, the audience scattered and blue-lipped. Those who endured the length of the ceremony shook beneath umbrellas that directed slush onto the coats of whoever stood next to them.

Franklin didn't feel any of it.

There was a distance between his physical self that stood and spoke, and his inner self, which was nowhere near the steps of the Capitol. That part was with Bennie. And from this remove, he heard his voice begin to speak the words he'd written for the nation and realized they were addressed to Jane.

> *It is a relief to feel that no heart but my own can know the personal regret and bitter sorrow over which I have been borne to a position so suitable for others rather than desirable for myself. . . .*

It was closer to eulogy than celebration. He heard himself go on while feeling himself split wider into two men. One the reluctant president. The other lost in an immense darkness, refining his case against God.

He was never strongly religious, but he was a believer. Now he didn't see himself as belonging to any church. None that was ruled over by a god that would push a train into a culvert and pluck just one life, the dearest soul among all its passengers, to join him in paradise.

The difference between Bennie's death—all his children's deaths—and the deaths of other children was that his had been *taken*. The world was full of loss, random and senseless. He knew it and accepted it. But his boys had been pulled from him for a purpose.

His standing there was proof of it. To deliver the words he was speaking, to be chiseled into the marble of history, required him to be free from the distractions of children. Maybe other men could be fathers and president at the same time, but he'd been judged to lack the focus to do both. Franklin Jr. gone before he had a chance to lay eyes on him. Franky pushed into the dark by the stranger in the smooth-skinned mask. Then Bennie. What explanation could there be other than the workings of a cosmic malice? A selection and destruction God alone had the power to enact.

Franklin Pierce was only the second American president not to swear his oath on a Bible. The first was Adams, who refused it out of principle. Franklin's reasons were assumed to be the same, but the truth remained undeclared.

The snow came down, the parade canceled. When Franklin was finished the applause was a sparse thudding of gloved hands, voiceless and brief. It sounded to him like spades biting frozen soil.

2

Franklin Pierce wasn't a slave owner. But Millard Fillmore was.

Fillmore, Franklin's predecessor, was bitter at the idea of a Democrat taking his place and indulged his pettiness by leaving most of his belongings in the White House after the inauguration, so that the last possessions to be taken away were the human beings he owned. It meant the new president's first day in office was consumed by overseeing a rotation of labor. Those who had attended to the residence's upkeep—the men who kept the furnace burning in the room directly beneath the similarly oval-shaped Blue Room, the women who reached the mops into the corners to rid them of cobwebs—all of them walked off under the watch of guards, their jobs replaced by those who were free, at least in name.

Franklin couldn't stop himself from watching Fillmore's people go. He was transfixed by the way that, despite their numbers, they were the only ones who worked in silence. He imagined he alone could see them.

It was their aura of nonexistence that lent them the purgatorial aspect of apparitions.

By midafternoon they were gone. So was most of the furniture.

When night fell, Franklin's room at the northeastern corner of the second floor's long central hallway possessed neither mattress nor frame. He considered ordering a bed to be brought to him but was concerned about starting his tenure with complaint. So he settled in a chair before the uncurtained windows, slipping into sleep before snorting awake, over and over.

In the morning his back refused to let him stand straight. His bad knee throbbed. He went about the business of setting up his office and chewing on a boiled egg in a haze of discomfort. Over the course of the day, he felt there was more to it than the troubles of his body. The building was unnaturally cold, for one. It had been a timid and soggy spring even by Washington standards, but this was something worse than dampness. The cold seemed to come from within the walls, not outside them.

He asked his secretary, a fussy but reliable man named Sidney Webster, if he would see to it that the furnace be stoked.

"My apologies, sir," Webster began when he returned. "You set me to a task more difficult than I would've guessed."

"Why's that?"

"I had a time *finding* the men who work the furnace. And when I did find them—well, one of them, anyway—he was reluctant to enter."

"Reluctant?"

"Yes, sir."

"Was he asleep? Drunk?"

"It appeared he was frightened, sir."

Franklin feigned exasperation and announced he would tend to the matter himself before starting the day's work. The truth was, it wasn't frustration that made him want to get away from Webster but the unsettled look on the man's face.

As Franklin moved through the hallways that remained dusky even in the middle of the day, he searched for something Jane might like. An offering to mention in the day's letter to her that could lure her back to him.

The first floor seemed to hold the most promise. He liked the Green Room's wallpaper, which was sprinkled with gold stars leading up to a dark blue ceiling, all of it creating an illusion of being adrift in the cosmos. The East Room was the most impressively immense, his footfalls echoing in every direction so that it sounded like a hundred men approaching. He was also intrigued by the curved walls of the Blue Room, and the false door Webster had previously told him about. Once Franklin had located the small crack around it, he pushed hard at its corner. A narrow piece of the wall swung inward. He poked his head in to find a short hallway that appeared to lead to an exterior office.

"Escape," Franklin whispered.

Back in the Cross Hall he headed left. The drama of the space was undercut by repairs started by Fillmore that had been left incomplete, so that the floors were partly carpeted by canvas sheets, the walkway interrupted by ladders and buckets holding plastering tools. This wasn't the only off-putting aspect. As he went along, Franklin had to endure the gaze of the presidents before him whose portraits hung between the holes in the walls. Washington. Adams. Jefferson. Madison. Each of them hung at a taller height than Franklin, taller than any man, so that they looked down at passersby with cool indifference.

What would his look like when the time came? He couldn't imagine it in any detail, but knew the setting of his frame that he would hold: wide-shouldered, his expression darkly troubled but with eyes ahead, showing he was more than capable of meeting whatever challenge was to come. Would any of it be true? The dark troubles, certainly. The rest of it, he feared, would only be a pose.

He quickened his pace and made his way down to the ground floor. It smelled of soap. Usually this was a scent Franklin liked, as it made him think of Jane. But in this case it was too strong to be inviting. This was the smell of the hospital, or the funeral parlor. The effort to mask one odor with another.

"Ah," Franklin said with a wave when he came upon a man outside the furnace room. "You must be the one committed to our deaths by freezing."

"I'm sorry, sir. We'll get back to it in a moment and have the place warm as July before you know."

Franklin was astonished. This man—short, old, black—was being directly addressed by the president about shoveling coal into the boiler and his answer was to refuse him. But then he saw it. The look on the man's face that wasn't defiance but profound disturbance. It could be fear, as Webster had guessed. Or what Franklin thought he could see just beneath it. A mournfulness.

"What's wrong?" Franklin asked.

The man looked down the hall as if hoping for the arrival of some-one who was already late. When the two of them remained alone, he looked at Franklin directly.

"They come to get warm," the man said with a glance at the furnace room door. "I give them the time they need."

"There's *people* in there?"

"I believe so."

"Who?"

"The ones before us."

"Fillmore's men?"

"No, sir. The ones you can't see."

So this was a man who believed in ghosts. Franklin was aware that the idea of the dead inhabiting the world was often taken to quite literal interpretations in the churches he assumed men like the furnace keeper adhered to. He'd certainly seen a good many maids and caretakers over the years speak directly to invisible aunties and fathers. On one occasion he'd been sitting on a settee in his own house in Concord when a young girl they'd hired to help in the kitchen came out to utter a startled laugh at the sight of him.

"I would appreciate to know the joke too," he'd said, but the girl didn't seem to detect the seriousness of her overstepping.

"It's my sister, Mr. Pierce. She's right next to you."

"Oh?"

"Yes, sir. She went home last year."

Franklin knew that some of the servants referred to passing on in terms of homecoming.

"And you say she's right here?" he said, pointing his chin at the vacant air beside him.

"She surely is."

"Well. What is she doing that's so funny?"

"She likes your hair," the girl said, breaking into giggles again. "She's *stroking* your *hair*."

In a reflex, Franklin's hand rose to his head. Before he could rebuke the girl he felt the briefest touch of warmth. Soft as a child's skin.

"If I opened this door," Franklin said now to the man outside the furnace room, "would I see them?"

"I don't think so."

"Why's that?"

"A person only sees things like that when they're ready to."

Franklin was annoyed. But he was aware of the moment possibly being part of a story someday, an anecdote shared by this man with others and taking on mythic resonance, perhaps even finding its place in a history book. A telling illustration of the understanding and patience of President Pierce.

"Once they're gone then, would you please fill the boiler's belly with coal?"

"Yes, sir. I surely will."

Franklin smiled at the man, a gesture of comradeship meant to convey that, despite their different stations, they both had tasks they were obliged to satisfy. Franklin was gratified to see the man's surprise. Then again, it may have only been his gratitude at not being made to go into the furnace room until whoever he thought was in there had left.

The ones before us.

Franklin was making his way back upstairs when it came to him. The furnace keeper wasn't speaking of ghosts who had worked in the residence in the past but the ones who had been brought here on the ships. Slaves. Ones he believed were in the president's house warming themselves around a dwindling fire. Their homecoming.

A person only sees things like that when they're ready to.

Up on the second floor, Franklin went past doors he hadn't yet opened. He paused outside the one he felt most likely would have been Bennie's. A smaller room across the hall from the bedroom he hoped to occupy with Jane.

He gripped his hand to the handle but didn't open it.

There would be nothing but an empty room on the other side. Yet some part of him felt he may be wrong about that. Wrong about any of these empty rooms being empty.

He drew his hand away from the handle.

Franklin wanted no revelations to be delivered in this place. Not after the train accident that replayed in his dreams every night. Not with his wife so far away she couldn't wake him when he called out to his sons in his sleep.

3

The First Lady went straight to the second floor upon her arrival a fortnight later, claiming the bedroom on the southwest corner, the farthest from Franklin's.

When he emerged from a cabinet meeting and was told Jane was upstairs he was stricken with nerves. It came from eagerness to see her. It came from dread of the same thing.

★   ★   ★

When Franklin Pierce first approached Jane at a social held in her grandmother's house in Amherst, more than twenty years ago, he intended to introduce himself as he would to any other girl. Yet something about her—her hair covering all but the pink lobes of her ears, her fingers interlocked in front of her as if they contained a tiny bird—emboldened him. All that mattered was that she see him as unlike the other young men scuffing through the hallways holding cups of punch. He wanted to raise her downcast face to his. He wanted to awaken her.

"You're meant to be the gloomy one of the three sisters," he said. "But I see now they are mistaken."

He was twenty-three, studying law under the tutelage of an established solicitor in town. She was two years younger, living in the house her family had moved to after her father's death. Jane had heard of Franklin Pierce, mostly from his sisters, who commented on how handsome he was. But as he stood close to her that afternoon, she saw something in addition to good looks. She saw a man who would become important by virtue of competent talents combined with exceptional presentation. She saw a true American.

She blinked up at him before returning her gaze to the hem of her dress.

"You claim a special vision," she said. "Tell me. What is it you see?"

Her voice was not what he anticipated. There was grit in it, and bass notes he could feel in his chest despite their being hardly audible. The voice of someone who had shouted for hours the day before.

"I see a rebel," he said.

"Oh?"

"You're not pleased."

"I wouldn't say that."

"What *would* you say?"

"I thought rebellion was only for militiamen."

"Or fallen angels."

He came partway to winning her right there. The other part would take more time. But in that moment, Franklin could see in the way her fingers untangled themselves that he had passed an outer barrier to her affections. He chose to believe that none had done so before.

"Now *that*, sir, is flattery," she said.

★   ★   ★

Franklin clung to the recollection as he made his way along the residence's second-floor hallway to Jane's room, resisting the thought of it being "Jane's room" when he wished it to be theirs. *What is it you see?* That had been her question to him, but he'd been drawn less by her looks than the sensation her voice inspired, the provocation in it, the illicit promise. What would he hear in it now? At her door he raised his shoulders straight before touching his knuckles to the wood.

"It's me, Jeannie," he said.

"A moment!"

He imagined her undressed. He pictured her spritzing rose water on her wrists or tying up her hair. Yet every second that passed without the call to *Come in!* pulled these hopes away into greater and greater unlikelihood.

The knob turned, and Jane was there, dressed in mourning clothes. The delay had not been to welcome him but to dry her face from the tears that continued to make a map of her cheeks.

"You look well," she said in accusation.

"A performance. I've missed you."

"I've missed everything."

She studied him through the tiny holes of her black veil. And he looked back at her, or tried to. His wife behind a wall she carried with her and that only a show of real suffering—suffering he felt weakening his legs now, so that he had to throw a hand out to the doorframe to hold himself straight—would win a viewing of the woman inside.

Jane lifted the veil. She'd painted her lips red.

"Can we be alone in this place?" she said.

"We have no choice but to be alone in this place."

He entered the room and closed the door. It was unclear if she would allow herself to be embraced, so he opened his arms to see if she would come to him.

"How is it?" she asked, unmoving. "Being president. Is it as you dreamed?"

"I never dreamed of it."

"No. You only dreamed of being loved."

She said this without sarcasm. Because it was also true, he nodded in dismal confirmation and lowered his arms.

"Will you not hold me?" he asked.

"You have your duties, and I have mine. Is that it?"

"I love you, and I'm *breaking*, Jeannie. There's no duty in it other than your feelings for me, if you have any."

She went to him. And when her arms were around him he let his hands rest against her back.

"I don't wish to punish you, Franklin," she said.

Which crime would you punish me for? he wanted to ask, but feared her answer. One more than any other. The train. The deceptions that led to his winning the candidacy could be overlooked. Perhaps they already were.

32

But their outcome—stepping into the railcar from the snow-drifted platform in Andover, sitting together, with Bennie behind them, his reaching for her when he should have reached for him—was why he was deserving of imprisonment outside of what remained of his family. Outside of her.

"Do, if it will bring you back to me," he said.

"You don't need to be brought back. Don't you see? You're *here*."

She squeezed his arms hard enough to hurt. He wasn't sure what she was trying to tell him. But there was life in the pain he felt, the message she was sending through it.

"Where does it go now?" she whispered.

"Where does what go, my dear?"

"Our love for him."

The question struck Franklin as impossible to answer. He had loved his son more than he loved Jane, more than his father. Bennie's memory gnawed at him, strangled him, tossed him on waves of unbearable sadness and, intermittently, a swell of gratitude for his having lived. He wasn't *gone*. That was the problem. What Franklin couldn't know then was that Jane was haunted too, but in a different way. For her it wasn't the memory of the boy that plagued her but the injustice of his not being with her in body as well as thought.

Don't you see? You're here.

"You're tired," he said, though it was his own voice that was shattered with exhaustion.

She pulled away and looked around the room as if for the first time. The bed. The curtains visibly thick with dust. The chest with its drawers pulled halfway out like a beast with four tongues.

"Yes, I'm very tired," she said, and sat down in the room's only chair.

"There is a small dinner this evening. A half-dozen congressional Democrats to discuss—Lord God I don't know what they want to discuss. Will you join me?"

As she considered his invitation he noticed she'd been holding a book in one hand the entire time. A Bible. The leather-bound edition that had been Jane's father's before she'd given it to Bennie. She turned it about in her lap to make sure he'd seen it, as if a weapon she was prepared to use if necessary.

"I don't believe I'm able," she said.

"Of course. You'll want to get settled."

"It may be some time before I'm ready to face the world. More than the time it takes to 'get settled.'"

"It sounds like you're proposing a remedy."

"We're too far gone for that," she said. "But I had in mind something that might be of help to you. A substitute."

Franklin understood now. It was not unusual for Washington widowers or "dedicated bachelors" to employ the services of a "substitute"—a woman who attended events, curated the social calendar, negotiated conflicts with other women performing the same function. A replacement wife.

"You have someone in mind?"

"My cousin."

"Abigail?"

"I have written to her, and she's open to the arrangement."

Franklin knew her, in the long-standing but superficial way of extended family. Abigail Means was Jane's aunt, but since childhood went by the title of cousin, given her closeness in age to Jane. Abby entered the family through marriage to the much older Robert Means, who died a decade earlier. She and Jane had been close before their marriages. Abby was someone who always wanted to help. And Jane always needed help.

"She is a sound choice," he said.

"Good. She will arrive this afternoon."

"You sent for her?"

"I didn't anticipate disagreement."

"Where will she stay? Not here, I should think."

"No, not here. She has found an apartment nearby."

"Well. I had no idea you've been so busy."

"She could attend tonight in my place."

"But you're right in front of me."

"Are you sure of that? I'm not."

He felt the heat of anger at the back of his neck and wondered if one could see it if standing behind him. A redness of the skin or curling of the ends of his hair.

"It's difficult," he said, his voice held to a willed softness. "It's not what we hoped. We are both of us in great pain, Jeannie. But we must endure, do our best. For each other. And—you'll not want to hear this—for the country too."

She pushed the Bible to the edge of her knees. It tottered there, back and forth. He watched it and soon felt not only his anger drain away but also his ability to meet his wife's eyes.

"Endure," she said finally, as if plucking a random word from the string he'd just spoken.

By the time he was out of the room there was a full moment in which he'd forgotten where he'd just been, where he was now, or what had brought him to this hallway lined with portraits of men who had the bearing of having always known which direction to take.

4

Jane stayed on in the guest room. She attended no formal events, took no visitors, refused to hostess the Friday drawing-room gatherings that had been held continuously by every First Lady going back to Martha Washington.

It wasn't rebellion alone that fueled Jane's denials. It wasn't illness nor idleness either. In fact, she considered herself well occupied over her first days in the residence. She was busy making a room for Bennie.

She chose the room directly across the hall from hers—the same room that Franklin imagined would have been Bennie's. The difference was that Jane was unafraid to open the door.

She called it the Grief Room.

The servants brought up the items she'd arranged to be delivered from Concord. Using a seamstress's tape she measured out the dimensions in relation to the corners and two windows, directing each piece be placed as close as possible to the same position as they had been in the Pierce house.

Once on her own, she spent the next hours adjusting the placement of everything. These were relics. Holy things.

There was what he called his "little boy bed." His crib too. The three-foot-tall tin soldiers he loved that had swinging legs and arms that lifted rifle butts to their shoulders. The chair she sat in when breastfeeding. The honorary sword Franklin had been given after the Mexican War and that Jane had secretly let Bennie keep in his closet to be taken out at night, polished and admired.

When Jane was finished she sat in the feeding chair. She felt the ribs of its back push against her spine with familiar discomfort. From a sewing bag she pulled out a leather journal and placed an ink pot on the arm of the chair.

As she wrote, she spoke her words aloud.

My precious child, I must write to you, altho' you are never to see it or know it. How I long to see you and say something to you as if you were as you always have been: near me.

The room had grown cold. Her breath exited her nostrils like gray smoke from the end of a barrel, one firing south, the other north.

She checked the positions of the furniture, the tucked-in sheets on the bed, the tiny lace-trimmed pillow in the crib. Nothing stirred. But something had altered from only the moment before.

Oh! how precious do those days now seem, my darling boy—and how I should have praised the days passed with you had I suspected they might be so short—Dear, dear child. I know not how to go on without you

Jane put down her pen.

"Ben?"

She asked it with equal parts hope and horror. Only once it was spoken did she look up from the page.

One of Bennie's tin soldiers sat on the floor directly in front of her. The general. His uniform lined with painted medals, circles of rust around the screws. The legs obscenely spread. A grin on its face Jane felt sure was wider, toothier than before. Its rifle raised so that its one eye stared down its length. Aimed at her.

"What do I do?"

She asked this not of the general, nor of Bennie's spirit, which she knew wasn't there. The boy wouldn't have set his toy on the floor in such a crude manner. He wouldn't have tried to make his mother as frightened as she was.

"I came. I brought you," she said, louder this time. "What do I do?"

It was her own voice that replied. The end of the echo thrown back by the cracked plaster walls.

Do.

★　　★　　★

For Franklin, Jane's isolation was becoming a problem. The Whig opposition, desperate for ropes that might pull them back into relevance, had begun murmuring about the president's mad wife. A good woman driven over the edge by actions on her husband's part.

"What actions?" Franklin demanded from Webster in his office. "What imagined injuries have I inflicted on her?"

"They are *imagined*. And all the more potent for being so."

"It's not fair to Jane. She doesn't deserve such vile gossip."

Webster shrugged. "It *is* Washington, sir."

Franklin vowed to visit her room with greater frequency but found himself putting off going down to her end of the hall. He came to imagine dreadful deformities. Bennie's Bible now fused to his wife's hand. The hairs from his dead sons' heads growing out from the closed locket around her neck. Her shoulders folding inward so that, in her black mourning clothes, she came closer in appearance to a beetle.

He chastised these products of his mind, looping through the reasons such grotesques were undeserved.

Jane had lost her children. She was living in a house that wasn't hers, in a city she loathed, with strangers outside the windows expecting her to lie about her acceptance of all of it.

And he'd deceived her. He'd let his famous friend, the author Nathaniel Hawthorne himself, talk him into putting his name on the convention ballot in Baltimore. Not to *win*, but to prevent a fracture within the Democratic Party. The compromise on the matter of slavery was showing itself as anything but. There were those who feared the selection of Buchanan or Cass would lead to disaster, committing the party wholly one way or another, north or south. What the moment demanded was a peacemaker. The hope was that the addition of Franklin's name would create a space for such a person. His presence at the convention wouldn't be required.

Jane hated the idea. She understood the tactic but dreaded even the remotest chance of having to return to Washington, a city she found stomach-flippingly gaudy, full of theaters announcing the basest spectacles and magic shows, along with tavern after tavern, all of it fed by a spring of whiskey and the pronouncements of men. She also feared the place, and told Franklin so.

"I feel terrible things await us if we follow this path any farther than we have" was how she put it.

He felt he knew her meaning. The work of politics could draw husbands away from wives and children. She was hinting at losing him to drink, to meeting rooms, to a mistress. Yet why did she speak of these conventional problems in such an oblique way? It was as if what troubled her about the thought of the presidency was a danger unique to the two of them, mysterious and unnameable.

When word came that Franklin had been selected as candidate, Jane had fainted and dropped to the floor. He worried that she would never revive. He worried that she would.

Knock, knock.

He was in bed in his second-floor chambers after deciding it was too late to visit Jane after all. The sound of shoes clipping to the door once more pushed aside his guilty thoughts of what he'd subjected her to. In their place was the distress of spotting new evidence of her turning from the woman he'd danced with in New Hampshire church halls long ago into a monstrosity, her voice lost to hisses, her back a shiny shell.

"Anything else, sir?"

It was Webster. There was no need for these evening farewells of his, but Franklin appreciated how the two of them had entered into a substitute marriage of a different kind. A sexless coupling fueled by fidelity from the one side, and the reward of kindly morsels from the other.

"Nothing, thank you, Sidney."

"Good night, then."

"Till the morning."

The shoes clipped away. Franklin tried to sleep. Failing, he sat up. Forced his thoughts away from work and toward Jane's substitute.

When Franklin met with Abby earlier in the week to formally thank her for agreeing to help "on social matters," she presented herself as a widow, not old, lively and practical. In appearance she was a less pretty, less troubled version of Jane. And was there a veiled promise in her smiles to him? A willingness to serve spilling into a more general availability? Over the days since, he couldn't stop from thinking of her as the physical manifestation of a wish. *Were my wife to be the same except for this, and this, and this.* Improvements to a gown that fit well enough but could always be bettered by a tailor's cuts and stitchings.

He lingered in wakefulness. Part of him troubled by the nation's forebodings of calamity, another part flashing images of his wife's appalling metamorphosis. Still yet another quadrant of his mind was willing the substitute to approach his room and whisper her request to come in.

That night, he heard it.

The feet bare, sliding over the rug that ran the length of the central hall. He sat straight against the headboard to better conjure the sight of her on the other side of the door. Abby in a nightshirt. This is what he wanted his mind to draw but it betrayed him. Instead, it sketched a beast. A creature made up of multiple parts—goat, rat, snake, Jane—that approached with its tail swishing behind it.

"Abigail?"

His voice barely pierced the murk. There was no way whoever stood outside could have heard him. He was about to speak again when his breath stopped hard in his throat.

Scr-rrrr-aammfff.

A palm drawn down the wood. Reaching inside without opening the door.

He didn't speak even when he was able because the word he was going to say again—*Abigail*—didn't make sense anymore.

Whump.

A solid weight brought against the door. He felt the restraint behind it even as he felt the floor shudder under the bedposts at the force of it. It wasn't trying to break in. It was showing him what it could do if it did.

He waited for it to go but he never heard it leave.

The dawn seeped through the curtains to signal his first entirely sleepless night in the White House. He remained there, cold and headachy, not daring to pull back the sheets.

The world came for him in the form of Webster. His knock light and harmless.

"Sir?" his secretary said. "Shall we begin?"

5

Jane was prepared to be impressed by the mansion's grandeur, but with the exception of some of the paintings and the books in the curved-wall second-floor library, she was astonished to find the White House a wreck. She would've never guessed it from the exterior, which suggested a country palace that had been lifted from Versailles and dropped into the marshland next to the Potomac. Then she went inside. And the palace turned into an asylum with better art.

There was the cold that even the ground-floor furnace at full fire could only nudge into the corners. The floors warped by humidity. The furniture scarred by pipe smoke and ash. It almost made Jane grateful for the curtains that so completely shielded the interior from light that to open them a crack sent a blade of yellow slicing through the air.

Then there was the odd rhythm to the house's activity: the halls echoing with the clipped boots of congressmen and servants and various head-lowered clerks during the day, followed by the muffled quiet of night, the rooms and parlors overgrown, foreboding, empty.

She didn't complain about any of it except the odor.

"It smells of wet peat," she'd tell Franklin when he came to her room in the early evenings. *Of a pig barn. Of meat left out on the cutting block. It smells of an undressed wound.*

He resolved to make improvements. His first decision was to install a dazzling convenience just down the hall from Jane's room: a bathroom with running water. Once completed he had to insist she come and see it, watch the billows of steam rise from the tub.

She looked up at him. Her nose pushing against her veil.

"I would prefer to be alone," she said.

He rushed out in shame without another word.

His next appointment was to hire the famed designer, Thomas Walter. Within days the crates and paint cans he brought in went beyond the president's instructions to "make it more of a proper New England home," instead installing love seats and satin cushions everywhere and brightening every wall by several shades. Worse, every minor repair on the first floor only brought the discovery of more serious damage. Tradesmen carrying planks and saws and ladders became a regular feature of any walk through the meeting rooms and salons. Not to mention the man-size holes they left in the walls.

The one change Franklin approved of were the new draperies held to the sides by gold ropes, so that sunlight became less alien to the place. In

Jane's room, if he came by during the day, he would open them only to have to do the same thing again next time.

"The light will do you good," he said.

"So I can see?"

"So you can feel its warmth."

She startled him by touching his jaw with her free hand.

"You are trying, aren't you?"

"I only want you back to what you were," he said. "Or half that, for now."

Her fingers traced around the edge of his lips.

"You need to be warmed too, don't you, my husband?"

The gratitude at this small tenderness was so great he worried that to say anything in the moment would trigger a flood of tears.

"Then perhaps we can shed the cold from each other," she whispered.

That night he waited for her in his room. He placed his hands on the mattress on either side of him to sense the vibrations of her approach. Listened.

Less than nothing. As if a presence had drawn all sound into another dimension altogether.

Franklin pulled the sheets off his legs and went out into the hallway. It was empty save for a lone sentry standing at the top of the stairs. Franklin saluted him, but whether the guard didn't see in the dimness or whether he'd been ordered not to enter into any exchange with the president, he remained still at his post.

There was a line of light coming from the bottom of the door across from Jane's. The room he wouldn't let himself enter. The one he thought of as Bennie's room.

He could just make out the orange flickering of candlelight over the floorboards from where he was. It grew brighter with each passing second. This is how he came to see that he was walking closer to it.

Franklin hesitated before knocking. Even he found this odd. It was almost certainly his wife in there. He could be with her if—

How do I know it's her?

He asked this from outside himself. And he answered from outside himself too.

She's talking.

Jane's voice coming from inside. A low, serious questioning.

She's talking with someone.

A man. He could hear this too. The sluggish delivery of words he couldn't quite make out. A sound that came from deep inside a cave, distorted by curving its way through tunnels and over black pools.

Something about the two voices held him there. There was a sense of wrongness about whoever was inside and, in turn, a sense of wrongness about him hearing them. He felt certain it wasn't infidelity he'd discovered but a blasphemy. An unspeakable act or communion beyond all understanding. Witchcraft, perhaps. A grotesque crime. He couldn't picture what Jane and the man might be doing, because he was sure, even as he tried to detect the words they parlayed, that it wasn't a man inside the room.

He hoped only not to be noticed. And then they noticed him.

Jane's murmured questions and the other's slow explanations—they stopped at once. He felt them look at him through the wood.

He started back toward his room. His walk quickening to a run that caused the sentry to turn his head. The president was sprinting away as if pursued, although he was alone in the long hallway. There was nothing for a guard to protect him from.

6

The president was obliged to attend the opening of the Exhibition of the Industry of All Nations in New York the following week. Given Jane's fondness for the city, Franklin was confident he could coax her to join him for a few days. She wouldn't go.

"You're disappointed," she told him. "But as you can see, I'm not up to the travel."

In fact, Jane looked better than she had since her arrival at the White House. The black veil had been removed, her hair pinned up to show a complexion pinkened by a walk in the sun or exercise he was unaware of.

"I could make time for us," he said.

"We'll have time when you return. Take Abby with you. God willing, I'll be stronger four days hence."

He was going to ask what she was doing in the room across the hall the previous night talking to herself—it *had* to be an exchange between

51

her Jeannie voice and the other, mischievous self that produced her oddly deep laugh—but she prevented him by offering a cheek to be kissed. When he lingered she turned her head and met his lips with hers.

Franklin could feel the excitement thrumming within her slight frame. It took some doing to convince himself that he was the cause of it.

★　　★　　★

On his last night in New York, Franklin met with lawmakers who argued over whether to purchase Cuba or invade it. Abby went out to see a show on Broadway.

Abigail Means was aware that she was the perfect choice to act as substitute for the First Lady. Once widowhood became her lot, she worried that the rest of her life would be spent husbandless, a fate she was prepared to face with dignity. And then her beloved cousin Jane was pulled to Washington when Franklin took the election, and even before the letter came asking her to come, Abby knew the role she would play. Pretend wife. Celibate mistress. It provided half the life she'd lost. But there were times she yearned for the other half as well.

It's why she constantly reminded herself that this was her part in the play. She was to *act* as spouse to the president, not become her. Yet being in New York with Franklin—rooms on separate floors, of course, and dining together only when formalities obliged—nudged her closer to confusing her role with reality. By the end of the trip she was grateful for the distraction of a night out on her own.

It was a musical revue that veered from sentimental ballad to idiotic skit. There was, however, one moment that stood out from the rest. A chilling tune that told the story of the two Fox sisters who could speak with the dead. The performers who played the parts of Maggie and Kate Fox portrayed them as sultry seductresses, astonishing their female clients and leaving the men so flustered they stole the ladies' fans to cool their passions. The program listed the number as "The Rochester Knockings at the Barnum's Hotel."

Abby had never heard of the Fox sisters. But the next morning, she found a newspaper story about them being the sensation of New York, holding spiritual readings in which rappings were heard, tables levitated, and canes, Bibles, and hats were flung across the room by unseen forces.

She intended to bring it up with Franklin after breakfast before departing for Washington, but when she arrived at his suite she was surprised to see the rooms filled with wooden crates.

"I was hoping you would give me your opinion," he said, his usually guarded smile stretched wide.

He pulled off the lid of the nearest crate. She had to come close to see what was inside.

"It's stunning," she said.

"You think so?"

"How could one not?"

He picked a dinner plate out from the top and smoothed his finger around its edge.

"Hand-painted. Made in France. And do you see the little stars? I thought it patriotic."

"It's lovely, Franklin."

"There's two hundred and eighty-seven pieces, I'm told. Which makes me wonder, if each place setting is composed of an even number, what's the two hundred and eighty-seventh? I suppose we'll just have to dig through it all to find out."

"The White House is lucky to have a president possessed of such good taste."

"In point of fact," he said, "I purchased it not for the White House, but for you."

"Well."

"Seeing as you're the only one eating off the old plates as much as me. I consider it service—friendship, whatever it is—deserving of recognition. And my gratitude."

It was an innocent speech in its wording. But one that bore additional meanings and invitations in his speaking of it.

"Jane will love it," Abby said.

Franklin heard it clearly enough. He'd come to a boundary.

"Yes, of course," he mumbled, lifting the top back onto the crate. "They're her colors, after all."

7

When the carriage rode past the gate Franklin's first thought was that black vines had burst from the ground to grow over the mansion.

"What is this?" he asked walking up the steps where Webster was waiting for him.

"Bunting, sir."

"I have eyes. Why is it here for all of Washington to see?"

"Come inside," Webster said. "See what Washington *can't* see."

Black ribbons. Yards and yards of it tied and looped around every pillar and post all the way along the central hall. Mourning bunting.

"Jane did this?" Franklin asked.

"She's been out and about since your departure and only returned to her quarters today."

"To avoid me."

Webster puckered his chin, which was his way of indicating mutual suffering. "In my experience, a wife can sometimes leave bread crumbs to be followed instead of saying a thing plainly," he said.

"Oh? And where does the trail lead?"

"A locked door, as often as not."

Franklin touched his hand to the nearest ribbon and, before he knew he was intending to, tore it off the wall.

"Have this taken down," he said. "Every inch. And if there are bread crumbs sweep them up before the goddamned mice find them."

★   ★   ★

Upstairs, Jane was not alone.

Abby had rushed to greet her before Franklin could because she wanted to calm whatever impulse had prompted her cousin to decorate the place like a mausoleum. If she were to be honest, Abby also wanted to alleviate the lingering guilt she felt about Franklin's "gift" in New York. Her plan was to be the first to tell Jane her husband had bought her the most thoughtful surprise. To keep things breezy, she would mention the show she went to and the song about the Fox sisters.

But once Jane heard this last part she asked about nothing else. Abby replied as best she could based on her reading of the article in the *Daily News*.

"Bring them here," Jane said.

"What do you mean?"

"Invite the sisters. I'll write the letter, but I ask you to deliver it. I'd tend to it myself, but I would prefer the staff—the wretched newspapers too—not to know."

"Will you—"

"No, I won't tell Franklin. And neither will you."

"I don't understand," Abby said.

"It's not for you to understand."

"But if Franklin were to—"

"You are *my* friend, not his."

Was this true? In any other place, she was certain that a dalliance with another woman's husband—let alone Jane's—would be so far from possible it would hardly enter her mind. But here it was different. In this house, there was space that suggested one could be released from what they normally were.

"When will the letter be ready?" Abby asked.

Jane came close, and Abby expected to receive a hug of gratitude, but instead her cousin leaned her face to the side of hers without touching.

"Stay a moment," Jane said. "I'll write it now."

8

Abby was hardly gone when Franklin called on the First Lady. She asked him about the exhibition, and he reported on some of the amazing things he'd seen—a steam-powered elevator, seamstresses who used machines instead of their hands. He also climbed up the Latting Observatory, a wooden tower that was the tallest building in New York, from which one could see all the way across the Hudson. It was the sort of news Jane usually liked hearing about, yet he had the impression that her interest was feigned.

"I'm glad to see you've been up and about," he said. "You've made the White House into a proper tomb."

"I thought it was fitting."

"When will you attempt returning to the world?"

"You mean returning to you."

"You're right. When will you be my wife again?"

He'd lashed out in anger only ten seconds earlier but landed, with his final question, in a place of genuine misery. In return she offered him the look of a kindly nurse visiting a double amputee.

"I'm sorry," she said.

He almost accepted it. If he hadn't noticed the stack of letters on her desk he would have made a step closer. Instead, he picked them up, one by one.

"These are all addressed to Bennie," he said.

"Yes."

"Bennie's *gone*."

"I believe he hears me just the same."

Franklin opened the envelope at the top of the pile. Began to read parts of it aloud.

" 'My dearest love, I can feel you close to me. It is only a pane of glass that separates us. Come to me, my sweet boy. If you reach for me I will do the same and we will break the glass.' " He looked up from the page. "Where do you send these?"

"They aren't intended for the mail. My *thinking* them delivers them."

"This matter of the broken glass," he said with a baffled laugh. "It sounds like you're asking him to come back to you."

"When you grieve him, do you not sense that he is near?"

"Yes. But that is—"

"What if you could take that grief and push it further still? Extend it to where he is now so that he might grab hold of it and follow it home."

"Stop."

"He isn't far."

"This—"

"He's right *here*. And if you help me reach—"

"*Stop* it!"

He didn't shout, but she recoiled as if he had. His fury visible beneath the surface like a red leaf in a frozen lake.

"Is that who you were talking to?" he asked.

"When?"

"Before I left for New York I came to the room across the hall. You were speaking with someone. It sounded like a man."

Jane looked at him without expression. "A man?"

"I guessed it was you, conversing with yourself."

"Really."

"You've always been capable of sounding different on occasion. As if you were two people in one."

"That would make me a very strange bird."

"Good Lord, don't you *know*? You are the strangest bird of all!"

There was a moment when they both came close to laughing. If they had—if one of them had—their course might have altered.

"There was no man in my room," she said.

"So it was yourself."

"I'm not saying that."

"What *are* you saying?"

She appeared to consider one way of responding before choosing another. "I'm not a madwoman," she said.

"I'm glad of it. Tell me, then. What is going on in this place, Jane?"

Even Franklin wasn't clear what he meant by *this place*. This room, this house, this space between them.

"I am being a good mother," she said, so deliberately it gave her time to walk to where Franklin stood and take up the stack of yellow letters, including the one he held, and press them to her breast. "I am doing all I can."

"As am I."

"When the time comes, will you do even more?"

He had no idea what she meant. Yet he had a sense of her implications, how they were straying off into—did it have a name? Sorcery, perhaps. Sacrilege.

"I wish I believed in prayer. I would pray for us both."

"Say the words anyway," Jane said, turning her back on him. "You might be surprised who hears them."

9

Jane found the pendulum game in the bottom drawer of her father's desk in the Bowdoin house. It was autumn of the first term of 1818. She was twelve years old.

The clapboard mansion at the edge of campus was the only home Jane had ever known, but there were still secrets about it, unseeable things she felt peeking at her from around corners or hovering inches from the back of her neck. She couldn't tell if these apparitions were connected to the building itself or the people who lived in it. As she aspired to be a holder of secrets herself, she wondered if the house recognized a talent in her that might be of use.

Jane's father, Jesse Appleton, a Congregational church minister, had been appointed the second president of Bowdoin College after being passed over for professor of divinity at Harvard. He and Jane's mother, Elizabeth, had their daughters—Mary, Frances, and Jane—prior to moving north to Maine from New Hampshire, but both of their sons were born in the house where the college president resided. Jane was the middle child. Understudy to her outgoing, teenaged sisters. Nanny to her indulged brothers. Pretty, but not widely designated a beauty. Bright, but not exceptionally enough to overcome the barriers to scholarship that came with her sex. When her father sermonized about purgatory Jane heard it as the dimension she dwelled in, though unlike the souls who suffered there, she appreciated its advantages. Privacy. Camouflage. A gray-skied immortality.

Jane Appleton would be an overlookable sort of girl if not for an inner quality detectable to only a few, and even for them it was hard to say what it was. An old soul's gravitas. The quiet that came from witnessing the unspeakable, so that one wanted to show her the small redemption of sunshine or the protection of a walled garden.

For her part, Jane was conscious of these perceptions, and of the people who held them versus those who simply saw her as sad. But Jane didn't think either were right. Her hidden aspect, as she saw it, was curiosity. A hunger for knowledge, transgressions that would break the minds of others but heal the fissures in her own. She assumed it to be a complex attribute, sophisticated and interesting. But there were also occasions when Jane worried that it was no different a thing from malice.

The college president's house was, on its surface, full of activity: the children shuttling between the rooms (all of them schooled at home through childhood) along with the social events that came with Jesse's position, the faculty gatherings and suppers with visiting scholars. On another level, Jane experienced the house as a place of solemnity. There was a gloom that followed her up and down its stairs and along its creaking hallways. It was so constant a companion that she never experienced loneliness there, which was funny, because she was aware that the thing that pursued her was loneliness itself.

Even at her age she knew these feelings were inherited from her father. He was given to headaches just as she was, ones that filled their skulls with colors and unbearable lights. Like her, he suffered from frequent illnesses the physician could diagnose no more specifically than "nervousness" or "fatigue." Jane felt another commonality between them that was confirmed in silence when she met her father's eyes. The shared vision of something bad coming their way, a calamity only they could apprehend but were helpless to stop.

It was her sister Mary who told Jane about the pendulum game.

Mary was five years older, openly mischievous in a way Jane wasn't, physically sturdy, and liked by boys. She had whispered to Jane lying next to her one night months earlier about finding "magic things" in their father's desk. Jane had guessed her sister meant items whose purpose she didn't understand but whose discovery their father would disapprove of. In fact, the house rule was that children were not allowed in his study. But why would their father, a man allergic to foolishness, keep a *game* in his desk? And if he did, why would they be forbidden from playing it?

Mary never mentioned the magic things again, but the thought of them enflamed Jane's dreams every night.

Jane entering a room locked to all but her, the door opening at her touch.

Jane floating to a cabinet, or a vault, or a sealed box.

Jane speaking a word that opened its door with a bony *pop*.

The dreams would always end before she could see what was inside.

She decided to enact the dream. In truth, there wasn't much of a decision in it. She *had* to do it because she *wanted* to do it. It was as if she was caught in a loop of desire, an inquisitiveness she felt around her middle like a leather belt, and only touching the magic things would let her carry on with her life.

The September day outside was bright. Walking along the main floor hallway she heard students heading to class on the other side of the windows, felt the vibration of their guffaws, the effort of boys trying to sound like men. But the brightness and the laughter might as well have been taking place in someone else's mind. The last of it sucked away the second she turned the knob and entered her father's study.

As in her dream, she drifted to where she knew she must go. Except this time, she opened the bottom drawer without having to speak a word. It required only her hand to grasp the brass handle and pull.

At first, her rummaging produced disappointment. A pair of white leather baby shoes. Stray checker pieces. A silver bracelet engraved with a dedication that had been worn away. She was going to leave, but her finger became entangled in thread. When she pulled it up the pendulum came with it.

A tripod of copper legs. The thread tied to the apex. A black marble with a needle's point fused to the bottom.

Jane set the tripod down on the desktop and freed her finger. The marble swung to one side, pinging off a copper leg and wobbling back toward her fingers, grazing her knuckle with a cold kiss.

She returned to the drawer. This time she pulled all the items out to find what might be buried beneath them. A board. Square, freckled with knots, the size of an unfolded linen napkin. She flipped it over. A circle of letters painted in an ornate style Jane associated with the illuminated Bible her father displayed on a lectern in his lecture hall.

As quickly as she could she put everything back into the drawer except the pendulum and the board. It would be madness to play with it right there, on the rug in her father's study, though she wanted to with a nagging urgency like the need to pee. She slipped out of the room and closed the door behind her, expecting to be discovered by one of her sisters or little brothers who were constantly searching for her—*Jane! What've ya got there?*—but the hallway was empty.

She headed to the kitchen, where the door to the cellar was. It had been left open by whoever had last come up with the jar of peach preserves they'd eaten for breakfast, and now Jane stood at the top and stared down into the wavering dimness beneath the house.

Later, she'd insert a voice into her recollection of this moment. A whisper of her name coming up from the bottom of the stairs, luring her. But there was no whisper. She was compelled to venture into the darkness that smelled of axel grease by something within herself, as direct and inarguable as thirst would draw her to a stream.

Her bare feet on the wooden steps, pinching at her toes where the paint was flaking off. A discomfort that reminded her this was real. That the cold, more intense than a cellar ought to be at this time of year, was unnatural, but also real. To Jane the moment was the least like the rest of her life.

There were crates down here, tools her father never used, shelves that held the chinaware for suppers she wasn't allowed to stay up late enough to join. She knew where the banner they tied over College Street on the first day of term was, rolled up and standing against the wall to her right, and she kept her eyes on it, waiting until she could make out the white *B* and *O* stitched onto the black cotton, before shuffling to a bare spot where she sat on the earth floor.

Jane was aware that the pendulum was a device designed to be a conduit to the spirit world, and therefore a sacrilege against God. Was this knowledge whispered to her by Mary? Was it intuition? She felt it wasn't something she'd figured out on her own, but rather someone had told her. Not Mary, now that she considered it. Neither of her sisters, who were more interested in collecting ribbons for their hair and reciting the names of all the Bowdoin boys they had ever spoken to. And not her brothers, who were too young to be interested in offenses against God.

It was impossible, but it seemed that the pendulum and its implications would be the sort of topic her father would share. A lesson of the kind he would bestow on her before bed instead of a story. The deviations from the righteous path that led to damnation. Fatal temptations. They were warnings, often horrifying in their consequences. Yet Jane heard her father's voice in the darkness of her room as offering her a different way, an alternative to the hair ribbons and dance invitations and smothered piety that would otherwise be the fate of an Appleton girl.

She set the tripod atop the painted side of the board and shifted it level as best she could, then poked the marble on its thread, pretending this alone—a swinging shiny ball—was the sole point of the game when she knew it wasn't really a game at all.

For a minute she watched the marble lurch back and forth between different letters on the board. When it tired, she held it between her fingers, pulled it back, and sent it swinging again. It was calming, in an unpleasant way. Like riding in a carriage and feeling at once sleepy and ill.

Her mind noted the letters that the marble's point swung to, putting them together into words. But they weren't words. It's because she wasn't playing the game yet. To do that, she had to ask it something.

"Who am I?"

She squeezed the marble. Eased it back, keeping the thread tight. Let it go.

The ball swung as it had before. Yet this time its point touched a letter before changing direction, its former randomness now determined by an invisible influence.

J-E-A-N-N-I-E

There was no way it was an accident. The point at the bottom of the marble swung to those seven letters and only those, settling back to its resting position when it was finished. It spelled her name. Except there was only one person who called her that. Her father.

"Is there someone here?"

The marble felt warmer between her fingers this time. Softer.

Y-E-S

"What are you doing?"

In the instant before she let the marble go she felt it turning into something else.

W-A-T-C-H-I-N-G-Y-O-U

Jane looked into the grayness of the cellar's corners. She was alone. But at the same time some part of her confirmed she was not.

"Not fair. You can see me but I can't see you."

She pulled the marble back and it warmed and softened even more. Still a hard ball in appearance as it swung between the letters, but against her fingertips it felt like skin.

A-S-K-M-E

"Ask you what?"

The marble wobbled between three letters, then stopped dead.

A-S-K

"All right," Jane said, and slid her bottom over the dirt away from the pendulum. "Come out, come out, wherever you are."

She was certain nothing would happen. She was certain it would.

There was no sound that drew her eyes to the farthest corner, but once they focused there it was where her attention was fixed. At times over the years that followed, she would wonder if it was this focus and attention that caused its emergence. Perhaps she was more than a witness to unspeakable things. Perhaps she was their creator in the same way that making the marble swing and asking questions of the air was the only way to make the pendulum speak.

The shadows moved.

Not something within them but the shadows themselves. It remained some distance away and yet she was enveloped by it. Embraced by layers of mud, suffocating and cold. She was terribly afraid. But her stimulation was louder than her terror, and she stayed where she was to see its becoming.

The darkness took a step out of the darkness.

It assumed the appearance of a man, but there wasn't a moment Jane thought of it as such. Nevertheless, its presence was unquestionably masculine. Not human but, like some men she'd walked past outside of taverns or loitering in the town square, the entity blazed with an aura of threat. She recognized that she should try to escape it. She also recognized its authority. Whatever this being was, it could do things that were uncanny, magical.

"This is my house," she said.

"You would have me leave?"

This reply came at once. It startled Jane more than the fact it was here, as its voice proved it was no longer—if it ever was—a product of her imagination. And there was the nature of the voice. Low, unhurried. A thickness to the way its tongue curled around its words as if slightly drunk. She'd heard men speak this way at receptions her father held, occasions when beer and tumblers of whiskey were served. The men looking at her sisters and Jane in a way she didn't like but was shamed to be also stirred by.

"You shouldn't be in my father's house."

"But you said it was yours."

"It's—"

"You asked me here. Which makes me a guest. Would you cast out someone who has only just arrived? And at your invitation?"

It spoke plainly and deliberately. Yet the words spun in Jane's head, turning simple phrases into riddles.

"I didn't invite you."

"That," it said, and without it gesturing Jane knew it meant the pendulum. "That's like a knock at the door. Yours and mine. And both of us answered."

The thing was an outline of darkness, the merest sketch of a man. It reminded Jane of the time she'd stood on the banks of a bog at the corner of her grandparents' property in Amherst and saw something moving just beneath the surface, thick as tar. She never saw what it was. It slithered through the water and caused it to bulge upward, suggesting the form of a turtle or snake without revealing any actual part of it.

"What are you?"

"There is no answer to that."

"You could come forward. Show yourself."

It paused for the first time. Jane thought it revealed a limitation. How the thing was still bound by rules of some kind, though it was already manipulating the space it occupied to make those rules disappear.

"That would only frighten you more than you are."

"I'm not frightened," she said.

It made a swallowing sound. A single, wet gurgle, as if a morsel of food—she thought of her mother's boiled whitefish—was sliding into its stomach. It looked at her with eyes she could now make out from what she guessed was its face. Eyes she felt draw the fear from within her, pulling it up her throat like the campus doctor had supposedly done for a college boy who'd had a tapeworm removed by way of his mouth, baited by a bowl of milk.

It made the swallowing sound again. This time, Jane heard it as laughter.

"I can do things," it said.

It was wrong to want to know what it meant. That's what the particular darkness of the cellar was. Wrongness.

"Show me," she said.

"We need to be friends first."

"I don't have any friends." Jane was surprised by the honesty the thing brought out from her even as she detected the shade of a lie in its every word.

"You will never need another," it said.

She reeled back at this, or wished to. But she felt like she was sinking into the earth, so all she was capable of was leaning a few more inches away, her body stretched so that made her feel vulnerable, as if she would soon be lying flat on her back.

"Are you a magician?"

"No," it said. "But I can make people see things."

"An oracle?"

"No. But I do have a vision of the future. And you're in it, Jeannie. We are there together."

It wasn't a haunted house. Jane was sure of it now. There was nothing foul buried beneath its wood-frame walls, no profane spirit that had been lying in wait. In a way she could never explain, she knew the haunted spirit was herself. And the foul thing came to her because she had called for it.

Could she be blamed for that? She was a child. The last girl before the prayed-for boys of their big family were born, stranded on an island between her strapping sisters and toddler brothers. Bookish, solitary, with an inclination for the morbid. She'd only wanted a companion, an end to her loneliness. But this too was a lie she'd thread into her memory later. The truth is that Jane Appleton summoned a living shape out of the cellar's shadows because she wished to bring back the dead.

"What's your name?"

"Name," it repeated, and seemed to ponder the nature of her query.

"What do I call you?"

"You," it repeated again. "You may call me Sir."

It was a trick. *Sir* wasn't a name. It was how she'd been taught to refer to the professors at the college or a gentleman stranger she might sit next to at church. But not laborers or those she could detect by their clothes or place of residence were below her station. The thing in the cellar was not a gentleman. And yet, by calling itself Sir it wished to fool her into lending it a superior position in their relationship. For that's what it was now. There was a bond between them even if she wished there wasn't. A friendship. One that was the opposite of what the term meant in all respects except its intimacy.

"I am the one you asked for. Aren't I, Jeannie?"

"Yes, Sir," she said.

10

Four days before Franklin and Abby departed for New York, Sir had come to Jane in the Grief Room.

Upon his return, when Franklin told her that he'd been standing outside the door, she was privately relieved. She'd always known Sir was real. But if his voice could be heard by someone else, it meant it wasn't just in her head anymore. Which meant something else too. He was stronger now—stronger here—than he'd ever been before.

She was careful not to lie to her husband. She said it wasn't a man who was speaking. This was how she thought of Sir: something he was not. To think of what he might actually be made her light-headed. It was like imagining the darkness past the end of stars.

When Sir came to her four days ago he didn't emerge out of nothing as he had in the past. She was sitting on the edge of Bennie's tiny bed and then he was there, next to her. His leg touching hers.

"Jeannie," he said.

His eyes were dark, but the second she glanced away she couldn't recall their color. She looked again, noted it, looked away, and once more their particular hue was lost. His details could change even as she watched him, as if he was the embodiment of a false memory.

He had a dimpled chin. His chin was flat.

The tops of his ears poked out through his hair. He had no ears.

His lips were pink as if from kissing. His lips were white as if from tasting ash.

The one aspect that didn't alter was the complexion of his skin. Unfreckled, pale as cake.

Considered as a man, she found him handsome without feeling the faintest attraction to him. Still, she experienced an unpleasant thrill in being near him. The closest sensation she could think of was the time as a child in Maine when she'd watched a hawk come down on a hare. The predator tore its prey apart with its talons, the hare twitching its legs at the same time it was dismembered and eaten. It was awful. It was impossible to turn away from.

"You've been very good," he said. "You've been faithful."

"Not to you."

"To your son. But also to me."

She wouldn't call it faithfulness. Sir was a parasite she had asked for. And she was convinced that, as he had said in the Bowdoin house's cellar, he could do things. But she had no loyalty to him, which was remarkable, because she felt a trace of at least some empathy for everyone, strangers included.

"Yes," she said.

"You have taken me so far, Jeannie. But I want my freedom now. My own room."

Jane was trying to follow him. As it always was with Sir, it was hard to stay with his thinking as he spoke. It was like he was teaching her to read his thoughts instead of hear them, and she was halfway between the two skills.

"Soon an opportunity will be presented to you," he continued. "You will see it when it comes."

"And you would have me accept it?"

"I would have you control it. You don't see yourself as strong, but you are. For Bennie, you have always been. Use that strength to help me come through. And I can bring him with me."

A creak in the floorboards. Jane scanned the room, but there was no one but the two of them on the bed. Someone had come to stand outside the door. Listening.

The idea of a maid or sentry or Abby or—most unthinkable of all—Franklin turning the knob and coming in to find her sitting next to this unnaturally perfect man filled her with terror.

Go.

She directed this at whoever stood outside.

GO.

The weight outside the door shifted. Walking away. *I would have you control it.* Sir was right. She was stronger than she thought.

"What do I—"

She turned, but he was gone. Only the smooth depression his legs had left in the sheets proved he'd been there.

11

For the first years they were in Amherst at the same time they saw little of each other. There were sightings on the streets as they made their way to shops or church, nods from Franklin and gloved waves from Jane. But they spoke only at the gatherings at Jane's grandmother's house. Polite updates on each other's activities, which, given that Jane spent her time mostly reading and playing piano and waiting for what she called, in her private thoughts, an "occurrence," the conversation quickly petered out on her end.

Discovering what interested Jane Appleton fueled Franklin's curiosity. He found himself thinking about her more than most of the young women he encountered, replaying their first meeting over and over and wondering what it was that had made her show that glint of mischief.

Now that, *sir, is flattery.*

He was able to speak at greater length of his accomplishments after his election to the New Hampshire state congress. He returned for four consecutive years, the last two as Speaker. All this well prior to his thirtieth birthday.

Jane was small. Every part of her miniaturized, so that one only noticed her size in comparison to something else. Her eyes were dark, hair parted in the middle and drawn over her ears. A fine nose, animated by flares and twitches, each breath an inquiry. People called her lovely, and she was, but in a way that inspired sympathy as much as desire.

Franklin's attraction to Jane felt to him less of a compulsion than finding himself caught in a spider's web, its threads sticky, inescapable. There was her place as one of the Appleton girls. There was the Amherst house with its respectability and order. There was the way he wished to repair her as if a miraculous, delicate construction, her thousand tiny screws insufficiently tightened. There was her mother's discouragements, which made Jane a jewel in his mind where she might otherwise have been only another pearl from a good family.

He told himself he was freely considering all these factors even as the web tightened around him. And so, when Franklin was finally bound, he decided on her.

It was only when history was watching them, during the time they lived in the mansion, that he wondered if it had been she who had decided on him.

When he recollected how they fell in love and calculated the costs, years on, he always thought of the day they sat on the banks of Caesar's Brook. It was Jane's idea to walk as far as they did, a mile past the cemetery's stone wall after a Sunday service in August. She suggested they rest before returning to town, and he chose a patch of clover in the shade of a plum tree for them to sit.

She kissed him in the middle of his guessing aloud about the chances of rain by suppertime. In return he held her so close she slid onto his lap.

"I'm like a bird in your hands," she said.

"Would you fly away if I let you go?"

"I might. But ride on me and you would rise too."

She leaned into him, the warmth of her words blooming over his scalp. His hands lay over her back, and he felt the disks of her spine, the liquid shifts of bone. Her body, slight as it was, aroused him. It came to him with a shiver: She would be more than a wife if he chose her. She would be a conjurer.

Jane was aroused and frightened too. In fact, her experience of both—the way their power flared when combined—was more acute than his.

"Do you feel it?" she asked him.

"What?"

"Where we could go together."

He did feel it. *Where we could go.* She was speaking of their bodies and the pleasures they could take in them. She was speaking of marital adventure—babies and prosperity and the satisfaction of God's plan. But she was also hinting at something bigger. Hidden forces they could discover only in each other's company. Did all lovers think this? Likely so, Franklin considered. But those others were wrong. He and Jane could make something in their union that was more than romance or family or a good name. They could transfigure into a whole new being, mesmerizing and terrible as the unknown approaching from out of the fog.

"It would be like nothing else, wouldn't it?" he said.

"I think not."

"The question is, are we brave enough?"

"Bravery? I'm not sure that's what's called for."

"What is?"

"Passion."

"A yielding."

"Yes. Submission. Total and irreversible."

She was laughing, low and smoky. A nervous distraction from the precipice they'd come to. A height so great that if they took one step more they'd find they could either fly as gods or fall the same as any fools who'd gone too far.

12

Jane told the residence staff she was expecting guests. The president was not to be informed of the visit. Perhaps because they had so rarely been addressed by the First Lady directly, each of the sentries, service girls, and groomsmen she spoke to had accepted her terms without question, if only to escape her gaze as soon as permissible.

Franklin was out. A dinner that Abby was attending as substitute. Jane asked her to keep Franklin there as long as possible, which, if precedent held, meant ten o'clock at the latest. She asked the Fox sisters to come to the servants' entry at the east side of the ground floor at eight. It was a quarter past now. Jane regretted setting the time so late. Seven would have been better. Or six. If these two girls were going to bring her together with Bennie she wanted all the time she could have.

From what Jane had learned subsequent to Abby's initial reports was that Kate Fox was the quiet one, the younger at sixteen, and possessed with the most acute abilities. Maggie was three years older and had a reputation as a beauty among the husbands whose wives called upon their services, which is one of the reasons they were so often run out of town. Rochester, Albany, Syracuse, Cincinnati. In one place after another the Foxes would set up shop in a fancy hotel and do sessions by the hour. They were young, unmarried women living on the proceeds of witchcraft. It made them the objects of fascination and scorn in equal measure.

As instructed, it was Jane's dresser—a woman named Hany who plainly disapproved of what was going on but whom Jane regarded as trustworthy—who brought the Fox sisters to her door.

"Thank you, Hany," Jane said.

Hany was stout in the legs, lithe in the arms, black, and wore wire spectacles so tight they pinched the flesh at her cheeks and temples. She was not excessively warm or conversational, but Jane found her a comfort in their encounters. There was a patience in Hany—an understanding extended to her own imperfections, to Jane's—that was communicated through small shakes of the head or a *chit* sound she made between her tongue and the roof of her mouth.

"You may leave us," Jane said, and Hany pulled the door closed with a grimace.

When it was just the three of them Jane saw how young the girls appeared for their ages. Kate especially. There was something wounded about her, as if she'd spent the last hour being shouted at. It didn't seem to Jane that the older sister, Maggie, would be the one to do the shouting. She looked to be hardly aware of her sister, let alone angry at her. The elder girl observed Jane with undisguised frankness. Jane tried to believe it was part of Maggie's professional approach to measure people in this way, so that she and her sister could customize their methodology to each client. Yet it left Jane with the distinct impression that she was only gauging how much she could get away with.

"The White House," Maggie said, and sucked at her teeth. She heard the sound it made and straightened herself in exaggerated humility.

"Welcome."

"We've been reading up since we got your letter. Our condolences."

"Thank you."

"I must confess I never thought we'd find ourselves in this place," Maggie said, a strained formality to her speech as if acting the part of a cultured lady and, in doing so, mocking cultured ladies. Mocking Jane.

"Your accomplishments have been widely celebrated," Jane said. "I suppose there are many who would wish an audience with those who have left this life too soon."

"Oh, you can be sure of that, Mrs. Pierce."

"Well then. I don't want to hold you here any longer than you need to be. Is there a way we ought to seat ourselves?"

Maggie looked at the three chairs set around the table in the middle of the room as if for the first time. "Mr. Pierce won't be joining us?"

"No."

"That's unfortunate. I'm sure he has some interesting spirit friends."

"The hour is getting rather late. Would you mind if we—"

"Please, we mustn't rush things," the girl interrupted, winking. "This isn't like getting your future on a scroll at the penny arcade."

"Of course."

Maggie walked around the room, inspecting perfume bottles and powders on the bureau top and pouring herself a glass of ice water from the crystal pitcher next to the bed.

"Is there someone in particular you wish to contact this evening, Mrs. Pierce?" she asked once she'd returned to stand next to the table.

"My son."

"Bennie."

"His name was in the papers you were reading?"

"Oh, yes."

"I didn't know a child's death is worthy material for public gossip."

"With respect," Maggie said disrespectfully, "it's not just *any* child's death when the father is the president."

It had taken Jane more time than it should have, but she saw now that Maggie was drunk. She held her liquor well, which was part of why it eluded immediate detection. She also had a way of adapting her inebriation into an attitude, one that vacillated between amused and bored, so that one found oneself tempted to try to hold her attention by saying or doing something outrageous or aggressive.

While Jane could see how such a charm could work on others, she was immune to it. She wasn't offended that a woman of Maggie's age had chosen to present herself aglow with liquor at the presidential mansion. It was the lack of seriousness she brought to her extraordinary vocation. If Jane could do what it was said Maggie Fox could do, she would devote herself to refining her powers, not dulling them with gin. It angered Jane to think of such squandering—she could speak with Bennie now, herself!—so she tried not to. Yet within minutes of

Maggie stepping into her room she found herself seething with jealousy. *This* cheek-painted, smirking harlot? *She* had the power to communicate with her Bennie, her poor father too, with all who had passed and left the ones who loved them cratered by loss? It filled Jane with an urge to slap the child's cheeks redder still.

"I'd like to begin now," Jane said.

She sat in one of the chairs at the table and smoothed the lace over its top. Maggie seemed to consider making another provocation, but whether she couldn't think of one or she considered the risk of losing their double-the-usual fee, she held her tongue and took her seat. A moment later Kate did the same.

"It's done through rappings and knocks," Maggie said, launching into what was her standard explanation of the procedure. "We'll ask the spirit a question, and they will answer by choosing letters of the alphabet according to the number of raps. One is *a*, two is *b*, and so on. A pause between means a new letter. Are you ready, Mrs. Pierce?"

"Yes."

"Then what is your question?"

Jane had been speaking with Bennie in her mind, writing letters to him, dreaming of him for so long that now that she had the chance to address him directly she didn't know what she wanted to know first. Was he in pain? Would he wait for her so they could be together when her time came? Did he know that she loved him, would always love him?

All these queries and others jostled to be front of her mind. But there was one piece of knowledge she dreaded the answer to, yet was most desperate to know.

"Bennie?" she said. "Can you see me?"

The sounds came right away.

. . . *pop, pop, pop, pop* . . .

Hollow raps in a steady sequence that none of them counted aloud, but Kate silently mouthed the number to herself. Twenty-three, twenty-four, twenty-five. A pause.

"*Y*," Maggie announced. Then the raps started again.

It was so plainly one or both of them cracking a joint in their legs—an ankle or knee under the table and therefore undetectable—that at first Jane almost laughed. *Pop, pop, pop, pop.* Her piano teacher at Catherine Fiske's Boarding School for Girls made a bigger noise bending back her fingers to "open the knuckles" before attempting Bach's French Suites. It was astonishing that anyone seated farther back than the fifth row in the theaters these two had performed this trickery in could detect any sound at all.

"An *e*," Maggie said, feigning excitement.

Jane listened to the raps start up again as if from a great distance, her disappointment pulling her out of her body, out of the room.

"And a *s*. That's *yes*! Mrs. Pierce, I believe your child is present with us!"

I believe you're a vulgar charlatan, Jane wanted to say but didn't.

This was now an occasion, like so many in her life, that she had to make it to the other side of. Throwing these children out after being scolded by the First Lady wouldn't do any good, and might end up insulting them enough to report the episode to the press. Despite their assurances that this session was to be kept confidential, and the extra money paid to ensure it, Jane had little doubt that Maggie Fox was the sort who would break a promise if she felt she'd been crossed.

"Remarkable," Jane said.

Kate, who'd been silent to this point outside of their initial introductions, sat forward in her chair and regarded her with open pity. She saw that Jane wasn't fooled. She also saw how this disillusionment hurt her more than the waste of an hour and a hundred dollars.

"Sometimes it helps if we join hands," Kate said.

Maggie shot her sister a look. It was hard to be sure, but Jane interpreted it as a warning. As if Kate was venturing somewhere that had proven dangerous. As if the girl was proposing to make the game real.

"Like this?" Jane asked, picking up Kate's hand in hers before Maggie had a chance of preventing her.

"Yes," Kate said. "Maggie? You too."

Maggie wrinkled her nose. Jane read it as an attempt to appear indifferent to what was happening now, but it didn't entirely mask something else that changed in the elder sister's expression. A stiffening of her back, the formerly slouched shoulders now high as if she'd been told to sit properly by a teacher. But it wasn't a response to authority. It was a response to fear.

"Hands," Kate said.

Maggie took Jane's and Kate's free hands in hers.

"Mrs. Pierce?"

"Yes?"

"Forgive me, but I'm going to ask you to do something that may be a trial."

"Ask it."

"Think of Benjamin."

"That's not a trial. I think of—"

"Don't *remember* him. *Bring* him."

"How?"

"See him."

"I *always* see him!"

"Not from the past. Here. Now."

She felt foolish playing along with such an obvious ruse, but Jane found it hard to deny the younger Fox girl. Partly because she was a child. Partly because there was something more convincing—some buried intensity even the girl herself was uncertain how to contain—that made Jane curious to see what might be revealed if she went all the way to the edge.

She focused. Brought up Bennie's face, let her mind conjure the tiny wrinkles and dimples of him as a newborn. And then those same markings as they deepened or shrank over time. A microscopic scan of her son's face.

"I see him."

"Now bring him to us," Kate said.

"I don't know how."

"Ask him. Pull him. Order him."

"How do—"

"*Make* him."

Jane exhaled for so long that, when she breathed in, it was like she had broken the surface of a lake after nearly drowning.

"Come to me, Bennie," she said.

"Clear as light so he can follow it to you."

"Come to me!"

"Good. Now open yourself to the other side."

As vague a command this was, Jane knew exactly what the girl was asking. She had been waiting to be given permission to let herself try since her children's passing. And before that too. In some way Jane had been waiting to yield herself to the realm of death all her life. If Franklin's fate was the shouldering of power, hers was this: to be a bridge between the underworld and the living world she only half-inhabited ever since she took her father's pendulum game from his desk drawer.

"Please, my sweet boy!" she cried. "I am here!"

"You are the door. Open it."

"Come to your mother, Bennie!"

"Open the door *inside* of you," Kate said, her voice rising. "Open it wide to your lost child. To all who wish to enter!"

"Bennie!"

"Open it *now*!"

Jane pulled her hands away from Maggie's and Kate's to swing her arms out to her sides. It expanded her. As if the smallness of her body had sprouted new appendages, a metamorphosis from woman to spider. When she spoke her voice was altered. Even Jane heard it, and would have screamed if she wasn't so far away, so open.

It was Sir's voice.

Come . . . through . . .

The temperature dropped with the abruptness of stepping into the ocean. It wasn't a mere sensation either. Jane exhaled, shuddering, and her breath reached out to Maggie and Kate in gray billows.

"He's here," Jane said.

There was a shape advancing from out of the shadows in the corner of the room. Clear, material, unmistakable. She was used to seeing things that others didn't, so when she looked to Kate and Maggie she expected the blank, trancelike expressions they wore as part of their theatrics. But they saw it too. Maggie's mouth hanging open so wide her spittle made the inside of her lower lip shine. Kate's neck stretched so long it was as if she was about to float up from her chair.

What Jane also noted was the sisters' differences of expression. Maggie's was astonishment. Kate's was recognition.

"He's come home! He's *come*—"

Jane was cut off so abruptly it was as if she'd been struck. In fact, her head spun to the side, though nothing visible had touched her.

Each of them watched the thing come out of the corner as if there were a door there without a hinge or handle, and each of them, for their own reasons, saw that they had been wrong.

"Splitfoot," Kate whispered.

It was different now. Jane felt it.

In his previous visits, even the ones when he had been most physically detailed, most manlike, he had given the impression of something wearing a costume. But this was what it really was. And while it was more faint in its particulars it showed itself in how it warped its environment. The density of it was so great it bent the floorboards under its weight. It stole the air from the room and left them gasping. The revulsion it brought was as sudden as taking a turn on the trail and coming upon a fly-buzzed corpse while on a walk in the woods.

All of it made clear that it was not a complex, self-contradicting thing as a human being was, but elemental. Malice. Hate. Violence. It was the thing such words are meant to refer to but can't dig deep enough to reach the thing itself.

Boom.

A clap of thunder. Except it came from below, not above.

BOOM. Boom . . . BOOM-BOOM.

It rattled the windows and shook dust from the ceiling plaster. It wasn't a sound in their heads but the vibrations of something—multiple things—smashing against a part of the building's wall. To Jane, the increasing desperation of the knocks spoke of people not trying to get in but trying to get out.

People. She was sure of it.

Coming from somewhere on one of the lower floors. The furnace room. People bringing their knees and feet and fists against its oval walls. Its door.

Boom-boom . . . BOOM!

The thing in the room liked the sound of it. The panic, the terror. Jane could feel that too.

"Oh Jesus Christ!" Maggie shouted. It sounded like nonsense. "Holy Jesus help us!"

The presence wasn't repelled by Maggie's words. If anything it savored the helplessness with which she spoke them and lingered a moment to witness the evaporation of the smugness she displayed mere minutes ago. Then it moved. Pulled away to the interior wall and passed through it to the hallway on the other side.

Once it was gone the three of them returned to themselves.

Maggie started sobbing. Kate was saying the same thing to herself, over and over, too quiet for any of them to hear. Jane was listening for where the thing had gone. Because it hadn't left the residence. It wouldn't leave, not now.

Jane rushed out into the hall. To the right, at the far end by Franklin's offices, members of the staff were collecting, asking what the noise could have been. When they saw Jane none of them called to her or came to her aid. They were as frightened of her as of whatever had been smashing around in the basement.

The door to Bennie's room was ajar.

Jane crossed the hall to it. It seemed to take an hour or more. The incalculable length of a dream.

Behind her, she heard Maggie and Kate run past, both of them wailing. The hallway's width and height a perfect magnifier of their distress, sending their voices backward and forward and reaching down the stairwell as they made the turn.

When Jane got to the bedroom door she was exhausted. Her arm was too heavy to raise to the knob, so she just kept walking into the wood, nudging it wider with the toes of her shoes.

Everything was as she had left it when she last came in. Yet something had just been there. Something still was.

There were the tin soldiers lined up against the baseboards. The paint-chipped crib. Her boy's little bed with the marigold headboard, the lace-fringed pillow, the sheets so tightly tucked in she could see the mattress's lumps of stuffing push against the cotton.

"Bennie?"

She hoped he would come running to her from out of the walls, out of the air, the same as Sir had appeared. The boy would hear his mother's voice, the depths of her love, the lengths she had gone to and the risks taken to provide him a way, and he would complete the last part of the crossing himself.

Nothing stirred. The thunderous knockings from below had stopped. Even the presence that had manifested in her bedroom—the thing that had made Kate Fox whisper *Splitfoot*—wasn't there anymore, if it had been the same force to open the door.

"I'm here," Jane said.

She stood there long enough that she discovered she was not trying to hear anything but detect the source of an almost imperceptible change in the room's temperature. A new warmth. One that she remembered from other rooms in her life, spaces that were similarly chilled and, when she entered, would push against the cold through her own breathing and the beating of her heart.

The crib.

There was a reshaping of the blankets behind the narrow wooden bars she hadn't noticed when she first entered. She wondered if an animal could have done it. A mouse or rat. But vermin don't change the smell of a room like this by their breaths alone. Only a child does that. Only a baby.

She went to the crib and bent over it, drawing back the quilt with gentle tugs of her fingernails.

A boy. Maybe two months old. A baby she didn't recognize, though it was like her own boys in many respects: square-featured, blue-eyed, a general resemblance to their father, which was to say good-looking without any particular beauty marks or aberrancies or exoticism.

"Who are you?" she said, already slipping her hands under its back and lifting it up to her face. "Do you have a name?"

As Jane looked into its eyes the baby's eyes looked into her. A communion that altered the infant's appearance in minuscule ways. The baby transformed into Bennie in the moments she held it as if drawing from her memories, the motherly times of being in the nursery, cold and tired but happy, seeing the child in her arms as forever hers.

The baby's face soured. It didn't change its features the way babies normally did—there was a mechanical aspect to it, an expert fakery, as if an enchanted doll—and Jane saw it. She didn't mind. She told herself precisely: *Don't pay any mind to that.* The baby may not be fully Bennie, not yet. But she was on a journey and this was the beginning. In any case, wasn't she a mother? Wasn't a moment like this when she felt the most secure, strong on her feet, her sicknesses held at bay? Didn't she always see the nursery as the place where the doubts and hauntings of the everyday couldn't touch her?

The baby cried.

Its eyes remained placid. The cheeks uncolored. Its body still in her hands. It *sounded* like a hungry infant. But in every other respect, it was the same doll-like surrogate to an actual blotchy-faced, blinking baby that it was a moment ago.

"There now," Jane said, and it hushed by a degree.

She carried it over to the feeding chair. It took only a minute to pull down her dress with the infant waiting on her lap and then lift it to her breast. Its mouth found her nipple easily and suckled in even draws.

"There, there," she whispered, and felt herself emptying.

13

"Jeannie?"

Franklin's hand was on her shoulder, gently rocking her awake.

"I fell asleep," she said, and discovered she was still in the feeding chair.

"Are you all right?"

She remembered the Fox girls. The younger one urging her to open a door within her. The true presence that Sir's skin had always hidden coming into the house. The baby in her arms.

"Is he here?"

"Is who here, my love?"

Jane looked around the room. The infant was neither on her nor in its crib, though the blankets remained tousled just as they were after she lifted it. Her dress had been pulled up. Had Franklin done that when he found her and was choosing to discreetly not mention it? If not him, she stiffened to think of Sir being the one to slip the buttons into their eyelets at the back of her neck.

"Oh, Franklin," she said, answering nothing.

"You weren't in your room. I looked up and down. And found you here."

"You don't like this place."

"I wouldn't say that," he lied. "I just don't know what it is."

"These are Bennie's things."

"I can see that."

"This is Bennie's room."

Franklin had expressed varying degrees of worry over her for as long as they had been married. But Jane saw a different type of concern on his face now. It was as if she were dying. Or worse. As if she were dead and had come back a different creature altogether.

"It's late," he said. "Can I help you to bed?"

"Perhaps you can help me to yours?"

There was no promise in it. It was a request for assistance and nothing else.

Franklin offered his arm, and she held fast to it.

They closed the door to Bennie's room behind them and started down the long hall to Franklin's quarters. She tried to find the anger she'd held for her husband, but whether it was the disorienting events of the evening or a new resolution of her own making, she couldn't find any.

As they walked, he tried to turn the moment toward the normal by talking about his dinner and its tedious guests, the husbandly sharing of the day pouring out of him after so long on his own, and Jane half listened to him. The other half heard the creak of a handle turning behind her and Bennie's door pulling open an inch.

Franklin didn't hear it. Just as he didn't notice her touch a finger to the top of her chest where she felt a dampness.

She drew the finger away. Sticky and wet. The yellowish white of milk.

14

When they were first courting, Franklin fantasized about saving enough money to buy Jane a piano of her own. She loved to play, and could read sheet music but preferred her own compositions. Melodies that sounded at first like one heard before, a hymn or nursery song that lay just beyond memory, before shifting into a murkier key. Some called them "original," while others said they gave them goosepimples, or brought on bad dreams.

In the end her uncle Amos, whom Jane adored and Franklin loathed (his contempt of his suit all too obvious) beat him to it. A polished Pirrson was delivered to the Amherst house addressed to "My Most Talented Niece," and Jane wept as the men heaved it up the steps. Everyone gathered to hear her play Mozart allegros and *Für Elise*. She followed this with an improvised piece, childish and light, that Jane dedicated to her deceased brother John. This brought on sustained applause from all including the delivery men, though Jane's grandmother later took her aside and asked her to never play the tune in her house again.

Her grandmother was not at home when, a few months later, Jane played it for Franklin.

They weren't alone in the sitting room—Jane's sisters came and went—but the music, once started, blotted out everything but the two of them. The melody was sweet but almost gratingly so, like an infant's burbling that prevented one from sleep. Nevertheless, Franklin was undone. The sensation he had was of deep recognition, a glimpse of himself in a mirror that was truer than others precisely because of its blemishes and distortions.

When she was finished he was astonished to touch his face and find his fingers glistening with tears. It was as if they belonged to a future version of himself, a phantom looking back at this moment and mourning it for reasons he couldn't possibly know.

He crossed the room to place his hand over hers, still hovering over the keys.

"Marry me."

"I thought we already were," she said. "Shall I play it again?"

She didn't have to. He would remember it always. There was the sense that, for better or ill, her composition was their love song, a theme to be repeated over time. He couldn't say that he liked Jane's music. But it was theirs.

"Please," he said, and stepped away without moving his eyes from her back. "If you would do me the kindness, Jeannie. Yes, please."

★   ★   ★

Their wedding was held in the Amherst house. Green bunting hung over the door as Franklin approached with his father, the only other guest on the Pierce side. The old man was dressed in his military finery, medals polished, mustache so heavily waxed its tips drooped like tubers feeling their way into his mouth. He was also slightly drunk ("Resolved," as he put it) from the sips taken from a flask allegedly handed down by Washington himself. In the carriage, his father had offered a drink to Franklin, who declined with a shake of his head, though in truth he wished for the resolve of whiskey to burn in his own belly.

Inside, the Appletons and people of local importance greeted the Pierces with relief. Franklin was shuffled into the parlor, given instructions by the minister, and handed a crystal glass of cider all so swiftly he had the impression there may be another wedding after this and they were running behind schedule. Then he heard the real cause of everyone's haste: Jane was crying upstairs. Deep-throated sobs that everyone in the house wanted to be free of as soon as they were able.

Franklin stood listening to the impressive anguish of his wife-to-be with the rest of the guests. He was grateful for the cider, the sipping of which gave him something to do. In time, Jane's cries were joined by the calming voice of her mother. What was happening now would prove a pattern for his wife: the dread of a forthcoming event, the summoning of will, and finally the steely execution, the sharp Appleton chin raised in a show that others referred to as brave. Franklin regarded her as such too. And yet sometimes—on *this* day, his *wedding* day—he couldn't entirely prevent a bitterness at the wailing upstairs. Why was her struggle with everything, even with happiness, a sign of courage, and his reaching for that same happiness a proof of selfishness?

It was so quiet when Jane stifled herself they could hear the creaking of the stairs as the bride made her way down. Because Jane was the musician of the family there was no one to play the piano for her entrance, so that they listened to the gritty scrape of her heels on the boards as if they signaled the approach of a midnight specter.

The brave chin came first, followed by puffy eyes and mouth alighting at the sight of her groom. Franklin felt the need to take her away to somewhere safe. He would never have guessed Jane was having the same thought about him.

The secret she held as she stood next to Franklin and spoke her vows was that her tears in the dressing room upstairs weren't caused by anxiety over the marital bed, nor bidding farewell to being an Appleton girl and becoming the wife of a congressman. She had grieved about those things on other occasions. Today, before her mother demanded entry, she wept out of fear as she listened to the things Sir told her.

He appeared in fully realized human form, though Jane was unable to look directly at him. Like the reflex that turned one's gaze from the sun she could only take in the details of his appearance in glimpses. His face refined, but unnaturally so: lips too thin, nose too pointed, all too white. She would say he wore powder on his skin except the powder *was* his skin, crumbly and bleached. His tongue didn't fit his mouth so that as he spoke it reached out with a predatory intelligence, stealing tastes of air.

She had been looking at herself in the standing mirror when she noticed a movement behind her, quick as a sparrow flying past the window. When she turned he was there. Already speaking. Already making his way to the bed where he sat straight-backed on the edge and looked at her knowing she couldn't match its stare.

"Jeannie," it said.

She couldn't answer. The thing's indifference to her horror compounded her horror. As it calmly formed its words she cried louder and louder. The words reached her nonetheless.

"I thought it was a proper occasion for me to be clearly heard," the voice explained. "You have done so well. And I have come to celebrate with you. Our day of union."

He wasn't naked, but his clothing lacked the wrinkles or dye of any fabric she'd seen before, so that it was a part of his being, a way of matching his surroundings as certain lizards can alter their color. Black jacket and trousers, starched shirt buttoned to the top. No belt, no tie. She took note of these details to avoid looking into its eyes.

"I am your *friend*, am I not?"

She didn't think this was so in any way.

"Yes," she said.

"This man—Franklin. I chose him. And I was right to choose him."

"Why?"

"He will deliver us."

In the cellar of the Bowdoin house Sir had been a line of darkness. In subsequent visits it had been notions in her head. Now it was a man, but at once more distinct and less real than any man. In its progression it was like a dream moving from the night into the day.

"You are special," it went on. "Ready to see and feel and learn."

"What do I do?"

"Let him love you. Love him in return if you wish."

"I wish—"

"It will be difficult. But I promise there will be rewards."

"For Franklin too?"

The thing cocked its head an inch too far.

"He will have his own campaigns," Sir said.

Jane's mother knocked at the door. Before the echo of it silenced, the being was gone, leaving behind a wordless message like perfume on a pillow. It would never leave her. Her husband was intended for a seat at a table set for gods. She would be witness to remarkable things.

It struck her as she creaked her way down the stairs and saw Franklin, bloodless and lost, that the happiest presence at her wedding was Sir.

★ ★ ★

A half hour after the service Jane and Franklin boarded the coach waiting to take them to Washington.

"You've made me a beautiful promise today," she whispered to him, so near he could taste her words. "Would you make me one more?"

"I can only know the answer if you ask me."

"Will you promise to abstain?"

He blanched, and Jane interpreted him as understanding her to be speaking of sex.

"From drink," she corrected.

Franklin was so happy not to have to debate his conjugal privileges

108

that he promptly accepted. It seemed an easy vow to honor. He liked whiskey, and imbibed it publicly with political men and clients from time to time. In private, he kept a bottle in his office to dull the longest days. But Franklin wasn't his father. Drink was something he could walk away from if he chose.

"Soon," she said, offering her hand to be held.

He didn't know what she was referring to exactly—the start of their married lives, their bed, the arrival of children—but all of it delighted him. He took her hand. So wonderfully small in his.

Franklin knocked his fist against the carriage's ceiling and the coachman *click-click*ed the horses into motion. With her free hand, Jane waved out her window facing the road, and he did the same toward those who remained standing on the porch. It was then that he saw a strange thing.

Next to his father stood a younger man he hadn't noticed at the wedding. In fact, it was someone he was sure he'd never seen before in his life. Tall, straight, his skin shining as if from some internal fire that emitted gray light but mostly smoke. His suit well pressed but plain, like an undertaker before he'd had a chance to put on his vest and tie. The features of his face individually fine—the word *lovely* came to Franklin—but together had the appearance of a mask designed to hide some wriggling horror beneath it.

Franklin's hand froze. His father didn't look his way. It may have been from too many glugs from his flask, or perhaps the bittersweetness that was visiting him upon witnessing his son's last step into manhood, but Franklin had the distinct impression that he was ill. *Lost.* His decades of self-certainty bled out of him from his contact with the stranger, whose arm, Franklin saw, lay resting over the old man's shoulders.

A moment on and the carriage was wheeling distance between themselves and the wedding party, turning his father and the others on the porch and the roadway into porcelain miniatures. Yet he was sure of it nonetheless. Before they were around the first bend and the Amherst house was swept out of view, Franklin saw that the only one still waving at him with his swan-white hand was the stranger.

15

In the morning, once Franklin had left her with a kiss to her forehead, Jane returned to her room on the residence's second floor to write a letter to Kate Fox. A request to know the girl's interpretation of the previous night's events.

"My curiosity is greatest," Jane wrote, "concerning the word you uttered in the midst of the queerness. Or was it a name? I heard it as *Splitfoot*."

Three days passed. Jane supposed she would never hear from either of the Foxes again. And then Hany brought an envelope that hadn't come by regular mail, but was hand delivered by a boy who'd been given a dollar to do it.

Dear Mrs. Pierce—
I have read your letter several times. I have also thought about the
night at the mansion more times still. There is so much to say, yet

great difficulty on my part to find a way to say any of it. I will try. For you. But also for the good of the country, given your husband's position and the grave possibilities that have come into it.

We are much alike, Mrs. Pierce. I don't know the precise nature of what we share, but I write in the anticipation that you will recognize the unwanted gifts of my life as something also bestowed upon yours.

I will tell you a story.

I had a secret friend as a child. This was back in Hydesville, a fine enough place but of no significance whatever. Many children have imaginary playmates—a talking dog or guardian angel who fades away as the years pass and reality finds a firmer footing in their lives. In my case, the friend never went away.

It wasn't a fellow child or singing pony. It was a man. His skin so white it appeared to be brushed with flour. Eyes a color that could be seen but never recollected the moment you looked away. His voice was low and dirty and made you feel low and dirty too. He said he would be the only friend I would ever need. He said he'd never leave me, and in truth, up til the other night, he never has.

He first came to me when I was five years old. I was playing with a dead bird the cat had brought to the door. It's a stupid thing to think of now, but I was stretching its wings out, trying to help it fly again. This was behind our house, my older sisters arguing inside, so they hadn't yet noticed what I was doing.

I heard something. Like somebody had whistled a note on a bent flute. I looked up and a man stepped out from behind the big oak at the back of the yard.

"Hello, Katie," he said. "Do you like that bird?"

I said that I did. He said the mean kitty killed the bird and that maybe it was the mean kitty that should be dead.

These were strange things to say to a child, but he said them so naturally it seemed honest and fine. It was later that I realized that what he was saying was exactly what I had been thinking to myself.

I asked his name.

"Mr. Splitfoot," he said.

When he didn't join me in laughing I became frightened for the first time. He asked what was funny, and I said the name he'd given himself was the nickname for a demon. Other children had been given thrashings by their fathers just for saying it aloud.

"It's only a word. What harm can come from saying a thing? The truth is in what you can see. Look at me. Do I not look more like a man than a devil?"

I told him he looked like a very nice man. What I didn't say— what I <u>couldn't</u> say, Mrs. Pierce—was that a nice man is just what a demon might try to look like if he was to visit a little girl and tell her he would never leave her. I thought to point this out but worried it would make him angry, and although he was as calm as a surgeon, I didn't want him to be angry.

I swear to God I knew one thing. He could do things. Awful, amazing things.

Like that time in the backyard.

Before he stepped behind the oak tree again, he whispered something I couldn't hear. And when the whispering was done, the dead bird flapped its wings.

It was alive once more! It hopped and thrashed away, bitterly tweeting. I watched it throw itself into the hedgerow. In its broken state, it would soon be food for a fox or possum or the cat.

It was brought back just to die again, a worse death the second time. He could do <u>that</u>, but he couldn't do the beautiful thing. He couldn't make it fly.

He came back many times over the next years. Sometimes he had something to tell me, other times it was only to watch me.

When I was nine, Mr. Splitfoot told me what the dead were saying from the other side. The raps and knocks act came later. For that's what it was—what it is. An act. Maggie's invention. We both have ankles and toes that can make loud cracks with the merest adjustment, and my sister proposed we employ the talent to play tricks on our neighbors.

Maggie was cheeky. I wanted to have fun too. But she couldn't hear the spirits, only I could. And I heard them only when Splitfoot whispered their answers in my ear.

It took us further than either Maggie or myself ever guessed. Theater performances, stories in the papers, meetings with people paying good money to hear us crack our toes under the table and spell out how their uncle Willy still loved them or that their momma was so proud. Sometimes I got tired of that and asked Mr. Splitfoot to join the proceedings. That was when people learned things from the dead that went beyond any trickery. The name of the child who'd died as a newborn and was buried in an unmarked grave, or the date when a lost husband first saw his wife with her knickers off.

Trouble was, Splitfoot could be unpredictable. Sometimes he didn't just answer the questions. Sometimes he threw plates against the wall or released odors so fierce they made people sick or growled like a beast that had leapt out of the walls.

But it was different in the White House. It was like he was there for you, Mrs. Pierce, as much as he was there for me.

I'm very sorry for what happened. Your lost sons. My failure to bring you into communication with Bennie.

Yet I am left hopeful in this one respect—ever since that night in your room, Splitfoot has not returned to me. I have neither seen him nor heard his voice. Perhaps I have rid myself of this hellish companion for good.

Wishing you peace,
Kate

It left Jane shaking. The last paragraph more than the rest of it. What it meant for her.

Along with the memory of her father it returned.

★   ★   ★

After little John's passing, Jesse Appleton's physical decline was a spectacle the entire college couldn't turn its eyes from. The president's once stiff-backed strides across the quad crumpled into arthritic shuffles within the space of months. It was like watching a walking suicide.

When he took to his bed one afternoon for a "good sleep" he never left it again. He asked to speak with each of his children. They came to him one at a time, closing the door behind them. Jane last. As she waited her turn, she couldn't guess if this position of being her father's final visitor was an honor or a punishment. What if he succumbed before she had a chance to sit in the chair by the bed and say whatever needed to be said? She feared what her father might share with her more than the prospect of her failure to provide any comfort.

Mary came out of the bedroom in tears just as all her siblings had. It made Jane resolve to be the only one who left dry-eyed when she exited. Brave Jane. It was important that her anguish be understood as greater than all others so that it could be seen as being endured with the greatest forbearance.

Her mother squeezed Jane's shoulder harder than necessary. Every one of her touches was harder than necessary. To Jane it seemed that her mother was always trying to wake her from a troubled dream.

"He's waiting," Elizabeth said, an unmistakable alarm stretching her features. Jane took it to be her mother's apprehension at losing her husband. But as she closed the bedroom door behind her she saw it as dread of something about Jane herself.

"Come here."

Jane's father was thin as a birch branch, but his voice arrived from a greater distance than the bed. It seemed that he was speaking from the woods that surrounded town, already drawing back into its leaves and soil.

She sat on the hard pine chair. It was difficult to look directly at him for any length of time. She was unsettled by his appearance and lonely at the idea that she would soon be without him. What upset her most was the prospect that he was about to say something that would reshape her, put her in a condition beyond her capacities to hide or repair.

"Are you comfortable?" she asked.

"I'm cold. And full of sleep. Yet these are only God's hands showing the way home."

She tried to imagine where her father was going. A frigid place where one felt ill and sleepy for eternity. She didn't think it sounded welcoming at all.

"I will miss you, Father."

"I will miss you too. But I will take condolence in my memory of you, as I hope you will take condolence in your thoughts of me."

Jesse Appleton was a kind man, if not warm, and these words were the most tender he'd ever spoken to Jane. She leaned back in the chair, and it cracked as if in amplification of the breaking inside of her.

The bedsheet moved. A rolling mound coming up and pushing through to the air. Her father's hand. Its fingers flexing with invitation. Jane placed her hand in his palm and the fingers closed around it.

"It's a paradox, isn't it?" he said. "Especially for those like us. . . ."

His voice trailed off, as if he expected Jane to finish his thought for him. But which thought? What was the paradox? Why was it one with special meaning for the two of them?

"Our time here is so unbearably long, and yet so short there isn't opportunity to say what we need to," he went on. "I have been a poor father in this respect, and I'm sorry for that. But here we are. Our last words. And you are my only child whom I wish to hear those words from, instead of you to hear them from me."

He stared at her from the sweat-soaked pit of his pillow with a look of expectation she thought must be a misreading, a side effect of his pain.

"My only words are that I love you, Daddy."

"Yes. Yes," he said, blinking. "What else is there you need to tell me, my daughter? We aren't members of the Roman faith, but think of this room as a confessional. A chance for forgiveness, and also for counsel. For both of us, I hope."

"Is there something you wish me to speak about?"

His hand tightened on hers.

"Please don't lie to me," he said.

"No, sir."

"Don't call me that!"

"I'm sorry. I—"

"Don't call me what you already call another!"

He knew. *Sir.* She heard him say it without him saying it.

He knew she was the one to take the pendulum game from his desk, that she played with it the way he had also done himself, that someone had come to her, claimed a small but essential part of her as it had claimed him. She understood exactly. They both did.

"I don't understand, Daddy," she said.

His face softened. This time it wasn't another increment in the gradual disappearing act of his passing but a show of sympathy. She was aware that her father loved her. But in this instant she grasped how much he did, how unique this love was for her and only her.

"I'm worried for you, Jane. Desperately so," he said, and eased his grasp of her hand without letting it go. "I know a little of what you know. About the—otherness. But there are only the two of us who share this knowledge. We're curious kitties, aren't we? Devoted to God but also devoted to knowing what he keeps from us."

Her father was speaking to her in the way of a sermon. Indirectly, seriously. In church, this kind of communication bored her. But now she not only comprehended what was being said, she was also riveted by it.

"Who did you lose, father?"

He winced. It was as if her question was the poke of a needle to his back.

"I tried to bring back someone who'd passed on a long time ago," he answered. "Someone who hurt me when I was a boy."

"So you could hurt them back."

"No. That wouldn't be possible. There was never anything I could have done or said that would have left a mark even when they were alive. Nothing they could ever feel."

He shook his head, and she wished he wouldn't because it showed the bulging tendons in his neck, the fluttering pulse against the inside of his skin.

"Why did you want the person back?" she said.

"I wanted to ask them why."

"Why they hurt you."

"Why he chose me."

Jane heard the shift from *they* to *he*, but she already knew it was a man her father was speaking of. She was of an age of intuiting that only men hurt in the way her father was suggesting, even if she didn't know the precise nature of the offense.

"Did you?" she said. "Did you get the chance?"

"Someone came back, yes. But it wasn't the person who hurt me. It was . . ."

He squeezed his eyes shut.

"Are you all right?" she asked. "Can I get you any—"

His eyes opened. His hand tight again. Pulling her closer as he spoke, inch by inch, so that there was no way for her to breathe without inhaling the mildewed onion scent of his skin.

"We are made of our losses, Jane. Sorrow is God's will. To look for ways around it is to open a pathway for the devil. It is unholy not to suffer as we are meant to suffer. Do you understand?"

"Yes," she said, but wasn't at all sure that she did.

Her father let go of her hand and she brought it to her side quicker than she meant to. He seemed not to notice. There was more activity under the sheets, more waves moving upward, and Jane worried that more hands were about to appear, some belonging to him and others not. He was propping himself up on his elbows so he could rest higher on the pillows stacked against the headboard. It took some time. She didn't offer to help him. When he was done, she could see all of him from the ribs up. A whiteness made whiter by the interruption of nipples and moles and hairs.

"The Bible is a book of teachings. But it's also a history. Not parables, not children's tales. Real occurrences. Most of us, even the devout, don't see the other world that lies"—he slapped his palms together—"atop our world. But some of us remain open. You are one, aren't you? You've seen the unseen?"

She didn't want to reply but felt her head nodding the affirmative.

"Now here is what you must remember. Just because you can see a way from this world to another doesn't mean you should travel the course between them. It is the serpent's temptation as often as it is a vision of the spirit. And we have no way of knowing which. Do you hear?"

"Yes," she said.

"Will you promise me?"

"Promise?"

"Promise me that if a passage opens you know to—"

The door opened.

Jane swung around to see her mother entering, cheeks flushed. She'd been listening through the wood, or trying to. Even if she hadn't comprehended most of the phrases, she'd heard enough.

"Your father is tired," she said.

Jane went to the door without looking back at him, not even when he whispered *promise* once more. She didn't want the way he looked to be the way she remembered him. More than this, she didn't want to stop so that she'd be forced to deny his plea for her word.

★　★　★

Once she was able to still her hands Jane folded Kate Fox's letter twice, dropped it in her wash basin, and touched a lit match to its corner. The flame rose. Its orange tongue lengthening, bending, like the outstretched arm of a lover reaching to touch her face.

She took a step back and watched the flame chew through what was left of the paper's white.

16

Bennie's birth was the only one Franklin was present for. The first bub-
bled cry. The body in his hands. The cord attaching the child to Jane in a
way he would never equal.

Neither Franklin nor Jane declared a favorite child, but the truth
they were equally aware of was that they loved Bennie most. Franky
was cheeky, ravenous, and loud. But comparison with Bennie put him
on the losing side in every instance. Where Franky complained, Bennie
endured. Franky blew his nose on his shirt and Bennie reached for the
handkerchief his father had given him.

Both boys contracted typhus within the same week. Jane took Bennie north to care for him at her sister's house. She wasn't able to look
after two ill children, and the choice of which she would focus her en-
ergies on was a matter of choosing the younger between the two. This
is what they said aloud. But it was known to all that a preference was
being expressed.

Franklin hoped that in his delirium Franky wouldn't notice, but in the way his eyes slid shut whenever it was his father who entered his room and not his mother showed the boy knew where he stood.

Franklin sat next to the bed. There was nothing to be done but he still wondered what he could do. A paradox that invited prayer.

He cast his thoughts heavenward with little hope of them being received. Because of this, he decided to be honest in what he put before an unlikely God. He prayed for Franky's recovery but added a clause. He asked that if one of his children must be taken, let it be the one in the bed before him and not the other miles away. It was a hideous thing to think, and he regretted it instantly. Still, it lingered in the room, in silent verification that he had thought it.

At first he assumed it was his guilt taking shape outside of himself. But it came not just from outside of him, but the house, the world.

There was something there. Not a person he hadn't noticed before. Nothing he could see. A presence that occupied a space at the end of the bed, dense with ill will.

Franklin couldn't say what it was. He could only be sure of what it wasn't.

Not a ghost. Not a shard of his imagination.

He was certain of the second of these because Franky sensed it too. The boy squinting at the same emptiness as his father and sliding his head up the pillow to get away from it.

"I'm sorry," Franklin said.

The boy looked at him. Franklin saw that he knew. He *knew*. That he was on the borderland between dying and living and it was even odds which side he'd be on at the end of the hour. That his mother wasn't there, because she loved his brother more. That his father was as afraid as he was.

Franklin's talents were limited to providing the child with assurances. *It will be all right. The fever will soon break. There is hope if you hold to it.* He rehearsed these lines in his head but knew he couldn't speak them without his voice cracking.

"I'll get some fresh water," he said, and stepped out into the hallway.

He stood there fighting for breath almost as loudly as Franky was. *Courage,* he told himself aloud. It came out sounding like a question.

Drr-eeee-tip. Drr-eeee—

It was the oddest thing. A weight on the floorboards moving in the boy's room. But there was no one there except the bedridden child.

"Papa?" Franky said, the voice clarified by terror.

Franklin spun around in time to see the bedroom door move. The boy saw it too.

The door slammed shut.

"Franky!"

The doorknob wouldn't turn. He noticed that first. And then he noticed how cold it was, his skin sticking to the brass.

Drr-eeee-tip. Drr-eeee-tip. Drr-eeee—

The movement inside the room heading away from the door, toward the bed. He could hear Franky's breathing tighten into squeaks. The heels of the boy's feet thudding the mattress as he struggled.

Franklin shouldered the door. There was a dull bump each time he did, but no give, no cracking. He might bring it down if he kept at it another twenty years.

"*Son!*"

He pressed his back to the hallway's far wall, held his arms out straight—

The door pulled open.

It took a moment for the room to be wholly revealed. Once it was, it took another moment to understand what was there.

Franky lay faceup in the bed, his eyes to the side, trying to find his father and, once they had, holding on him.

A man stood over the boy on the opposite side of the bed. His eyes were fixed on Franklin too.

Franklin went for him at the same time he recognized who it was. The tall stranger he'd spotted from the carriage window at his wedding. The one with his arm over his father's shoulder, drawing the life from him.

It was perhaps a half-dozen feet between the doorway and the bed, a distance covered in an instant. Yet it was time enough to watch the man sink into the floor. The stranger lowering with the speed of a man who'd broken through the ice of a frozen lake.

Franklin fell to his knees and laid his body protectively over his son's. Franky was still alive—Franklin could hear his heart popping in his chest, wavering, as if unsure whether to make the next beat its last.

"You're safe now," Franklin whispered. "I won't leave you alone."

Franky appeared to shape his mouth around a word. Something intended for his father, whether gratitude or grievance or farewell it couldn't be known, though Franklin had the idea it might have been a warning. And then the child's breathing stilled in his throat, and it was Franklin who was alone.

17

Nathaniel Hawthorne was the first guest to stay at the White House during Pierce's tenure. The author, Franklin's best friend at Bowdoin, was to come for a week, maybe longer if he felt like it. It was a show of gratitude on the president's part for Nate having written a glowing biography of the candidate in the run-up to the election. It also came from Franklin's need to have a friend to talk to instead of a general or senator or Jane, who was hardly speaking to him anyway, and when she did it was in her unsettling riddles about a damned path they couldn't stray from.

"Would you do me the honor of signing my books, Mr. Hawthorne?" Franklin teased as he wielded a stack of leather-bound novels in front of the author's face the moment he stepped through the front door.

"Is this *all* of them, Frank? I would've thought a busy solicitor and congressman—the president now!—was denied the time to read modern literature."

"Did I say I *read* them?"

While the purpose of fiction had defeated Franklin in college, he had sampled some of Hawthorne's writing. The most fantastical of the early tales had appealed to him, but it was *The House of Seven Gables*, published just two years earlier, that halted any further attempts at his friend's work. The idea of a secret-riddled family and a haunted mansion whose wood and stone remembered the sins of its inhabitants troubled him to a degree he was obliged to turn his back on.

"I will sign all that our leader puts before me," Hawthorne said, "but not before a kiss upon the First Lady's cheek!"

Jane allowed it. She nodded at the author's condolences, and wished him a pleasant stay before retreating upstairs once more. The truth, known to the three of them, was that she wasn't pleased with Nate staying in the house, given his role in eliciting Franklin's name for the convention ballot. Yet she insisted it wasn't her grievances about that, only the return of one of her "color headaches," that prevented her from joining the two of them for dinner on the first night.

After they'd dined, Hawthorne and Franklin stayed up late drinking whiskey in the Crimson Parlor, confident that Jane wouldn't venture downstairs to find them. They spoke little of politics, Franklin asking after Hawthorne's children; his wife, Sophia; his literary triumphs; and the state of works-in-progress. When Nate attempted similar inquiries after Jane, Franklin waved them away.

"For this evening, let's pretend this is the old tavern in Brunswick, not the president's house."

"Not a difficult request," Nate said, filling his glass from the crystal decanter. "I am, as is often stated, a master of the imagination."

Franklin and Nate had met in the Bowdoin debating club. Even at only seventeen, the latter introduced himself as "Nate Hawthorne, author." Before he became the most renowned American novelist of his generation, Hawthorne was Pierce's tutor. Each was the other's first best friend. Franklin was about to comment on their remarkable ascendancy when Nate spoke. "I knew this would be your place one day," he announced, finding himself, then Franklin in the Tiffany mirror over the fireplace. "You've always been a man other men will follow."

"But you can see through that bluff," Franklin laughed, sensing a joke at his expense.

"Me? I've been following you from the start."

Franklin lowered his glass. He inspected his companion's face and found something unreadable there, a blend of teasing and affection and weight.

"Why?"

"Other men are bound to forge their ways," Hawthorne answered, taking his time, as if lines he'd written in one of his stories. "But you are bound to have great things happen to you."

"*To* me?"

"Like a flame. And consequence is the moth."

Hawthorne loved him—loved in the awestruck way of an awkward younger brother for his elder—but now Franklin recognized the selflessness in his friend's feelings. Nate had a high regard for his own capacities, to say the least. But when it came to Franklin there was no competition, only the ceding of the stage to his perceived better.

"You're drunk," Franklin said.

"Not yet. Not completely. But perhaps another glass and we can speak of true things."

Franklin knew what he meant. The puzzle of marriage. Lonesomeness. Fear. *True things.* It had been so long that he'd been in the company of a friend, free from the surveillance of politics, that he almost doubled over with relief.

"I am heartbroken," the president said.

"At Jane's condition."

"Of course. But I was speaking of myself."

"You are grieving, Frank. What happened to poor Bennie—"

"Not only him. I'm grieving for the family I lost."

"Yet you are still here."

"Jane and I are still walking and talking, it's true. We *appear* to be living. But what we were together has been stolen from us. It's as if the death of our sons has left us dead too."

There was the sound of choked weeping, and Franklin assumed it was coming from himself. Then he raised his eyes and saw it was Hawthorne, his face oily.

"More whiskey?" Franklin offered, already reaching for the decanter.

"Has it ever been wrong to say yes to that?" Nate answered, his empty glass raised high.

Later, the two of them stumbling and leaning into each other in a frail balance, Franklin put Nate in the guest room down the hall from his, right next to Jane's. Before parting, Franklin pointed to the light coming from under her door, and the two of them broke into giggles, as if they were college pranksters sneaking back into their dormitory with the dean still awake.

*   *   *

In the morning, Franklin awaited Nate at the breakfast table in the state dining room. He thought it would be amusing for the two of them to eat their oatmeal in the grand chamber beneath the glinting chandelier. But when Hawthorne entered and took his seat Franklin could see his friend had lost the humor of the night before.

"The whiskey was good, though perhaps we swam too deep in it," Franklin said in sympathy.

"I slept poorly, it's true."

"Oh? There was a disturbance?"

"Yes." Hawthorne poured himself coffee from the silver pot but didn't drink it. "A remarkable disturbance."

Franklin saw his friend's upset through the lines of his face that had been deepened overnight. Penciled striations etched in his forehead and temples as if from the effort of holding his eyes tightly shut for hours.

"This sounds like the sort of thing one of your narrators would say before embarking on a wondrous tale," Franklin said.

"There's not the form for a tale. It was an occurrence."

"What sort?"

"A noise."

"Ah. So a yelp? A whinny? A cry of—"

"A child's voice. Coming from the bedroom in the northwest corner."

Franklin placed his cup down so hard he was surprised the saucer didn't crack.

"There are no children here," he said.

"That's why I rose and went to the door where the sound was coming from. When I entered—" He caught himself from speaking something he was not prepared to say aloud.

"The furnishings," he went on finally, choosing a different course. "They were Benjamin's, weren't they?"

"Jane brought them here."

"I'm not certain that's all she brought."

At this, Franklin suspected a joke. The hangover, the buried rivalry between Nate and Jane, the setup of breakfast in the mansion's finest dining room. It must be a continuation of last night's teasing. Because if he was describing an actual "occurrence," it wasn't Nate's way to talk around a thing, even if he sometimes brought an excess of poetry to the point. So the president waited for his friend's piqued expression to melt into laughter. But Hawthorne's unease only doubled as he struggled to bring his mind to where it didn't want to go.

"There was no child in the room," Nate said. "But it wasn't unoccupied."

"Who was there? The staff have been forbidden to enter. I will take it up with Webster."

"There was no *person*, Frank. Yet there—"

He stopped. Sipped from his cup. Winced as he swallowed.

"It's not my place to tell you what to do," Hawthorne continued. "But I wouldn't enter that room. Never. I certainly wish I hadn't."

"For God's sake, you're jabbering like one of the bloody witches in the Scottish play!"

Franklin was hoping this would, at last, pull a laugh out of Hawthorne. But the author remained severe, his pallor bleached.

"I've forged my vocation on the translation of experience into words," he said. "But there are no words for what I experienced last night. Or if there are, I choose not to speak them. I'm sorry."

This was absurd. Franklin tried to convince himself of it. He was mostly successful, as he was now concerned for his friend's state of mind, given he was saying such nonsense as this. He sounded like Jane. And yet a part of Franklin thought he understood him, believed him. Just as part of him understood and believed Jane.

"I'm sorry too," Franklin said, shaking his head. "I realize this is a strange old house. And I feel even stranger for having to live in it."

"You are committed to these walls," Nate said, rising from the table. "But I'm not. I won't stay here another night."

Franklin was astonished. Hawthorne was serious. More than serious— he was leaving. Running away.

"Dear Nate, don't go. We drank too much last night, and you slept poorly. Dreamed poorly. But we're not *children*."

"No, we're not," Hawthorne said, and took another step away from the table. "We're fathers. Which is why I must go."

"You miss your little ones so much after only one night?"

"I cannot explain this to you. But it's not just that I miss them. I feel that I must be near them. Protect them."

As you failed to do for yours. Franklin heard this, even if it went unsaid.

135

Hawthorne started for the door. At the sight of his retreat, Franklin felt at once a powerful sadness and stirring temper.

"You came here at my invitation!" the president shouted. "To leave like this—you couldn't blame a man for taking offense."

"I don't blame you for it," Nate said, looking back at him.

"Then make it right." As abruptly as it arrived, the anger in Franklin drained away, leaving only a gutted desolation. "Stay on, my friend."

Hawthorne didn't move. Even this plea wouldn't draw him back, though the regret of it knotted his brow and shrunk his frame.

"There's no way I will risk another hour here. I apologize for that," he said. "Not for the impoliteness of it, which I know you will forgive, but for my cowardice."

"Will you not speak directly of what you saw?"

"I won't. For my sake, for yours. For Jane's."

"And what of Jane? Why do you speak of her?" Franklin said, his voice rising again. "Your condescension toward me is one thing, but to direct it at my wife is another. Once Jane is well, I will be sure to bring this up with—"

"Jane is no longer of this world! I'm not sure she ever was!"

Franklin lurched in his chair as if he'd been punched. Nate had insulted his wife. No matter how troubled their union since coming to the mansion—no matter how right Hawthorne might be—he would not stand for anyone to hurt her.

"I believe you were right," Franklin said, standing himself, fists clenched. "You must go. And I ask you to do it now."

Hawthorne left the room and was gone from the premises before Franklin could find him to take back the threat in his tone, if not the words themselves. For the rest of that day the president hoped, after some conciliatory correspondence, his friend would return and stay longer his next visit. But the first letter came from Hawthorne. While it made clear his fondness for Pierce, it made clearer his intention to never set foot in the presidential mansion again.

Despite Franklin's repeated invitations, he never did.

★   ★   ★

Within the fortnight, Pierce awarded Nathaniel Hawthorne a choice post: United States consul in Liverpool.

"He will like it there," Jane remarked, not unkindly, when Franklin told her.

"I hope that he will."

"Yet I fear he will never write anything of consequence after this."

"Why would you say that?"

Jane blinked at him, her eyelids thick and slow.

"He told you, didn't he? The night he stayed?" she said. "He had a disagreeable encounter."

She must have been listening outside the door of the state dining room at breakfast. That, or she enlisted the steward to eavesdrop. How else could she know?

"You seem to know all about it," he said. "Perhaps you can tell me."

"It's not for me to tell. I only heard him from my room."

"Yes?"

"Thumping up and about. Then he rushed back into his room, locking the door. I believe he had a fright."

She was enjoying this. He didn't want to consider too long as to why.

"How does this lead to your conclusion about his writing?"

"It doesn't. That's only a guess," she said. "A whisper in my ear."

18

Over the days that followed the Fox sisters' visit, Jane spent most of her waking hours in Bennie's room. She liked to read there, sitting in the hard chair. Listening to the baby breathe in its crib.

Sometimes she would close her eyes and hum one of her melodies, the one she composed herself on the piano in the Amherst house and later sang to each of her children. The music was mischievous, sportive, a prelude to a fairy tale. But as with all fairy tales, it revealed something else beneath its surface as it went along. Even in Jane's own ears it eventually curdled, and she would stop, always with the sense of being watched by a presence behind her, outside of view.

When she sang she kept her voice quiet, especially when she felt the footfall of one of the staff pass by in the hallway, though she knew they heard her nonetheless. She was certain they would never enter. They had been ordered not to, for one thing. For another, they were too frightened to attempt it, given the way they slid along the wall opposite to Bennie's door on the occasions they had to venture to the west end of the second floor. Only Hany lingered there sometimes. Pacing back and forth along the middle of the hall. Waiting for Jane, wishing for her to come out of the forbidden room, but not daring to come within arm's length of the door.

Jane checked on the infant only when she first came in, confirming it was asleep. The head smooth and warm. The little fingers clenching and unclenching. The mouth pursed as if withholding improper laughter. She picked it up the first day, but not again after that. There was a stillness to the way it lay in her arms that was distinct from sleep. As if it didn't know how to receive affection. As if it was tolerating her.

She would sit in the feeding chair in a state between waking and sleep. Look to the crib, return to the thoughts she'd already lost.

Once she looked and found the child staring at her. Its face pushed against the bars of its crib as if attempting to slip through. She looked away, then back again. The baby was on its back once more, unmoving. She would have doubted she'd seen it in any other position had it not forgotten to close its eyes.

It never needed to be fed after the night of its arrival. It never soiled its diaper. It never cried.

On the sixth day the baby was gone.

Jane entered the room midmorning as she usually did. Franklin was safely out at Congress, the residence busy downstairs where Thomas Walter's workmen continued renovations in the public rooms, but relatively still upstairs where the improvements were complete. She closed the door behind her. This was what she'd done every other time she considered announcing herself in some way, or saying her son's name, but decided against it. She didn't want to hear herself declare the one thing she wanted most—*Bennie*—and for the quavering in her voice to allow admission of any doubt.

Her feet took her to the crib. A mother's obligation. It had to be that, as every other part of her wanted to leave. Jane's mind was able to convince itself that a baby appearing out of nowhere that resembled her own was acceptable, fortunate. But her body knew better.

The blankets were curved upward into a tent as they had been since she'd swaddled the child in them days ago. Yet now the child inside them was gone. The blankets hollowed out as if a tortoise had abandoned its shell.

Someone had stolen the baby. She thought this for only a second or two before dismissing the possibility. This was the White House. Who would have gained access to do such a thing? And then, more uncomfortably: Who would want it once they picked it up and felt how it didn't respond, didn't open its eyes, kept sleeping with a vacancy that was less than sleep?

She pulled back the blankets. Got to her knees to look under the crib. Nothing but pearls of dust. She lay flat to scan the entire floor. Under the bed, the chair, the dresser. That's where she saw the feet.

The dresser had been pulled out from the wall, leaving a gap between. Too small for an adult to hide. But sufficient space for a child.

One of the feet rose, drifted to the right, stepped down. The left did the same. It had been hiding. Now that it was detected, the game was over, and it was time to show itself.

Jane started for the door on hands and knees. Kept her eyes straight ahead, scuffing in orderly locomotion before tumbling forward, a desperate series of leaps and clawings.

She heard the sounds she was making on the floor. She also heard the child shuffle out from behind the dresser.

"Momma."

Her forehead was touching the door. She had only to raise a hand to the knob and she could scramble out, kick it closed once she was in the hall. But her son's voice held her to the spot.

Jane turned her head to the side. She did it slowly so that her neck wouldn't click, as if any sound from either of them would violate a rule.

Bennie stood there. A boy of the age of six or so, perhaps ten feet away. He had clothed himself from what he'd found in the dresser: pinstriped short pants and a white linen shirt with a lace collar. What Bennie wore to church on hot midsummer days.

"Are you cold?" she said.

Even to Jane this struck her as an odd first query to ask, but the truth was she wanted to know. Was he hungry? Was he hurt? All of these preceded what she knew ought to be of greater relevance. Was he Bennie? Was he returned? Was he dead?

Nothing in the boy's stance or expression altered. Yet she knew he'd heard her question. He just had no interest in it.

"Don't go, Mother," he said.

She grabbed the knob. Turned it.

The boy started for her as she pulled the door open. It was harder, at the low angle she was at, for Jane to swing it wide enough for her to fit through than if she'd been standing. She could only tug at it and wait for the door to come back at her before jumping forward.

"Let me . . . *out*!"

The boy slammed into the other side of the door the same instant she closed it, so that the two sounds came together in an echoing boom that traveled the hallway's length.

She waited for Bennie to plead with her, or cry, or screech, but the boy made no sound. He could easily open the door himself, and Jane flipped onto her back, watching the handle, waiting for it to turn. It didn't move.

Her breaths, taken in clicking gulps, was too loud to hear if another was breathing inside the bedroom, so she held the air in her lungs and slid close, her ear an inch from the wood. Listened. A silence sustained longer than she could deny herself from inhaling.

She had to get up. It was good luck alone that had prevented anyone from seeing her crawling out of what was known to be an empty room. She was aware that it was one thing to indulge herself inside it, on her own, but quite another if she was observed acting this way in front of staff, no matter how they'd pledged their discretion to her, no matter how they wished to avoid her altogether.

But she had to check. She had to.

Before she got up, she lay flat on the floor. Put her cheek to the frigid boards. Looked under the door.

He hadn't made a sound because he hadn't moved. The bare feet so close she could make out their odd lack of details. Veinless, the nails rounded as if filed, the rest unmarked by blue as the cold would've stained skin exposed to the chill as long as his had been.

She rolled away. Scrambled to her room. Locked herself inside.

Once she was there she stood at the threshold the same as Bennie stood at his. Feeling for any trace of a vibration from him. Her prayers that he remain where he was equal to those asking him to come out, come to her, be hers.

19

In the morning Jane mounted an assault against the day. She washed. Dressed. Tied her hair in the twin tails that was her custom before she came to the White House and gave up on tying it at all. Then she went down the main stairs and joined her husband in the private dining room.

At the sight of her, Franklin laid his spoon down in his bowl and rose so abruptly his legs slammed the table's edge.

"Careful," she said, "you'll hurt your sore knee."

"I can't feel a thing."

"It's the shock of seeing me."

"Not shock. Relief."

Jane felt it too. The thought that she could reenter her life, partial and marred as it was, by the application of powders and perfume and ribbons, was thrilling to her. She knew better though. There was the boy in the room upstairs. There was Sir. There was what she'd come down here to say.

She sat next to Franklin at the broad table and shook her head when a steward entered. When they were alone again, his hand strayed toward her. She took it. The memory of his strong fingers and thick palms on her body came simultaneously with the recognition of having missed several meals in a row.

"This is an unhappy place," she said.

"Is it the place or us?"

"We're unhappy too. There's something here with us though, making it worse."

Franklin nodded. "Tell me."

"It hasn't a name. The closest I could come would be to call it a thwarting from goodwill. Forces that constrain us, tell us we have roles now."

As was often necessary in speaking with Jane, he gave up on thinking through her words and swam with them instead, finding meaning through the quality of their temperature and touch. He wondered if this was the way it was between other husbands and wives.

"Like actors in a play," he said.

"But in the play, despite the palace we live in and its thrones for king and queen, we are powerless."

"And you've come to tell me you'd like out of the performance."

"No. I couldn't leave even if you allowed it. But I wanted to see if we could try to be who we were. If we could resist."

She looked at her husband and caught a flash of it: the way they once knew each other. A foundation of decency they reinforced together. The concession that while she would never totally know this man, she knew enough. Back then, when she encountered the rare reports of murder in the gossip of Amherst or Concord, she wondered the same thing: Was the killer's wife surprised? Did she know a shard of malevolence existed in her husband but had pushed it aside until the day he thrust the blade through the overbilling blacksmith or bickering neighbor or disloyal child and she saw that she'd been uselessly correct? Even in the thrall of courtship Jane was aware that Franklin wasn't guided by principle alone. What man was? The important thing was his goodness. A muddied form of it, to be sure, but one free of meanness or cynical calculation. He was uncomfortable when he lied, soothed when he confessed. His crimes were the fruits of passivity, not action.

"Be who we were," Franklin said, as if recalling the same time himself. "How would that be done?"

"By reaching beyond these walls. Doing the Christian thing."

"You're speaking of something in particular."

"Anthony Burns," she said.

All the newspapers were bursting with the name. Burns was a twenty-year-old man who escaped his slave-owners and made his way to Massachusetts, a free state. He'd recently been arrested in Boston and ordered to be returned to Virginia. Under the Fugitive Slave Act the matter was clearly settled, except that abolitionist protesters surrounded the prison where Burns was being held, demanding his release. In the melee, a US Marshal was stabbed and killed.

"You would have me let him go," Franklin said, pulling his hand from hers and reaching for his coffee cup before changing his mind, his stomach roiling.

"You are the president."

"It is the law, Jane."

"We're speaking of a single case."

"Cases such as these, if mishandled, can lead to others."

"Then handle it rightly. Release the man. And if it leads to other men being freed, then we're all the closer to a bad law melting like ice in June. You've said many times that you see the ownership of human beings as a practice that will retreat over time. Here is an opportunity to hasten its end."

Given her distaste for Washington, Jane's interest in politics was always surprising to Franklin. She read the newspapers as if preparing for an exam. She was especially alert to the human dramas that lived under the discussions of policy, such as the allowance of women to study medicine or the wagon trains of families headed westward under military escort, killing "all manner of Indian" along the way. For Jane, politics was fueled by the discernment between right and wrong. For Franklin, it was the way a nation remained united.

For the sake of their marriage, the slavery question was one they tried to avoid. Yet every topic seemed to find its way there eventually, forcing them to restate their views. Jane was sympathetic to abolition. While Franklin saw its philosophical merits, he believed it was a risk to national unity to impose on those in opposition to it.

Franklin looked down at the egg yolk smeared over his plate and saw it as a self-portrait.

"I am no advocate of slavery," he said. "I wish it had no existence upon the face of the earth. But as a public man I'm called upon to act in relation to an existing state of things."

"And what ought the president do when the existing state of things is in error?"

Franklin could be guilty of underestimating his wife on certain accounts, but he was always alert to her ability to find a way of knotting up the personal and the political. He preferred to see a space between the two, as his legal training had it: what a lawyer argued in court had no bearing on how easily he went to sleep that night. Jane never failed to point out the lie in this on the nights Franklin tossed and moaned in his bedsheets.

He pushed the toast rack her way. "Will you at least join me for some breakfast?"

"Will you consider my appeal?"

"Naturally."

"Then pass the butter, please."

★　★　★

That evening, when the congressional visitors and daytime staff were gone and the house was quiet, the hours when Jane was reading or weeping or writing letters to the dead or doing whatever it was she did in the room across the hall from hers, Franklin slipped down to the first floor, went into the Crimson Parlor, and poured himself a drink.

The whiskey was warm and alive in him. It felt like the only part that was.

When he wasn't occupied with his work, the residence closed in on him, stifling him with a combination of anxiety and heartbreak that sometimes left him gasping. He wasn't allowed to grieve his sons during public hours, and when he was in Jane's company he was obliged to be strong, show her what a recovery to normalcy might look like. The result was that he only permitted himself the full freight of his sadness in stray moments like these, always alone, always at night.

His tears made him cough so he cleared his throat with the rest of the amber in his glass. He took his time with the second measure, more generous this time. He sat in one of the straight-backed chairs that Thomas Walter had said was "traditional American design" but felt to Franklin like something churches made the choir sit on to prevent them from falling asleep.

He was drinking. Breaking his promise to Jane. But it was all right, because he was keeping another. In his mind, he forced his thoughts away from his boys to consider what his wife had asked of him.

It would be recklessness to make a decision of the kind she wanted him to. No matter the injustice of returning Anthony Burns to chains, this was a national issue, and he was the leader of the nation. Franklin had been chosen by his party to carry on in the predictable way he'd conducted himself as a congressman and senator, which is to say he would run the country by the same rules his father ran his tavern:

Appear to be in favor of both sides of any argument.

Business is always business.

If there were beatings to be done, one didn't hear them so long as they happened off premises and at night.

And it wasn't just the offense to Democrat insiders that made Jane's idea so imprudent. If Franklin Pierce were to start making freemen out of fugitives willy-nilly it would show a boldness he hadn't demonstrated in his career. History would note it, and as history tended to judge abrupt turns, condemn it. This is what made saying yes to Jane so dangerous.

It's also what made it appealing.

The party pleaders, the congressional flatterers, the New Hampshire fundraisers—they had all trapped him here in this sorrowful place, frigid as a crypt and with ladders and holes in the hallways from repairs that would never be completed. Now he had a chance to break out of the blinders they'd fixed to him. Stability, compromise, balance. They left him no room for change, for daring, for decision.

He took another sip.

He would do it. Letting Anthony Burns walk away from the stockade in Boston would be the closest he could come to letting himself walk away from the White House. And if they all saw him as reckless, at least they would *see* him. A president for once, instead of a custodian.

The glass was empty. Franklin didn't like seeing it that way.

He was about to get up to refill his glass when he spotted his father sitting on the satin banquette on the far side of the room.

The old man didn't appear as a ghost might. If anything, he was more real-seeming than if he were alive. There was a density to his presence, a particularity to his clothes, the shine of his boots, the filaments of hair reaching out from the tops of his ears, all the parts of him visible even at this distance. His face aglow not from fresh air or liquor but the over-stated colors of a painter's brush.

Franklin's father had started out a soldier. By the end of the Revolutionary War he was named a general, the head of the Eighth Massachusetts Regiment, a member of the Society of the Cincinnati. Honors that marked Benjamin Pierce as a man of bravery and distinction when in fact his primary accomplishments had been forging an acquaintanceship with George Washington and managing not to die.

Afterward, he turned his farmhouse into a tavern. It suited his disposition perfectly: the tolerance for lewdness, the capacity for roughness on the occasions a fellow had too much ale. Yet if one were to only listen to him one would assume that Benjamin Pierce was among the greatest heroes the Union had ever known. It was true that he had fought the English at Breed's Hill and Ticonderoga. But beyond that, there were questions the tavern patrons didn't dare ask. Had he actually killed Englishmen with his bayonet? His hands? How closely was he consulted by General Washington on tactics?

Only young Frank voiced these queries directly to his father. And he did it only once.

"There are some things men don't speak of," his father told him, which were precisely the same words he used when Franklin asked why some of the men took Caroline, the lunch cook, upstairs from time to time, only for both to return minutes later looking as if they'd beaten the dust out of a rug.

"Who are you?" Franklin asked the dead man now, his voice enfeebled by the room's size, the sudden arrival of drunkenness, and in the moment that followed his speaking, the panic that took hold of him.

"Are your eyes poorly, boy?"

His father had spoken without moving his lips. Franklin was sure of it. But when he spoke next, the mouth was in alignment with his words, as if a correction to an error he recognized on his first attempt.

"Speak up when your father's addressing you, Frank!"

"No, sir. I can see you fine."

"Then you know it's me."

"Not. It's—"

"What?"

"It's *not* you."

The man waved his hand in dismissal. "We can have a nice debate about that another time," he said. "I'm here to right your ship. Because you look ready to run her aground."

The whiskey's warmth was gone, leaving only a metallic taste in Franklin's mouth and a weight in his belly as if he'd eaten a handful of pennies. He was aware that he could get up and leave the room. It seemed impossible that the man who looked like his father would follow if he did. Yet he stayed where he was.

"This abolition business," the man across the room said. "All well and good. But you—"

"Who was that man with you?"

"I was *speaking*, if you don't goddamn mind."

Franklin winced at his father's sharpness. But the question had been tossing around at the back of his mind these past years, and now, unexpectedly, he had the chance to ask it of the only one who might have the answer as to the nature of the thing he'd glimpsed stealing the air from his poor Franky's lungs. So he asked it again.

"Who was the stranger next to you on the porch after my wedding?"

The old man nodded twice and sighed. In life, it was precisely the sequence of gestures he used to show he was addressing an audience he pitied.

"There's a lot you don't know," he said. "Most of it you couldn't understand even if you *did* know it. But I'm trying to *help* you here, son, and I don't have a lot of time. That all right with you?"

Now Franklin was nodding. "Yes, sir."

"Now then. This matter of bringing freedom to the enslaved. It will come in time. But rushing it? Like your skinny paddle of a wife would have you do? It's not the job for a man like you, Frank."

"I'm the president."

"And what's that? Someone for dullards to blame their failures on and patriots to pin their hopes to. You're like a painting of Jesus over a child's bed in place of Jesus himself—you hear the prayers but have no choice but to let fate have its way."

The more the man spoke, the more Franklin came to accept it was his father. Not the man dug free of his grave, but his counsel, his way of thinking being spoken through the too-convincing puppet seated under George Washington's portrait twenty feet away. It certainly was the sort of thing his father would say, and in his tone too. At once bullying and companionable, as if he was paying Franklin due respect by speaking to him with the hard honesty only afforded to friends.

"Wasn't Washington a president who made changes?" Franklin put to him.

"He certainly did. But it was easier for him. It was the *beginning*.

Now we're a going concern and there's no room for saviors. Not in this house."

"I want to go now," Franklin said, and was startled to find that he was crying.

"Y'see? Look at you! You don't have the bones to sit there and listen to your father, much less fix the country of all that ails it. You know *that* much, don't you? Maybe you learned it when you fell off your horse in front of your men and pissed yourself before fainting like a lady too fat for her corset." The old man nodded and sighed again. "You're not made for the hard stuff, Frank. Nothing wrong with that. You look good, talk good—you made it *here*. Now leave it be."

Franklin went to put his glass down on a side table, but when he let it go he saw there was no table there. The glass met the floor with a thump but didn't break.

"Pick it up," his father said. "You'll want a full one now."

Franklin bent over and hooked a finger under the glass's rim. When he pulled it up and looked across at the settee under the Washington portrait, his father was gone.

The glass slipped off his finger. This time, it shattered.

★　★　★

A plate of eggs, oatmeal, rack of toast. Franklin was alone in the private dining room when Jane came in. The same as the morning before, except this time she was smiling. Until he looked up and she saw him, read him, and she wasn't.

"You did it," she said. "Burns. You had him sent back to Virginia."

"It's in the papers?"

"I could tell from your falsely resolute face. It's the way you look when you're being most cowardly."

He absorbed her insult so readily she knew he was prepared for it.

"I was a fool to think I ever had a choice in it," he said.

"You're a fool to believe you don't have a choice in all things."

Jane intended this for him, but heard the way the sentence curled back to become a condemnation of herself. Franklin heard it too. She could see how he wanted to know what she had made a wrong choice about, but dared not ask directly.

He got up. Pulled back the chair next to his. She sat. He took his seat but didn't resume eating. The two of them looked at each other for a long while without doing or saying a thing.

20

"Bennie?"

Jane entered through an opening in the door just wide enough for her to squeeze through and closed it with her foot. The room was darker than hers, darker than any other in the house, so that she stood there waiting for her vision to adjust.

"Momma's here."

She kept her eyes on the orange in her hand and imagined it as a miniature sun, a piece of the sky smuggled underground. The boy never ate again after his first suckling, but she would bring him food anyway. An apple, a slice of buttered bread, a bowl of stew. Every time she would take the item away with her when she left, untouched.

Over the hours she spent in the Grief Room, Jane had forged a grounding for herself, a mental island of objectivity surrounded by the uncanny. It required the balancing of multiple paradoxes and was subject to erosion, but it held firm for the most part. For instance, she knew the boy was not Bennie, while maintaining the belief that he essentially was. The story she told herself was that he was her child but in a reborn state of some kind, returned from the afterlife but with differences attributable to his time away. He had seen inconceivable things. Of course he wouldn't be exactly the same today as he had been before.

She had answers for every question that demanded to be answered:

Why didn't he eat or drink? Angels had no need for bodily sustenance.

How did he grow from infant to crawling child within hours? For most, time inches forward like the hands of a clock, but for those who have been to heaven, it can also leap ahead.

If this Bennie was such a blessing, why didn't she share it with her husband? It would only make him afraid, and what men feared they destroyed.

As for his origins, she presumed Kate Fox had brought him back. Her, along with Jane. They had achieved a connection to the place where the recently passed go, the good ones, the innocent. They had done it through the power of Kate's talent and Jane's love. She tried to prevent Sir's role in the resurrection from entering her thoughts, but he did anyway, lingering there, a shade in her peripheral view.

She took pleasure in her time here, though it was of a queer sort. The closest experience she could say it was akin to were the feelings she would have for certain boys when she was young, Bowdoin students she found handsome as they passed by the house, whom she manufactured not only feelings for but a history too. First words, Valentine's gifts, first kiss. None of it was real, but even its simulation had a fizz of veracity to it, perhaps more than if she'd actually spoken with or kissed them. An image or two. The embrace of fantasy. The compensations of not being alone. That's all it took.

Jane and Bennie spent hours together over the late mornings and early afternoons, but it was time that was compressed while in the Grief Room. She would check the clock upon leaving and confirm the expired hours, yet remember only fragments of how they'd passed. The child crawling out from the corner to greet her. Her tidying his untouched clothes in the dresser. Offering him food that he would shake his head at. Sparse moments that amounted to half days.

She yearned to hold him. Sometimes she resisted this, anxious at how he might respond if she bent to pick him up, though whenever she did so he went voluntarily, if stiffly, into her arms. On other occasions it was the child who came to her. He would climb onto her lap when she sat in the feeding chair and let her stroke his hair or hold him against her with his chin resting on her shoulder. It made her wonder what expression he wore when he was facing away from her.

On the same morning Jane asked Franklin to consider releasing Anthony Burns, she stood inside the door of Bennie's room expecting to find him as she had before, sitting up in his bed, waiting for her arrival. When she lifted her eyes from the orange in her hand she found he wasn't there.

A different boy stood with his back to her, looking out through the curtained windows. When he heard her he turned and she could see that it was Bennie, though an older version of the boy. Not a toddler anymore. Eleven. As old as life allowed him to become.

"Stay back from the window," she said.

"I won't open it, Momma."

"It's not—I don't want people seeing you from outside."

He paused. A calculation of whether he was obliged to do as she said. After a measure of time, he drew back the finger that had parted the curtains and let it slide near closed.

"Nobody can see us now," he said.

She stepped closer but left enough space between them that neither could reach the other without taking further steps.

"You've grown," she said.

"I'm a *big* boy now."

"Too big to be picked up."

"Too big to play?"

"No, no. Never that."

He knelt on the floor and lifted one of the tin soldiers Jane had arranged against the wall. It was clear that prior to this the boy—whether as a toddler or as the eleven-year-old he was now—had never played with any of the toys when she wasn't in the room. They were always in the same position when she came, which was equally true of the covers on his bed. Everything untouched except the curtains he would part to poke his face through.

But now Bennie played with the soldier. The one decorated with the most medals on his tin chest. The general.

He didn't play the way other boys did. He made no voices for the toy or other imaginary characters, no interaction between the soldier in his hand and the others against the wall. He just moved it over the floor, one way and back again. Not guarding or marching or shooting. Pacing.

"It's not right, Momma," he said without looking at her.

"What's that, darling?"

"Keeping me in here. It's not right."

It hadn't occurred to her that that was what she'd been doing. Was it imprisonment to ensure a child was safe in his room at night? She was only doing what a mother would do in her own home. Yet she was not the mother of this being who was now staring up at her, the tin soldier still in his hand. He may not be a child in any sense that mattered.

"I'm not keeping you here. Not like that."

"Then am I free?"

She thought of Anthony Burns and all the men and women like him. This was her own son asking for his freedom, and she was denying him.

"This isn't a jail. I'm not a—" she said, and her thoughts became tangled in nuance. "You just have to stay."

"Why?"

"You'll get in trouble if you leave."

"I'll be good."

She swallowed and choked on it, her throat narrowed so that she had to concentrate to negotiate the passage of spittle and air.

"Are you good, Bennie?" she asked once she was able. "Are you my good boy?"

He stared at her with blank incomprehension. A half second later his face found its animation again, the sweet pout, the widened eyes, and Jane saw the answer to her question in the shift between the two. But just as quickly, when the child spoke again, she pushed what she'd seen from her mind.

"Of *course* I'm good, Momma," he said. "I'm yours."

She managed to fight off the reflex to step back when the boy approached her. He stopped a foot away. Closer than the normal space between two people who weren't embracing, even intimates, even mother and son. It forced Jane to cross her eyes when she looked at him, so that two half Bennies swam in front of her, trading places.

"There's no lock on the door," he said, reading her mind.

"No."

"So I could leave if I wished."

For the first time since entering, Jane sensed the lie in what the boy just said. If he could walk out on his own he wouldn't bother debating the point with her.

"Do you wish it?" she said.

"Yes."

"Then leave."

He glanced past her. Not to the door, but an angle off to its side, as if someone stood there prompting him.

"I'm a good boy," he said, looking back at her. "I do as my momma and papa say."

"I'm glad of that."

"Did you?"

"Did I what?"

"Did you always do what your daddy said?"

Her father in his sickbed. Confessing to the connection the two of them shared. *We're curious kitties, aren't we?* The promise he had tried to make her agree to.

"I was wrong when I didn't," she said.

Bennie stepped into her. He was tall enough now that the side of his head rested against the tops of her ribs, a small weight that doubled her efforts to draw breath. He was not her son. He was irresistible.

"You're perfect," she said. And then, correcting herself: "You look perfect."

She meant unharmed. There were no signs of the injuries he suffered in the train accident, or any scars or scabs of any kind. No dried sleep in the corner of his eye, no cold sores on his lips, no hair unaligned from the part combed into the left side of his head, though she had brought no comb or brush into the room.

"I'm born again," Bennie said, and did the first truly awful thing since coming back from wherever he'd gone. He raised his chin, tilted his head back an inch farther than it ought to have gone, and laughed.

The laugh, when the sound of it came out of him, wasn't her little boy's. It was hers.

PART TWO

RESIDENCE

21

There was a break in his agenda at lunchtime and Franklin used it to slip outside.

He found himself walking into the glass hothouse he'd never noticed in his carriage rides past from when he was a congressman peering enviously over the hedgerow. Inside, the wind was filtered out, leaving only the sunlight that warmed the vines and weeds in the pots. A quiet space, smelling of soil and the off-season memory of roses. Webster had called it the orangery. Franklin didn't know why it went by that name but it sounded right to him.

The calm allowed his thoughts to stray from duty for a moment. It let the memory of his boys back in.

Franky pleading for his mother in his final hours.

Bennie lying on the ceiling of the train car.

The two of them wrestling—Franky winning, Bennie letting him win—on the parlor floor of the Concord house.

Franklin's grief struck him with the force of a fist to the ribs, leaving him doubled over and choking.

"Sir?"

A man stood at the far end of the aisle between boxes of magnolias and crab apple blossoms. Franklin couldn't recall the gardener's name if he'd ever known it, though he appeared familiar.

"Good day," Franklin said, standing and swiping his face with the back of his hand.

"Are you in search of a cutting?"

"No, no. I just came out to—well, to be here."

The gardener nodded. "You aren't the first."

"Oh? Others have come to smell the flowers today?"

"No, sir," the gardener said. "Other presidents. I've worked here for some while and each of them has made their way to this place without accompaniment at one time or another."

"They must have liked the greenery as much as I do."

"Perhaps they did. Though I believe they came seeking refuge."

Franklin regarded the man. He appeared old, but he stood straight and strong. There was too great a distance between them to make out the expression he wore.

"I'll leave you in peace," the gardener said before Franklin could demand his name, and slipped out the hothouse's rear door.

Franklin pushed aside a pot of hibiscus and sat on the wood bench next to it. *Seeking refuge.* He closed his eyes.

His thoughts reached out to Jane. Given how far off she was from him now, it forced him to remember her in the past. Dancing in a Peterborough church annex, waltzing without the acceptable gap between their bodies.

There wasn't much to her, bodily speaking, then or now. Other girls offered a softness through their dresses. Jane's frame suggested only unwavering lines, boyish and taut. Yet it was her form that excited him most as he commanded his feet to slide with hers—*ONE-two-three, ONE-two-three*—and nudged close enough that his belt buckle left a fold in her sash. He wondered what it would be like to have her atop him, to submit to someone who, in her public manners, was always first to submit. He wondered what it would take for her to lose herself.

Even by the proper standards of the day their courtship was physically innocent. Held hands, his skin denied contact with hers by gloves worn even in the wilting July heat. Kisses like burns, brief and scalding and nursed for days after.

It was talk that took up their time together. Memories of childhood. Town gossip. Most of all they spoke of lost brothers. There was a strange excitement that accompanied their recollections of little John and strapping Charles, Franklin's older brother who was taken by fever. The passion for an absent body similar to what lovers feel for the presence of their beloved.

"There is nothing like seeing trust in another's eyes. The *real* thing," he recollected her saying one afternoon when they were walking on a river path that skirted under the willows.

"How do you know that's what it is?"

"Have you ever thought you've seen it?"

"I can't be sure."

"Ah, then you haven't," she said. "Because when you *see* trust, you know it."

He heard how certain Jane was, a confidence bordering on mania.

"When I sat by John's sickbed," she went on, "the two of us with full knowledge that he would not recover, he believed me when I told him it would all be right. That God would protect him. That I would never let him go."

"He trusted you even though what you said wasn't true."

Jane stopped.

"Of *course* it was true," she said. "I would *never* let him go."

"Say it to me then."

"What?"

"Tell me you'll never let me go. Look into my eyes. Read my trust."

She nodded several times as if counting the ticks of a clock in her head. Then she stared into him without blinking.

"I will never let you go," she said.

The gorgeousness of the words struck him like a line from a psalm, transporting and pure. And then the feeling that followed: a warmth in the pit of himself like the dawn of a tiny sun.

He had been in love with her for some time but only recognized the fullness of it now. In her eyes he saw that she loved him too, and more. She had fostered it from the beginning, made their love grow into the oddly beautiful thing she had pruned it into being.

"Yes," she said, nodding deeper this time. "I see it."

Franklin remembered the strange conviction of her face, and with its memory Franklin sensed someone in the orangery with him. He opened his eyes expecting to see Jane standing there, or the gardener. But it was neither. It was Abby.

"I knew you liked to hide out here," she said.

"It's a glass box. How could I be hiding?"

"Nobody would look for the president in a greenhouse."

"You did. You found him, too."

He didn't intend this to be flirtatious, but heard it as such. He could have said the exact same things to Jane and it would leave a ring of accusation, or self-pity, or resignation in the air. *How could I be hiding?* But with Abby, they were veiled provocations no matter his caution. *You found him, too.* He wondered if she heard it, and if she liked it if she did.

"If you would prefer your privacy—"

"No, please stay."

There it was again. His genuine want for her company coming through where he intended to convey mere politeness. Abby looked along the rows of pots and found the only possible place for her to sit was right beside him, so she remained standing.

She was struggling to find a way in to whatever she wanted to say. Franklin was content to wait, remembering the woman in front of him from the dinners she'd attended as Jane's substitute. She had a dress he liked. Dark violet, with a thread in it that caught the candlelight, sparking. He would look at her across the long table of the State Dining Room and always, at first, see her as Jane. And then, in the following moment, he corrected himself. What distinguished Abby from his wife was her cheerfulness. Attentive nods to whatever tired anecdote the man next to her was repeating, a warm smile for the guest of honor at the raising of glasses.

It may have only been a performance of her duties. What difference did it make if it was? A marriage often amounted to the same thing. Kindnesses offered when one least felt like it, providing an audience when one's mind longed to be elsewhere. Why couldn't Jane at least *appear* alive, even if her inner world was fixed on death? She could do it for herself, if not for him. Franklin had found that, sometimes, pretending to be something was the first step toward convincing yourself of it.

"I came to speak to you about— There is— I'm *concerned* for you, Franklin. For both you and Jane," Abby started, and touched her cheek, checking her finger as if to see if a cut had healed. "I'm concerned for my own well-being too."

"Is there someone troubling you?" he said, disappointed to see Abby so downcast, so much like Jane. "I'll remedy it if there is."

"It's not mistreatment. It's that I'm—such a *strange* thing to say—I'm losing myself."

A number of interpretations arose in Franklin's mind as to what she might mean. *She was dissatisfied with her work. She had diagnosed herself of unsound mind. She was falling in love with him.* He had always been hopeless at feeling his way to indirect meanings.

"Perhaps you're tired," he said. "Heaven knows that Jane found these dinners and luncheons exhausting to the point—"

"I *know* what Jane feels," she interrupted. "That's what I'm saying. It's like I'm not just her substitute anymore. I'm *her.*"

He saw it the same instant she said it. More than the similarity in appearance the two of them shared, there was a merging of Abby into Jane he could detect in the lines at the corners of her eyes, the too-tightly-pulled-back hair, the suppressed alarm in her voice.

"I'm asking too much of you."

"Please don't take this as complaint, Franklin. I don't mind getting dressed up and minding my manners at your events. What disturbs me is knowing with such closeness what it is for Jane to have lost . . . all she's lost. And knowing that now, in this place, there is nothing to stop her from getting a piece of it back."

"What piece? I don't understand."

Abby tapped her heels on the dirt floor, trying to think of another way of getting to where she wanted to go. She had said far too much already. But she wouldn't let herself turn around and go. So she decided on a direct query.

"Couldn't you and Jane live elsewhere?"

"It's the presidential residence. I'm the president."

"Of course. But there's nothing to stop the president from sleeping and working across the street, or in Baltimore, or Boston, is there?" She glanced over her shoulder at the building looming behind her. "Anywhere but there?"

Franklin wondered if Abby and Jane were working in concert. Or perhaps what Abby was saying was meant in the literal sense. She *was* sharing Jane's mind. And whatever illnesses dwelled there had passed over to her.

"There would be an outcry," Franklin explained deliberately, working for the balance of gentleness and authority he tried to hold with his wife in such discussions. " 'Not good enough for the Pierces? They've left a mansion so the rats can call it home?' You know better than anyone that half of what I do is pageantry. And having the man the people voted for live in that big house is part of it."

As he spoke, Abby came to a decision. She would tell him. About the revue she saw in New York, the tune about the Fox sisters she'd told Jane about, the invitation the First Lady made that brought the mediums to the residence to perform a ritual of some sort. How everything had changed since then. An enmity brought into the White House capable of assuming different forms. All of them delivering the same message of hopelessness, leaving your spirit depleted, disenfranchised.

She was lining up the sequence of details in her head when she heard someone call her name.

It didn't come from outside but directly behind her.

A-bi-gail.

A man stating one word, slow and clear yet with each syllable corrupted. It made her swing around. No man was there. But the house was. She saw something in it that held her, erased the confession she was composing like a wet cloth clearing a slate.

"Who's that?" she said.

"Where?"

She pointed. "There. Do you see?"

Franklin stood next to her. Followed her trembling finger to a window at the end of the second floor.

"A child," he said. "A boy."

"What's he looking at?"

"Us."

It was hard to make out much through the smudged windows of the hothouse, the glare of the sun, the distance between them and the mansion. Yet there was enough for Franklin to piece together. As his mind grappled with the impossible, the boy in the window stood still, gazing down at him, as if wishing to be observed.

The window he stood in belonged to the room across from Jane's.

There were no children in the White House.

The brown suspenders and lace-collared shirt the boy wore were Bennie's. His hair parted like Bennie's. His grin an unfriendly version of his son's.

"Oh . . . *Christ.*"

Abby swung around to find Franklin kneeling on the floor. Her first thought was that he was moved to prayer. Then she saw how the hands in front of his face weren't palm to palm, but covering his eyes.

"Franklin! Are you—"

"Is he gone?"

She looked up at the house. The boy was no longer standing at the window, though the curtains had slid shut to prove that, until a moment ago, someone had been.

"Yes."

"Are you certain?"

"There's no one there."

He pulled his hands away yet still refused to look through the glass. His eyes held to Abby's.

"I must return to work," he said, standing.

"You saw who that was, didn't you?"

"I saw a child, nothing more."

"Franklin. That's not—surely you—"

"I must return."

He moved past her, their shoulders meeting as he went. It brought forward the breath she'd held and he felt it against his face. Warm and smelling of licorice.

"Perhaps I'll see you tonight?"

Once more he was muddled by possible meanings. Did she mean a chance meeting in the hallways? Was she mistaken about a dinner scheduled in the evening's calendar? Or was she opening herself to another kind of intimacy altogether?

"Yes," he said, anything more risking misapprehension. But yes was enough.

22

When Jane's youngest brother, John, took ill at the age of three, he was assigned to a bed in the nursery. Jane discovered his dying offered her a new power: the observation of horror. She stayed at his side, tending to his fever as best she could, but mostly watching him. Death wrapped itself around her little brother, everyone's favorite, and Jane was at once panicked and awestruck.

She was there for it, closest to it, because she was her mother's "little helper." While she attended to her housecleaning and laundry chores with languor (her illnesses were most severe when asked to do things she didn't want to), Jane was a devoted caregiver to the boys. She hovered around the three of them with hands that wiped and stroked and slapped, calling them "my tiny ones," doting on them with a maternal passion that well surpassed their own mother's. In a practical sense, Jane *was* their mother. And she cherished the license that came with the position: the responsibility, the discretion as to who was fed or warmed first, the choice between offering or denying comfort.

John's passing—the moment itself—was transformative. For the boy. But also for Jane. The life in him undeniably there. Then undeniably not. A line between the two that most couldn't see, or turned away from. Not Jane. She saw it for the arbitrary thing it was. A rule that, like any rule, might be broken if you were possessed of the will and means.

Three days after John died Jane entered her father's study and took the pendulum game out of the bottom drawer.

That was why she was able to do it without being detected, why the house was empty except for her. It was the boy's funeral. All of the Appletons were gathered by the hole in the ground of the Bath Road cemetery, tossing earth upon the box. Jane was too ill to attend. Her stomach. Her headache. She offered her parents different excuses but they weren't really listening, ascribing her pains to grief.

The truth was Jane wasn't interested in putting things into the ground. She wanted to see what would come out of it if you asked.

★　★　★

Ever since she'd arranged her son's furniture there and Kate Fox helped deliver a child to its crib, Jane hadn't gone an entire day without visiting the Grief Room until today.

She made excuses to herself as to why. A fever that lurked in her chest. The need to sign off on one more letter to her sister, or finish one more chapter in her book. In fact, twice she had made the thirty-foot journey across the hall to stand by its door. And twice she had returned to her quarters, shivering, as if she'd walked the perimeter of the South Lawn in a nightdress and bare feet.

She wanted to see Bennie. It was her duty as a mother to ensure his comfort. He might be afraid. He might be hurt. While it was defensible to keep the boy safe inside, it was wrong to leave him there all on his own. These thoughts formed one side of the ledger in her mind. On the other were more troubling calculations. The child in Bennie's room was a danger to her and anyone else who came close. He was a creature that was in part hers, in part Sir's. He would try to get out if she opened the door.

In the evening she left her room and kept to her side of the hallway. She made a point of not looking at Bennie's door in case she could see the shadow of his feet on the other side, or if it was ajar, or if her looking triggered his voice to call out. There was no one else in the second floor's central hall. While her intention was to find Franklin in his office or in the room where he slept close by, when she came to the top of the main staircase she abruptly turned and started down.

She knew there were other people currently in the White House with her. During the day there were sentries, maids, stewards, the women who cooked and baked, the men who tended the furnace, along with the workers on the first floor inching forward on the structural renovations. But the political business and carpenters' work was over now, dinner served and cleared, so many would have left. In fact, the White House at night was a mostly empty place. How many remained? Six, seven? Ten? Whatever the number, they would most likely be on the ground floor. So long as she didn't go down that far she could feel as if she was the only living soul in the mansion.

On the first floor the gaslights had been lowered so that Jane had to pause at the bottom of the stairs to orient herself. Perhaps it was because the ceiling was higher here than on the residential floor, but it felt to her that she had descended into a much larger building, or perhaps not a building at all. A living thing in the midst of transforming from a house to what now stretched out before her as an endless tunnel.

It made her dizzy. To find her balance, she walked.

Past the closed doors of the state dining room on one side and the pantry on the other. In her peripheral view she could see that the entry to the private dining room was open wide, but she refused to look inside. She was certain that if she did, she would find something awful there. A being—a *smudge* was how she thought of it—that watched her as she passed on and shuffled to the Crimson Parlor, where she appeared about to carry on before abruptly slipping inside, eluding the emptiness that pursued her.

The room was brighter than the hallway. Had the staff forgotten to shut off the gas? It seemed unlikely. Which made her being alone unlikely too.

"It's Mrs. Pierce," she announced, introducing herself to the unoccupied chairs and settees. "Is anyone here?"

No one replied. But something moved.

She didn't hear it exactly, nor see it. There was the room as it was, and then the room that followed her query, the two atmospheres distinct in the way of the sun slipping behind a cloud in the time you blinked.

She hadn't noticed the piano when she first entered. Could that have been the difference? A baby grand piano appearing between one second and the next? In any case, it was here for her. Certainly she had never heard it played. Perhaps music was what was missing from this place. It would be her holy water, or burnt sage, or whatever talisman she'd read that witches or priests used in the cleansing of befouled homes.

The bench squeaked when she sat on it. Once the quiet was restored, she lifted the polished lid. The keys shone like animal teeth. She set her fingers down to begin, then raised them. She did the same thing again without pressing a note. Her mind was clear of the sheet music she'd studied at Fiske's Boarding School, and she was unable to remember any of the Mozart or hymns she once knew by heart.

The only thing she could play was an improvisation. Once begun it came to her easily. More than easily—it was like she wasn't playing at all. The tune started out buoyantly, like a march. As it went along, it fell apart. The major chords interrupted by minor-key digressions, bass thuds breaking the melody into fragments. To Jane's ear, it was like the failure of music more than music itself, the revelation that it was only ever hammers striking wires.

You are the instrument, Jeannie.

Sir whispered this so close it was as if he was sharing the bench with her. She lurched to the side, but the broken tune continued. Her fingers kept playing even when she tried to pull them away.

She pushed against the pedal struts with her feet, threw her head back, any part of her that responded to the command to break free. For a moment her arms were stretched so far from the keyboard she felt a pop in her shoulders, first left then right, following by a searing pain in both. If she pushed any harder she could imagine her arms ripping away. But she couldn't listen anymore. There was madness in the music. That, and terrible pain, a wordless history of it.

She knew she was free when she opened her eyes and found herself on the floor. The bench tipped onto its side. The piano's lid shut.

No one had come to investigate either the music or the sound of her fall. Jane knew that the staff did their best to avoid her. If they attributed the piano playing to her it was probable they would have stayed away no matter what other sounds came out of the room.

She rose, rubbing her shoulders, and made her way to the hallway without looking back into the parlor. There was a worry that something would be there if she did. The same smudge she sensed in the private dining room, or maybe a different one. A whole number of the dead showing themselves, finding a way to be seen through her.

She paused in the hallway and thought of returning to her room. But she was no more protected there than anywhere else. And if she went back upstairs now she would be compelled to check on Bennie, something she could avoid so long as she remained shuffling along down here.

At the Cross Hall's end the oversize doors to the East Room stood closed. Jane remembered looking inside when she first arrived and being astonished by the size of it. A ballroom that could accommodate hundreds. She wondered, as she pulled one of the double doors open, if they would come spilling out, trampling her in their rush to escape.

The room was empty except for the woman.

Standing across the forty feet of floor, wearing a mourning dress, starved and with eyes yellow as custard. Jane waited for the witch to come at her. The woman matched her stillness, studying her, working out where she'd seen her before.

The otherness.

Her father's deathbed phrase came to her, and with it the recognition that the witch was Jane herself. A reflection standing at the threshold in the great gilt-framed mirror on the opposite wall.

She stepped inside. Her eyes moved to her feet, as if she was crossing a flood-rushed river while balancing atop a fallen tree. The darkness around her widening into pools. Bottomless, but not unpeopled.

In what she guessed was the middle of the ballroom she stopped. Looked up into the mirror.

The dead lay around her in piles. Not in neat stacks like firewood, but a chaos of limbs and heads that came up high as her knees. Unlike the smudges she had glimpsed earlier, these were exclusively the casualties of war. Those that had already occurred, as well as those to come.

The more Jane watched through the mirror, the more she could make out the individual men lying around her. Not all of them were still. Some shuddered, or writhed about, or raised a hand for help—all dead but for these final reflexes.

There were soldiers of the Revolutionary War wearing red waistcoats over their chests, their white pants soiled by blood or dirt or human filth. There were also bodies dressed as soldiers but wearing colors and garb she'd never seen before. Hats of smaller size, gray and blue, some shaped like boxes on their heads. These men made up the greatest number by far. Jane had the idea that they were those lost in a conflict yet to take place. Their torn bodies entwined with the dead that came decades or centuries before in an indistinguishable mass.

Some of them had more life left in them than others. Missing arms or legs or blinking through the blood that streamed into their eyes yet still fighting to crawl over the bodies beneath them. Their movements made Jane think of the bugs she'd watched her older sisters burn with a magnifying glass. Not to kill—not right away—but to scorch with disfiguring heat. Ants, wasps, beetles, spiders. They all died differently. That's what made her sisters laugh. Jane never used the magnifying glass herself. Yet she couldn't pull herself away from watching each of the insects curl or leap or drag themselves over the ground, a pointless struggle to find a hiding place she saw as akin to her own.

One of the soldiers found her leg.

She looked down. Saw nothing there. But in the mirror's glass he had pulled himself out of the vines of bodies to claw at her. He was one of the ones wearing a uniform she didn't recognize, a navy sack coat with yellow buttons undone as far as his heart. He was young, pimpled, weasel-snouted—an ugly boy made uglier in his terror. His hands wrapped around her thigh and attempted to pull himself up but the blood was too plentiful to find a dry holding. Each time he would slide down, his cheek resting on the side of her knee. On the third try he went down and stayed there, his eyes fixed on hers.

Someone was screaming.

She assumed it was herself. Then she heard it as a man, though none of the ones lying on the floor of the East Room. It was coming from the floor above. The voice familiar but its shrieking distortion new to her ears.

Her husband.

There was a pause for the intake of breath, then screaming again. Over and over until his voice broke and Jane was alone once more in the silent tide of the dead.

23

Franklin fought to stay awake. He wanted to see what Abby meant in the orangery.

Perhaps I'll see you tonight?

He lay there, waiting, his thoughts alternating between guilt and his rebuttals to it. He'd been abandoned by his wife. He was on the verge of collapse. He had never felt more alone in his life. The most persuasive excuse was the one he least wanted to dwell on: there were no rules in this house. Behind the whitewashed columns there lived a corruption, something secret and alive and ready to compensate his public propriety with private debasements.

He tried to push back against his shame by remembering Jane. It often helped to go back to the same night in his mind. Dancing together at the barn-smelling church annex in Peterborough. The vivid conjuring of *her*: the combination of voice and body that charmed him then, but that now offered him the sense of direction he had lost.

At some point he must have slipped into sleep because when he rose back into consciousness he wasn't alone in his bed.

Next to him was a warm body. It slid up against him, the fingers unbuttoning his nightshirt, laying the two halves aside, stroking a hand down from his throat to his stomach.

"Abigail," he said, and heard it as unnecessary. It was her. His gratitude and excitement made clear by his body. He resolved not to speak again.

Twice he attempted to rise up on his elbows to touch her as she was touching him, and twice she pressed him back down. She had intentions for him. It felt—what would the word be?—*ungentlemanly* to be so passive as this. Yet once her movements revealed a clear plan he was happy to submit to it and let her show him what she wished him to.

Abby was smaller than he was expecting, smaller even than Jane. And swifter too, her hands and fingers scrambling over him in a way that felt beyond the capacities of one person. He momentarily wondered at the source of her expertise. Did it matter? No. He couldn't think of a single thing that did.

He felt a heat between his legs and lay fixed by astonishment. His hardness had been taken in her mouth. It was indescribably lovely. In place of words, it brought a cascade of sensory memories: the mist from a waterfall in the woods behind the Bowdoin campus, a March snow he let fall on his upturned face, the first spoon of soup for supper after missing lunch on a long hike. What was happening had never happened to him before.

Her mouth held him and stroked him for some time before he noticed the music.

A jaunty march he didn't recognize being played on the piano. It sounded like it was coming from a keyboard rolled up to the grass outside his window. He wasn't really listening. As if to gain his attention, the melody soured, morphing into discordant plinks and chords of distant thunder. It sounded to Franklin like the music of nausea.

He fought to ignore it. It wasn't difficult, given the wondrous distraction Abby was providing. Even the fleeting consideration that it was Jane's playing failed to pull him out of the moment. Soon the music ended entirely—abruptly, with a thud he felt come up through the floorboards—and his mind returned to the sensations of waterfall mist and hunger.

Tap, tap, tap.

The knocks at the door lacked the urgency that Webster or a messenger would bring to it if there was an emergency. He lay there hoping he hadn't heard it at all.

Tap.

A delicate knuckle against the wood.

Abby had retreated under the bedsheet, leaving him slippery and cold. He almost asked her who she thought could be outside, but worried even their whispers would be detectable from the hallway.

That's when he calculated the time between the end of the piano playing from downstairs and the knocking. Enough, he thought, for someone to make their way from the Crimson Parlor to his room.

He swept the covers off and pulled his trousers on. With the blankets piled on one side of the bed he didn't think it would be immediately obvious that someone lay hidden beneath them. His concern was that Abby wouldn't be able to breathe under their weight for too long.

It took him three strides to reach the door. Each step bringing with it a conclusion built upon the one that came before.

It was Jane.

She had come to ensure he was alone.

He couldn't let her inside.

At the door he wondered if the thing that had been done to him in his bed could be smelled, or read on his face. Too late either way. Because he was pulling it open and she was there.

"Forgive me. I know it's late, but— Franklin? Are you all right?"

Abigail stood there.

"I don't—"

"I was on my way out when I heard the music," she said. "It was Jane playing. Did you hear it?"

"Yes."

"I went to see if I could provide her company and saw her go into the East Room. She's down there alone. I'm worried that—"

"I will see to it."

"It's just as I said earlier. There's something—"

"I will see to it, Abby. Good evening."

He closed the door before she had turned away. He pivoted on his heel, looking back across the three-step distance between himself and the bed.

The blankets shifted. They had been moving as he stood there, and now, with his eyes on the bed, they continued to rise and roll for the length of a hiccup before they went still.

He took a step. Another, and another. Each unveiling a new horror in his thoughts.

It is Jane lost to madness.

It is something dead.

It is the thing—not alive, but from a place deeper than the grave—they'd felt in the house.

He was about to leave, to start the long negotiation with his rational mind that he hadn't seen or felt anything over the past minutes that bad dreaming couldn't explain, when a spot in the blankets bulged upward.

His hand grasped the top of it. Threw the covers back over the vacant half of the bed.

The tin soldier lay on its back. He recognized it as one of Bennie's. The general. The toy's medals and uniform and bodily features the same as Franklin recollected. All except for the mouth. Closed in stern determination before, it was now open, the lips reddened as if with fresh paint. Glistening.

Franklin reached out his hand, expecting to be bitten, or have his fingers slashed by the general's sword, or have it utter a laugh at the string of spit swinging from his chin that he dared not wipe away for fear of losing his balance and falling forward.

It didn't move.

But when Franklin touched its metal cheek, it was warm as flesh.

24

Webster came to Jane's room in the morning.

"The president would like a meeting, ma'am," he said. "*Franklin*, that is."

"A meeting?"

"In the Blue Room. If you would be so kind."

"When?"

"As soon as you're able."

Webster continued to stand there with brows raised in what may have been an acknowledgment of his errand's strangeness. After an awkward stretch, Jane realized he was waiting to accompany her downstairs.

"I'll need to wash," she said.

"He's made a space in the calendar. This present space."

Jane considered making a remark, something to lower those furry brows of his, but saw there was no point. Webster was doing his job. In this building, in the whole of Washington, when someone took precedence over the will of another, it was only someone doing their job. And she was aware of her place in things. The First Lady. The wife.

Ever since she was a child Jane felt that she alone among the Appleton women saw the full injustice of being born a girl. Her sisters never seemed to notice it, or if they did, they embraced the rules and excelled within them, "getting along" as her sister Mary liked to put it. Her mother did her best to instill her daughters with a sternness that might preserve them. But whether through getting along or a cold heart, Jane didn't see a way of escaping the constraints of womanhood, at least not in the outside world. So she moved inward. Reading. Music. Daydreaming. She built a wall with a single door around herself.

This is how, as she grew older, Jane came to see love the same way she'd seen the occult: it was a way through the door. She lived inside her mind so much yet longed for the world, its exchanges and caresses. For a boy, such passing between the mind and the body was not only possible but cultivated. For a girl, it would require sorcery.

"Very well," she said now, tying her hair back in a tail and following Webster to the first floor, where he admitted her into the oval sitting room. Once she was inside, Webster shut the door with a firmness she heard as resentment at not being a party to the discussion about to occur.

A couple of things struck Jane at the same time.

The first was that Franklin stood opposite the door, as far from her as the dimensions of the chamber allowed, yet even from this distance she saw how bloodless his cheeks were, his hair a greasy nest atop his head.

The second was that he stood next to a walnut chair in which sat one of Bennie's toy soldiers. The general.

She started toward her husband but he raised his hand, as if there was something about himself he wished for her not to observe in any greater detail than she already had.

"Do you remember this?" he asked, and glanced down at the toy.

Jane glanced at it too. The crimson-jacketed assembly of hammered steel and bolts, propped up with its legs out straight, sword raised. Had it been in that position when she first entered? It must have only been the clarity brought by the few steps nearer she'd taken. Yet she believed she could see it grinning now. The slightest curls at the edges of its lips that were stern points before.

"It's Bennie's," she said.

"This may strike you as an odd thing for me to ask, but did you have a hand in putting it in my room?"

"Your room?"

"I found it in my bed. As whoever put it there intended I would."

"Your *bed*?"

"Stop parroting me and answer."

"It wasn't me."

"Do you know who it was?"

Yes, she wished to say, practicing it in her mind. *It was a spirit I've called Sir, and whom others have called Splitfoot, others still something else, though it has no true name. It brought Bennie back. It showed me dead soldiers in the East Room mirror, but what it really wanted was to show me the dead to come. It cannot enact change on its own, but it can change people if they let it. As it's changed me. Changing you now too.*

"No," she said.

He cast his eyes over the ceiling, raised his foot as if to advance, then brought both eyes and foot back to where they had been.

"I'm having the most miserable dreams," he said.

"Funny you say so."

"Why?"

"I'm not dreaming at all."

"None that you can recollect in the morning."

"There is nothing to recollect. My worst dreams are real here."

It came out sounding like wifely misgiving and Jane moved closer to him, not stopping this time when he brought up both his hands to hold her back. As she approached she shifted her gaze between her husband and the general, the former losing color with each footfall as the latter grew in vividness, the little face obscenely rouged and eyelashed as one of the whores of unguessable age that Jane had to walk past outside the theater at the end of a play.

"Oh, Jeannie," he said when she was close enough to be held, though he made no move to do so.

"You're spent."

"Do I look so poorly? It's true that the mirror is not my ally."

"And after a lifetime of such favorable judgment."

Once more her comment came out in a tone she hadn't intended, but Franklin let it go with something akin to a low chortle.

He shuffled backward to take one end of a settee that Walter, the designer, had reupholstered in blue velvet. Franklin's body sank into the cushions as if they were stuffed with water.

"Come," he said.

She sat next to him. As it appeared he was unwilling to reach out to her, she thought of putting her hands aside his face to show that she wanted to connect with him, not repeat their old quarrels. But at her approach he involuntarily leaned away and she saw how shaken he was. How he felt unsafe at the idea of her touching him.

"I'm sorry," he said.

"For what?"

"Bringing you here."

"You didn't," she said. "I brought you."

He straightened. Even in his agitated, underslept state, his pride was capable of being offended.

"You've made great sacrifices for my career that I appreciate, and you've been a valuable counsel to me over the campaigns," he said, wrestling his irritation down as he spoke. "But in fairness, I think I had a part in it."

"That's not what I mean."

"Please share what you do."

"We've been *used*, Franklin."

"That is politics. Everyone feels it."

"Not by the party. Used by a higher design."

"I don't believe God has a hand in determining who wins elections."

"Nor do I."

She needed him to see it for himself. There would be no way of outright announcing what she knew—the role that Sir had played in her life, their courtship, his presidency, their deceased child's return—without him rejecting the notion and her along with it. He had to be *closer* to knowing before she could reveal all she knew. She was confident now that he was halfway there. Jane saw Franklin's reflex to cling to her literal meanings yielding inch by inch to the mystical, the unspeakable.

"I believe I know what you're saying," he said. "I have been used—been an instrument—my entire life."

Jane recalled Sir describing her in the same terms as she played at the piano the night before. *You are the instrument, Jeannie.* She wondered if Franklin had heard the voice too. Perhaps he was now about to admit it, and she waited for it.

"Look at us! Here we are in the most powerful house in the nation and yet we're talking as if we're no more than pieces in a game!" He cast his eyes toward the general and lifted an arm to point to it, but decided against it, as if even an extended hand would put his fingers too close to the thing. "No more than toys."

He placed his hand on the cushion between them. She couldn't tell if it was an offering to her, or to buttress his unsteady balance. Whatever the case, she placed her hand atop his.

"I'm worried of the influence life here may have on you," he said. "And because I treasure you, because you're all I have left, I ask if you would consider living elsewhere."

"Leave you?"

"To be safe."

She pulled her hand away.

"Would Abigail stay on?"

"It wouldn't be proper if she did," he answered, his shoulder twitching as if tapped from behind. "I'll find another substitute. Or get along without one."

"I will not go."

"There are things I have seen in these rooms, Jeannie. The most terrible things."

"I won't—"

"The country has called *me*, not *you*."

"I'm not staying for the good of the country, nor for you. I'm staying for my son."

"Your son?" Franklin stood. He was shaking. "Your son is dead! All our boys are dead!"

Jane heard the accusation threaded through Franklin's shouting. He was saying she had lost her sanity, that this wasn't normal grief. She heard something else too: Franklin's phrasing was again almost the same as Splitfoot's when his voice came out of Bennie's mouth in the overturned train car. *All the boys will die.* Jane had wondered ever since if this referred to her own children, or some cataclysm to come. She saw now that it was both.

"You think the only way to resist the terrible things you speak of, is to escape," she said, as soft as she could manage. "And seeing as you can't do that until the end of your term, you're granting me the opportunity."

"Yes."

"But what if you're wrong?"

"On which account?"

"What if resistance can only be achieved from within? No matter the forces"—Jane moved her eyes about the room, its floor and ceiling, as if indicating the unseen presences all around them—"that seek to reduce us to our expected roles."

He moved away from her but when he bumped against the chair in which the general sat, he sidestepped farther from them both. It left him stranded in the center of the rug, the painted ceiling of stars cast over him so that he appeared as isolated as a man standing in a rowboat at night.

"You speak of idealism," he said.

"Perhaps I do. But what if the blather of policy and compromise and costs—what if all we give primacy to is only a distraction from the pursuit of our ideals?"

"This is an intriguing proposition, but there isn't—"

"Haven't I always been good counsel to you, Franklin?"

"My finest."

"Then hear it now: There is no escaping this place. Because to leave it as it is will only hand it over to another man to lose his way. Whatever darkness is yielded to inside this house, the nation outside will yield to as well."

Franklin folded his arms and it shrunk him by half. "What do you propose?"

"Change."

"To prove my independence?"

"To prove your humanity."

"And how is that done in my shoes?"

"By disregarding the machinations of party and electioneers. By the exercise of will. By choice."

"Change," he said, as if seeing a new meaning to the term for the first time.

"Of course it can't be arbitrary. It must be *moral*. An action taken according to the principles I know you hold deep within yourself."

Franklin looked down at the floor, and imagined he could look through it to the men who fed the furnace in the oval room directly below where he stood. *They come to get warm.* Spirits that came here, to America's house. It was the only way they could. Because outside these walls, in the lives they would live there, they would be required to either show their Certificate of Freedom upon demand or be returned to chains. *The ones you can't see.*

"I believe I'm aware of the issue you're referring to," he said.

"There is no other."

"It plagues every matter before me."

"Because it's not a matter. It is an offense against—never mind God—an offense against what is right. And so long as it is allowed to stand, whether under the name of respecting the powers of state legislatures or its assistance to commerce, there will be no ridding ourselves of what resides here with us."

They didn't say *slavery*. They didn't say *evil*. Not *ghost*, nor *demon*. But these inadequate terms passed between them now in silence. The things to which they referred rendered in specific images, a nightmare collage assembled in each of their minds.

"I feel it too," he said.

"What?"

"A wish for redemption."

"You may have it."

"That assumes my capacity to enact it. But I also feel the shackles that hold me from it."

"Politics."

"Not that. The ways that good intentions may be sabotaged by torments of a different kind."

He tapped a finger to his temple and she understood him to mean the realities seen and felt along with the other things manufactured inside his skull.

"Fight it," she said.

"Alone?"

"I'm with you."

"Ah! Then we're a full battalion!"

"Frank—"

"And what are the two of us armed with? The crusaders' banner of change? Change!" Franklin paused and cast his eyes about the room just as Jane had done. "It's as if this office—this very house—conspires against it."

Jane stood. Her body stiff with defiance. "That is why you *must* fight it."

He unclasped the arms belted across his chest and it appeared he might melt into a pool on the rug of stars and heraldic eagles. It wasn't helplessness this time that threatened his undoing, but gratitude. His wife was on his side again. His ally. Pushing him in an unfamiliar direction, to be sure, and possibly mistaken to a catastrophic degree. But in that instant of her standing, fists clenched, setting him to a bold purpose and believing in his capacity to carry it out—in *her*, he saw a way out.

She saw it too. But for Jane, her faith was less in her husband's strengths than the novelty of resistance. She had never really attempted to deny Sir's plans, as they were vague to her until only recently, and in any case his intentions for himself had seemed to complement her own prayers. Even now she wasn't certain what he had planned for herself and Franklin beyond their terror and chaos of mind. Perhaps that was sufficient. Yet she had an idea that Sir's greatest opposition was to courage. The individual push against the supposedly foregone conclusion that, when joined with others pushing the same way, could reshape the inevitable.

"Jeannie?" Franklin said, opening his arms to her.

She fought against rushing headlong into him, losing herself in the rules and hierarchies of marriage again. But as she drew closer to her husband her body reminded her of all the ways her preceding months of independence were merely isolation. Perhaps it was one of Sir's tricks to have her confuse anger with strength.

Right away she recognized the mistake she'd made.

She let Splitfoot into her thoughts. Now when she was so close to—

Huummb.

A stretched-out thud from the floor above. A roll of thunder passing over them between the plaster and boards.

A-hummmb . . . Boom.

Something of enormous weight had dragged itself over the floor before slamming into the door that contained it. Bennie's room. The weight not that of the boy's body but the mass inside of it, a malignant concentration of emptiness.

"Jeannie?"

The first time he said her name it was an invitation to be whole again. Now Franklin said it not to stand alone.

Hummmb . . . BOOM. Humm—

Jane rushed to him. To lend what comfort she could. To feel the thickness of his arms around her and believe there was force within them to shield her as she'd always tried to believe there was.

There was another reason she buried her face in the wool folds of his jacket. She didn't want him to look directly at her and see that she knew the cause of the noise. She didn't want to look at him and see that he knew it too.

—BOOM.

The two of them clung together in a fearful embrace. Exposed on all sides, the starry ceiling expanding, breathing ice down on them.

BOOM!

Jane turned Franklin around so that he faced the door. If something was about to enter she wished for him to see it first. But when she leaned her head away from him and looked back in the direction of the velvet settee, it was Jane who saw something horrible.

In the chair that Franklin was positioned close to when she first entered, the general was no longer sitting still, but shifting forward, rolling its hips closer to the cushion's edge. It wasn't just grinning anymore either, its lips ovalled to show two rows of teeth, jagged and tartared as a dog's. Its sword remained raised, the tip touching its shoulder. Its free hand held next to its temple in a salute to whatever master had called it to attention.

"They will come," Franklin said.

Jane couldn't guess if he meant the staff to ensure their safety, or the monsters he imagined upstairs, smashing their way through into the house's interior.

She didn't answer, her eyes on the general as it slid off the chair.

When its boots met the floor—*cle-Clink*—it started marching. The little sword shuddering lower until it was pointed at her knees. The mouth wide and stretching wider, the lips still metallic in appearance but the material pliant as flesh. Inside she could see the black gums and, behind them, the bone where a pink throat ought to be.

It wasn't that the boy's toy soldier was alive. There was something alive inside of it. The tin shell a skin for the softer parts within.

... Cle-Clink-cle-CLINK ...

Jane watched it come at her with the slaloming approach of a cat looking to be scratched. Top-heavy, wobbly.

It would be comical if she didn't know the nature of what it contained. She glimpsed enough through its mouth to imagine the rest of it: random parts of dead men stitched together into a dwarfish mongrel. Fingers to work the arms. Eyes goggling behind blue-painted pinholes. A purple tongue slapping about, learning to speak again.

"There's something at the door," Franklin said, and once more Jane couldn't tell what he meant, whether it be the portal to the Grief Room, the main entrance, or a figurative meaning of some kind, a way into himself about to be breached.

She held her shoulder hard to the middle of his back. He would understand it as her using him as a shield against whatever might enter. What she in fact wanted was for him not to turn because for Franklin to see the general too would confirm she wasn't mad.

Until this moment she hadn't realized the comfort thinking herself insane had brought her.

. . . Clink-cle-Clink-cle . . .

She remembered the scene in the East Room mirror. A future vision of human butchery. Now she had the idea that the general's steel skin contained some of those boys' parts. Grave-robbed. Or pieces that were never buried at all. Soldiers fallen in the field and left for the carrion and flies to dispose of.

The toy soldier stopped at Jane's feet. It craned its head back to look up at her, which allowed her to look down past its throat. Gray bones fused into a web. A bruised heart, pulsing. A pair of lungs squeezing out a breath she could feel before she could smell.

The Blue Room's door opened. She heard it over her shoulder and wondered, in the distant way one does about something that occurred some time ago, who was entering.

The general drew its sword back to its side. Readying for the swing.

Jane was moving too. Her slippered foot drifting back, tapping against the side of Franklin's knee. Then driving forward. Her toe meeting the toy's painted rows of medals.

Franklin remained facing the door. But he had to have heard the impact of Jane's slipper to the general's chest, its tumbling contact with the rug and hardwood as it fell backward.

"Ma'am?"

Jane pivoted to see her dresser woman, Hany, stopped mid-stride at the door. Judging by the look on the woman's face she'd seen at least something of the general's walking. Or perhaps more. The thing inside it.

"What was that?" Franklin demanded. It took a moment for Hany to recognize he was speaking to her, then another moment to interpret the question.

"I'm not sure I—"

"Did you *hear* it?"

Hany shifted her gaze from the general to the president. She hadn't forgotten her duty to the latter. But it was the former she feared more.

"Hear what, sir?"

"The banging! Coming right through the ceiling. Shaking the whole house."

"I heard none of that. Only the child."

Jane stepped out from behind Franklin. Her head moving between Hany and the toy that had come to rest in a twisted jumble against the chair leg in what she sensed was only a pose of brokenness.

"What child?"

"I don't know, ma'am," Hany said.

"How old? Was it a boy or girl?"

"Just a boy."

"What was it saying?"

"He wasn't saying anything."

It was Franklin's turn to shout at the woman, not from anger or impatience but the ravaging of grief finding its way to the surface.

"Then why in the hell did you think it was a child?"

"Because he was *laughing*, sir."

25

Franklin walked out without a glance back at Jane and for close to a full minute both she and Hany waited for his return. When neither heard shouted orders from the Cross Hall or the president's distinctive footfalls approaching—the crisp *snik* of his boot heels, the pace deliberate, self-aware—it settled on them that he wasn't coming back. His haste was so that neither of the women saw his distress. What Jane could only guess was whether this state was brought on by fright, or heartbreak. She imagined his face twisted into a similar shape in either case.

"Beg your pardon, ma'am, if I offended."

"You needn't apologize, Hany. But I would ask if you would keep this conversation—this entire episode—to yourself."

The older woman nodded so deeply the folds of her chin touched her chest. She knew what it was to be discreet. It was as much her job as the cleaning of gowns and stitching of holes. "Of course, ma'am."

Jane wanted to ask if Hany would take the toy soldier back upstairs but saw the problems such a request would create. The first was that Hany, as far as she knew, hadn't been inside Bennie's room, and her seeing the arrangement of furniture there—not to mention the possibility of her encountering Bennie himself—would test her loyalties. The second was that it wasn't fair to ask Hany to carry the general and the monstrous life within it upstairs when it was Jane who had, however indirectly, been the cause of its enchantment.

"Can I help with anything, ma'am?" Hany asked, her eyes on the tin soldier as if reading Jane's mind.

"I'm quite fine, thank you."

"Forgive me, but you don't look it."

Jane saw the kindness in Hany that had always been there, a sympathy that went well beyond the obligations of servitude. A tenderness that opened her.

"Shall we step into the hallway?" Jane said.

"If you wish."

The two women moved outside, and Jane closed the door behind her.

"I have no right to complain," Jane said in a lowered voice, though they were alone in the hall. "My husband is the president. This palace is my home."

"With respect, ma'am, I don't believe you see this as your home."

"Why do you say that?"

"No person who's ever known a proper house ever could."

Jane thought of the college president's residence at Bowdoin, the Amherst house where she played piano, the stately house in Concord they couldn't quite afford where she and Franklin sat together, listening to the music of their two boys' laughter before breaking into laughter themselves. Those were proper houses. This was a prison, no matter its splendor.

"I am bound to this place," Jane said.

"We have that, the two of us."

"Our fates are fixed, then."

"Fates? I don't know about *that*. But I know the jobs you're given to do, and the ones they'll never let you do. I know what's *expected*. Don't you?"

The truth of this—true for her, the two of them, perhaps for all women—struck Jane with the force of a freezing wind. *What's expected.* It's what Jane had resisted all her life in her nurtured illnesses, her unwholesome obsessions. Franklin had seen it in her from the start. *Fallen angel*, he'd called her. It's what excited him, and what made her feel truly recognized by the only man other than her father. But what difference had it made? She was here, transported to the White House, yet she was still a wife, a bereaved mother, a woman. Still trapped.

"May I share something with you?" Jane said, and before Hany had a chance to accept or decline—before Jane heard how far she was going—she told her almost everything. The pendulum game. Her life with Sir. The ritual with the Fox sisters in her bedchambers. The one piece Jane held back was how she had caused a monstrous Bennie to return to life. It was something she found possible to believe, but impossible to say.

"Well, good God," Hany said, and leaned against the wall, shaking her head as if at the confirmation of a privately held suspicion.

"You have expected this!"

"No, ma'am. I wouldn't go *that* far."

Jane attempted a throat-clearing laugh. "Perhaps I'm speaking only of ghosts. And ghosts have likely been here long before our arrival."

"There's ghosts in any place with a past. But you brought something new here. Or *not* new. Something very old."

Jane abandoned her crooked smile. "You've seen it?"

"The best way I could describe it would be to say it's made itself known to my feelings."

"I'm so sorry, Hany."

"I'm sorry for *you*, ma'am. Because that snarly dog? Sir? That what you call it? I know one thing. He doesn't like us being friendly. He wants you to be alone."

Jane's hunger for understanding had been so great, for so long, that it was everything she could do not to break into sobs at Hany's words. But while she took comfort in her dresser woman being here, she now had the task of clearing the general away. And to be a friend to Hany required Jane to do so on her own.

"I'd like to speak more later, if we could," Jane said. "But for now, could I ask for a moment?"

Hany didn't want to go but saw no choice in it. "Of course," she said, starting away as Jane opened the door to the Blue Room and slipped inside.

Now that that she was alone again, Jane dreaded even more the idea of putting her hands on the general. It waited on the floor for her to come. The arms and legs twisted around its head, its face framed like the centerpiece of a grisly wreath.

Jane decided to be brave. That is, she decided to act as if she were brave. She hoped that whatever it was that looked out through its pin-hole eyes would see she was ready to destroy it if need be, send it back to whatever shallow grave it came from.

She cradled the general in her arms and started for the hallway. Part of her wondered why she didn't just toss it outside instead of returning it to the room across from hers. The answer was emotionally simple, if practically nonsensical: the toy was Bennie's. Something her son had played with, had held, had loved. Now even more than before Jane was obliged to protect the true memory of her child against the incursions of the false one.

Yet the soldier reeked. She couldn't tell if it was from its ongoing exhalations or her memory of the odor from earlier. It didn't move. There was an additional weight to it that Jane didn't recall it having, but it didn't thrash about as she feared. It seemed to her that the general wanted to return to Bennie's room as much as she wanted to deliver it there.

Once she made it to the second floor she hustled off to the right. A steward was coming out of her bedroom, presumably from changing her sheets, and when he spotted her he did his best not to stare at the folded-up man held to her breast.

"Ma'am? May I—"

"No. Nothing. No." She cut him off as she passed, slipping into Bennie's room and closing the door.

The first thing she wanted to do was put down the general. The feeding chair? Atop the dresser? The bed? Tossed into the crib?

As she stood there, scanning between these possibilities, an observation arrived: the boy wasn't there. Not lying, waiting, in the big-boy bed. Not standing by the window. If he was hiding, there were few places he could do so. Behind the curtains? There were no telltale feet beneath them. Beneath the covers? The bed was neatly made. Under a piece of furniture? She bent to look under the crib and bed frame, but there were only gray shadows there.

Jane rose. The toy soldier shuddered in her arms. A doubling of its smell blown cold against her face.

She rushed over to the crib and half placed, half dropped the general on the floor. It tottered for a second. A motion of its own making, or simply the weight of it rolling, unbalanced, on its elbows and knees. She didn't speak until it settled.

"Benjamin?"

The silence mocked her.

He was gone. She didn't want to think of the possibility of his having escaped, so she focused on him simply returning to some netherworld. He did what other spirits were said to do—he appeared, then disappeared. There was nothing left behind but the experience of it, the doubt of its ever having occurred, and the collision of the two shaping themselves into a story.

She was talking herself into his never having existed even as she watched the hand slide out from under the crib.

It couldn't be happening, but it was. She had looked into the darkness there and seen nothing. Maybe that's what Bennie was, just as Splitfoot was, what every murderous idea was. The mind's sculpture of darkness.

The hand slid out over the floor longer than she thought his arm could stretch. When it stopped, the other hand came after it, extending an inch farther than the first. When they were side by side the fingers bent at the knuckles, gripped hard. The arms bending as they pulled the rest of him out.

Play . . .

The voice wasn't pretending to be her son's anymore. It wasn't Sir's becalmed tone either. She had never heard a voice like it, but it came to her as something she had always known.

Play with me.

A crash. Something heavy clattering to the floor. Jane looked up, expecting to see the place where a chandelier had detached from the ceiling, but there was no chandelier in this bedroom. She looked down. The general. Its knotted limbs still twisted around its head, but now lying on its back. Fallen over. That, or its first attempt to get up.

Don't go, Momma.

She backed away. Her eyes on the boy as he slid free and, without pause, pulled himself erect with the smoothness of a snake rising from the grass.

The general was moving too. Rocking back and forth.

Play!

Jane turned and rushed out to the hallway. She meant to head straight to her room but veered to the left, half running, keeping herself an equal distance from both walls as if the portraits of dead senators and Speakers of the House might reach out to her as Bennie's hands just had.

She was halfway along when she saw what had drawn her there.

On her left was the staircase, on the right the oval-shaped library that sat above the Blue Room below and, another floor down from that, the furnace. That's where she found him.

He stood alone in a roomful of books. His expression kindly, patient, suffering. The same surroundings and state of mind she had seen him occupy all his life.

"Daddy?"

He gestured for her to come closer. She remembered him doing that too, and in just that way: less a wave than a rounded clenching of his fingers, as if grasping an invisible cane. When he wanted to speak with her it was always a matter of significance. And because he didn't want to raise his voice—because so much of what he said had the aura of a secret about it—he needed her to be close.

Jane went to him.

She was almost near enough for him to reach out to her, touch her if he chose to, when she remembered she'd left the door to Bennie's room open.

26

He heard the banging from upstairs but felt it from below.

It's why Franklin headed down to the ground floor upon leaving the Blue Room. He wanted to fix the problem. He wanted to give someone a piece of his goddamn mind. The house was coming at him, an attack composed of the distortion of everyday things that he guessed was the way insanity presented itself. He wouldn't let himself entertain the possibility. So he decided: it was the house that was against him. And if it was the house, he would restore his place as its master.

There were a half dozen staff members in the ground floor's hall when he appeared. Maids, a brass-buttoned steward, an aproned cook. All but one of them scuttled into the kitchen or cellar or laundry when they saw him. The one who remained stood outside the furnace room. The same man who'd warned him against entering when he'd come down on his first day to complain of the house's cold.

"What's going on in there?" Franklin demanded, striding up to him.

"Sir?"

"All the noise. Likes fists against the walls. Didn't you hear it?"

"I've heard some things, but not that."

Franklin couldn't tell if the man was mocking him. If he had to guess, he'd say the fellow was protecting someone.

"Step aside."

"Sir?"

"If you won't stop this nonsense, I will."

"I wouldn't call it nonsense."

The man said this with a seriousness that even Franklin's stare failed to dissolve. At first it seemed he wouldn't move. And then, with a shake of the head of the kind one gives to someone who insists on drinking another glass of whiskey despite being unable to stand, he moved back.

Franklin considered the door, listened for movement or voices on the other side. When he could detect nothing he gripped his hand around the brass knob and turned to ask the furnace keeper another question. The hall was empty. Was it possible that the man had retreated so quickly as that? Franklin would have called out his name if he'd known what it was. He would shout an order now—*Come back!*—if he didn't want to hear the uselessness of it.

A person only sees things like that when they're ready to.

He was ready now.

Franklin pushed the door open and stepped into the wall of dry heat.

The first thing he noticed was the boiler itself: smaller than he would have imagined, a fat steel barrel with a dozen ducts stretching out of it like tentacles punching up through the floorboards. It looked to him like a crab on its back. He remembered peekytoes he found overturned by the tide on the beach at Boothbay, where he visited during breaks at college. Some were dead. Some only looked that way until you tried to pick them up and the claws would clamp on to your skin.

The second thing he noticed was that the room was unoccupied.

The man at the furnace room door was a believer. In what? Other worlds. Franklin hadn't been brought up that way, the world of his father—money, politics, war—decidedly the present one. And then, when Franklin was older, he'd been chosen. Picked out from the crowd to speak for the crowd. There was no room for other worlds in his.

He drew closer to the boiler. The mansion was big, but the heat blasting out at him was of a volume he was sure could heat all of Washington if the windows were opened. It would melt the ice on the Potomac. Tell the crocuses it was time to rise. Yet he knew that only a floor above the rooms were chilled as those of houses laid to waste by plague.

The ones you can't see.

Franklin felt something come up behind him.

More than one thing. Bodies. Doubling in number, coming not through the doorway, not previously hidden and now revealing themselves, but deciding the same thing he'd decided. It was time.

He turned.

He was encircled by men. A growing number of them squeezing together in rows. Staring at him, but not touching. They didn't speak, but in their looks Franklin was certain none of them were freemen. Or they hadn't been while alive.

They drew closer.

"I am—" he started, but had no way of ending the statement that would make any sense. *I am Franklin Pierce. I am a friend. I am the president of the United States.* Each utterance irrelevant, hollow, fictional.

The men didn't appear to hear him anyway. Franklin could peek over their shoulders to see that the entire room was now full, yet still more pushed out from the oval walls. The density of their bodies compounded the heat. Franklin couldn't breathe. He tried to step forward, but whether they refused to move or couldn't, there was no passage through them.

"Please. I need to—"

The child's cry traveled down through the vents. Franklin heard it. The dead men did too, their heads rising to look into the brick ceiling above them.

The voice shouldn't have been able to reach the furnace room, buried as all of them were in the foundation and surrounded by tons of timber and brick. Yet the cries found Franklin's ears with the clarity that comes from being separated by nothing more than a pane of glass.

"It's my son," he said.

There was a pause of a kind, the hush of people drawing breath. And then the men in front of Franklin stepped aside. Behind them, tight row after row, others did the same. A parting that left a space just wide enough for him to sidestep through.

He tried not to look at their faces as he went, an aversion he intended to communicate as respectful thanks. It didn't stop him from noticing the expressions some wore. They weren't letting him go out of deference to his position, nor pity for being the father to a mewling child. It was grim satisfaction at possessing knowledge he didn't. Knowing what awaited him upstairs.

Once he was out in the hallway Franklin closed the door. The furnace keeper was there again.

"You saw," the older man said.

"Yes."

"Do you know who they are?"

"By name?"

"By what they did."

"No."

The furnace keeper grinned toothlessly. "They built this house."

Franklin glanced back at the furnace room door. Imagined the dozens, hundreds of men on the other side.

"Why are they in there?"

"This is America. This house. You and the missus up top, the paintings and crystal in the middle for the men to do their bargains, and down here the ones who do the work. And the ones in there—" The furnace keeper tilted his head toward the door. "They *made* these walls. But once they did, they weren't allowed inside them."

"And it's cold outside."

"It's cold on either side, Mr. President, depending on your situation."

The child's crying started again. Not just alarmed anymore, but in pain.

"You hear that?" Franklin said.

The furnace keeper shrugged. "Hear what?"

A wave of illness washed over Franklin and he doubled over, sure he was going to be sick.

Papa?

Franklin jolted. The furnace keeper cast his eyes up at the ceiling too.

"I know who that is," Franklin said.

"Oh?"

"That's my boy."

"You don't say."

Pa-pa!

Franklin started away toward the stairs. With each step he felt less ill, less likely to spill his stomach onto the floor.

When he looked back he found the hall empty. The furnace keeper was gone.

★ ★ ★

The second floor's library was the same oval shape and size as the Blue Room below it. Yet from the start Jane found this space so much smaller than its twin, almost suffocating. Even more so now with her father standing at the center of it.

She had assumed the claustrophobia that limited her previous visits to a quick snatching of a new book to read resulted from the shelves that held the volumes, the towering weight of them all around. She saw now that her aversion had come from Sir being here all along. His presence hiding among the histories and atlases, looking back over the worlds he had traveled.

"You're not my father," she said.

"I thought it would be a solace for you to see me."

"You don't give solace. You can't."

The lines on her father's forehead folded like a plowed field, the lips gluing and ungluing. This was Sir trying to make a smile out of wet clay.

"Would you care to tell me what else I can't do?" he said.

"No."

"Then come in. Or do you want your husband hearing you talk to yourself?"

At the same instant he mentioned Franklin—*your husband*—she heard his distinctive step coming up the stairs across the hallway.

She closed the door. Moved just far enough so that her back wasn't touching it.

"Why are you here?"

"Dear Jeannie. You *wanted* me to come."

Had she? Jane struggled to work through the recent hours of her life and found nothing but a soup of unnatural images and sounds. Yet buried in it was the sense that there was a purpose to her being there. An attempt to prevent catastrophe.

"I would like to ask you to do something for me," she said.

"Something else, you must mean. Something in addition to all I've already done?"

"I've asked for nothing."

He approached her with small, sliding steps. The voice shifting from Jesse Appleton's to Splitfoot's word by word.

"I came to you because you invited me. I brought your boy back because you wished it. I lifted your polished shell of a husband to a mountaintop."

He stopped an arm's length from her. It let Jane hear the last of what he said as the partial lie it was. She also saw the distinction between ask-ing and wishing, and was about to present him with it, but as was so often the case when in his company, such nuance slipped away before she could speak.

"Take me," she said.

"You?"

"Let me be your compensation."

"For what?"

"Your leaving this place. In return, you may have what spirit I have left."

It was pathetic. Jane heard it. Sir did too. What seemed an enormous sacrifice, the offer of her everlasting life, struck them both as a pittance.

"I *like* it here, Jeannie," Sir said, restraining most, but not all, of the mockery from his voice. "It's like a church to me."

"A church," she repeated.

"Oh yes! There's blessings of the rich and commandments of the ones chosen to speak for them. There's the saints who'd waged war. Marriages of power."

She had to find another way to resist him. Discover a vulnerability in his composition that might be exploited. His pride. She thought this was the way. Yet with every query she put to him, the more convinced she became of his superiority. He revealed himself now with an openness he hadn't before because there was no need to conceal his intentions. He was here, where he had set out to come when he attached himself to her as a child, just as he had identified her father as a way to her before that. There was no vulnerability in him. He had already won.

"Why have you done this?"

"I am always looking for a path," Splitfoot said using her father's mouth.

"Where?"

"To your thoughts, your choices. To be the loudest voice in your head. And through that voice, to guide you to your ends."

Jane wished, hopelessly, that the man standing in front of her actually was her father. She didn't know how much she missed him. He would understand everything that had happened to her. They would have so much to talk about. But the man with her could provide no comfort. The very notion of his touch made her shudder.

Sir read her mind and encaged her in his arms.

"The thinking of a thing gives it a reality. Every cruelty, every murder, every lie. Even the greatest atrocities begin with a harmless musing," Sir whispered against her cheek. "Thinking a thing makes it want to *be* a thing."

"You want the world to end."

"I want it broken."

"You can't do that from here."

"It is the best place to do it."

"No. We won't—"

"From here I can break the world by breaking the mind of the man with power over it. How is that done? You break his heart."

He pulled her closer. He would never let her go.

Behind her, from the other side of the door, she heard someone running down the hall. The steps light and quick. A child.

27

The president rushed upstairs toward his dead son's voice.

He wasn't thinking. Not in the way he normally did, arranging his considerations by pros and cons and priorities. Franklin's mind was alive but in a different way, and he realized this place had been pulling him there since he entered it, opening him to senses and visions he didn't welcome but, once revealed, were impossible to dispel. It was the dead who did it. The house was full of them.

Including the man outside the furnace room.

It's cold on either side, Mr. President, depending on your situation.

It was also the way Franklin felt around these presences that confirmed they weren't living. The gut twists, dizziness, the fattened tongue. Speaking with the furnace keeper made Franklin ill. He had the idea that it was not inflicted on purpose but was necessary for the presence to make itself visible, and in the case of the furnace man, converse. Maybe all the dead were like that. To get from *there*, they had to ride on the shoulders of someone *here*.

If he was right, it would go some way to explaining why he hadn't felt properly himself since coming to live in the mansion. Then again, he wasn't himself in coming here. He wasn't Franklin Pierce anymore, a husband, a suffering father of lost children. Here he was president. Greater than a man, though one not permitted to be human.

He heard the door to the library close at the same time he came to the top of the stairs. It wasn't where the voice was coming from, which removed any curiosity he might have had as to who was in there. He started to the right. The second floor hall was empty in the way a space is following an act of violence. It was how his father's tavern felt after being cleared of a brawl.

He knew the door to the room across from Jane's would be open. It let him slip inside without touching it.

There was the neatly made bed, the crib, the dresser, the chair. He couldn't see anything out of the ordinary. But he felt it all the same.

"I was calling for you, Papa."

The boy was standing in front of the window with his back to him. Heavy curtains were lined against his sides so that Franklin had mistaken him for a high-backed chair fixed to let the moonlight in.

"Are you all right?" Franklin asked.

It was the wrong question. It wasn't what he really wanted to know. And it let the boy win the first point: he was here, being treated as a human being would. They were both acting now. Which was the initial step on the way to doing away with the difference between acting a part and being who you really are.

"I'm fine," the boy said. "I was just lonely."

He turned. The room was dark so that the only light came from whatever dusting of moon and lamp found its way through the window, along with the shaft of yellow cast along the floor from the hallway. But it was sufficient to illuminate two things. One was that the boy's turning wasn't the only movement, as there was something else, something to the right, that rose and seemed to unfold itself—*cle-clank*—at the same time. The other was that the boy's face was that of his son. His Bennie.

Fixing his attention on the boy alone was another mistake. It prevented him from getting a good look at the rising, unfolding thing that came at him.

Fif-fif-fif-fif-fif . . .

A dwarf. It's back and neck and shoulders so stiff it advanced in arthritic lurches. Low and fast as a startled rat. And like a rat, its very nature was repulsive.

The thing passed so close he felt some part of it graze his pant leg. Franklin moved deeper into the room to be farther from it in case it leapt on him from behind. But as he spun around to meet the attack, he caught sight of it. The general. Bennie's toy soldier banging its arm against the door, swinging it shut. The shaft of light from the hall skinnying to nothing.

"Don't be afraid," Bennie said.

Franklin didn't reply, didn't move. Another point won by the boy. He didn't mean to calm his father, just hold him there. That wasn't his only victory. By not denying the boy's claim that he was afraid only proved that he was.

The floor squeaked. It was the boy stepping closer. Franklin turned from the dwarfish shadow standing guard at the door. Now that the boy was away from the window it let more of the scant light in, silty and brown as a disturbed creek bed.

"Do you know who I am?" the boy asked.

"I know who you were."

"Were?"

"None of this is real."

"How best to show that you're wrong?"

The boy seemed to ponder his own question. And then Franklin saw it wasn't a question meant for a response from either of them. They both already knew the answer.

"Do you know who I am?" the boy asked again, precisely the same as before, a mimicry that smuggled a threat inside it the second time.

"Yes."

"Will you say it?"

"You are Benjamin Pierce," Franklin said, his throat on fire. "My son."

He was expecting it. The figure at the window he'd seen from the orangery. The cries that had traveled down through the vents. The calls for him that sounded so much like the ones that awakened him when he still had living sons, the shouts for their father to come and push away the bad dreams that invaded their sleep. And he had responded with the same reflex to help. To shield.

But what *was* it?

It was Bennie in the sense that its resemblance to his son made him remember his son. Jane carried the locket with the boy's hair for the same reason. Yet for all that, looking at the boy who kept his distance as if hiding the flaws that would give him away if he came too close, Franklin saw even less than a clipping of hair. He saw a betrayal. It was an agent sent here to build a bridge between where it came from and where Franklin existed using his love as building material. From what he could tell, it was almost all the way there.

"May I go, Papa?"

The boy took a step closer. He seemed pleased when Franklin neither retreated nor told him to stay away.

"Where would you go?"

"Not far."

"You wish to leave."

"No!" The boy giggled. "I'll *never* leave!"

The more Franklin kept his eyes on the boy the louder the second voice grew in his thinking.

Did the child *have* to be devilry? The dead rose from time to time in the Bible, did they not? Lazarus. Jesus. Couldn't this be such a case? He was aware of the facts against it. He'd watched his boy die, tried to lift him up and felt him come undone, his sweet head damaged beyond all fixing.

Yet here he was. Proof that questions lingered.

Was God real? Was he kind? Did he know how broken Franklin's heart was, how heavy the strain of keeping his country together when so much conspired to tear it apart? Who other than God had the power to bring his boy back?

"Why do you need my permission?" Franklin said.

"I only do as I'm told. I'm a *good* boy, Papa."

He saw it then. A part of this boy who truly was Bennie. How could that be? Perhaps it was that his son's spirit had been commandeered. Perhaps this *wasn't* a trick. It was an opportunity. A miracle in waiting.

It made him remember himself as a child, as a man, a father: Franklin had always tried to figure out ways to be loved. Yet his son Bennie simply loved.

Where did the boy come to it, this ease of feeling? Not from Franklin, certainly. And not Jane, who felt deeply but translated its excess into pains and aversions.

Now here was a way to go back. To love as openly as he ought to have done from the start. Not many men were lucky enough to stare at it as he was doing now. A second chance.

"Papa? Please?"

It was exhaustion that made him do it. He was tired of having people stolen from him. He was tired of being lost, sounding lost even in his most strident speeches to Congress and letters to foreign leaders. More than anything, Franklin was tired of not being a father anymore.

He went to the door. The general stepped aside. *Fif-fif-fif-fif.* Franklin opened it and looked back at his son. On his face a creeping smile yellowed by the lamplight from the hall.

A single word. Quick as a snapped finger.

Despite its brevity, Franklin wasn't finished speaking it when he heard the error he'd made.

"Yes."

28

Her father unclasped the hands at her back. Raised his lips all the way to the gums.

"Let me go," Jane said, but he was already stepping away from her.

As he went the particulars that made him appear as her father blurred. The gray brows became a line over his eyes, the veined hands a pair of white mittens.

She spun around. Opened the door.

Her dead son was running down the hall.

When Bennie saw her he paused. His face betrayed no feeling of any kind, the eyes not even assessing her, merely looking. It made her think of feral dogs encountered on the street: people had no way of guessing whether the dogs would walk on, or whine for food, or bite.

"Benjamin," she said.

The boy looked back down the hallway. Jane looked too.

Franklin stood outside the Grief Room. Even from this distance she could see how ruined he was. She recognized it from the image of herself she saw in every mirror now: a place beyond failure, beyond sorrow. He had been pulled so far out of himself there was no self to return to.

Franklin raised his arm. Pointed at the boy.

Jane saw what he was asking. She started toward the child. Not to hold him or speak with him but to capture him. Drag him back down the hall to his room. Lock him inside and never open the door again.

Bennie was too fast for her. He moved to the top of the stairs—not running, but skipping. He did it without turning from her, so that his body was faced forward and his head behind. The unnatural twisting of a boneless doll. As he descended she expected him to show her something of his nature, a grimace or snarl. But his face didn't change, revealed nothing, which was worse than if he had.

Franklin appeared next to her.

"We have to find him," he said.

Jane heard the way he bypassed all the questions he might need answered. *How is he here? Did you know? Was it you who brought him back?* Perhaps he already guessed the replies she would give.

"What will we do with him?"

He coughed in her face. It smelled of sourdough and bourbon.

"Let's find him first," he said, and started down the stairs.

★   ★   ★

The two of them searched every room on the first floor. The Blue Room, the Crimson Parlor, the State Dining Room, the pantry. The president and First Lady entered them all and peered wordlessly behind every settee and cupboard, murmuring vague explanations to the staff—*Just looking; Dropped something*—if they asked if they could be of assistance.

They encountered Webster on their way out of the Green Room.

"Have you seen a boy?" Jane asked him.

"A boy, ma'am?"

"He was running about."

"No. I've neither seen nor heard the running of a boy."

"Keep your eye out," Franklin said, and Webster turned to him.

They saw it then. The image of themselves in the face of the president's secretary. And in it, they saw too the only conclusion he or anyone could come to. The Pierces were more than grief-stricken. They had slid away from their sanity, and for those who worked around them in the residence, the question was now how best they be handled, contained, avoided.

"I will, sir," Webster said.

★　　★　　★

They talked through the dinner hour in Jane's room. When the candles guttered out she lit more and returned to sit on the edge of the bed across from the chair where Franklin was slumped. A dozen confused years had been added to his features. Yet Jane found he remained handsome, possibly more so, in the way that older men can tell heartbroken stories with the lines in their faces.

"Will you stay with me tonight?"

He went still at her question.

"In your room?"

237

"In my bed. Our bed."

"You must be very afraid to want that."

"I *am* afraid. But that's not the reason I'm asking."

"What is it?"

"We haven't had something together, something to share, for a long time."

She offered her hand. He took it. Let himself be guided to the mattress next to her.

"I just wish—" she began.

"That none of this was real."

"That it *was* real. That the boy was real—our Bennie."

Given all that she'd told him over the preceding hours—her invitation to the Fox sisters, the summoning of Bennie's spirit, the infant that had leapfrogged in its growth in the room across the hall—she would have granted Franklin the right to be angry for her making a remark like this. It was her "just wishing," after all, that had led to a sweet-faced ghoul moving about the mansion. Not to mention the other presences. Their fathers. The enslaved dead in the furnace room. And then there was the way she'd kept from him the presence that had followed her out of the Bowdoin president's house of her girlhood and walked alongside her all her life. It was like an adultery, shaming and selfish. In this case something worse than that, as it was born of an offense against God.

But Franklin wasn't angry at her. He had a sense of the power of the shadow she called Sir from his own encounter with it at Franky's deathbed. How could a being like that be shaken if it was decided in its interests? He didn't blame Jane for keeping it a secret from him, because he kept what he'd seen a secret from her now. He told himself he was doing it to protect her from knowledge that could only cause pain. The same reason, she'd tried to convince herself, justified her deception of him.

As for her calling Bennie up out of the soil—he couldn't fault her for that either. He felt it too. The longing so deep it would do anything, break any law, for the briefest reunion with the lost. The way the heart could be fooled by a likeness. The closeness of the thing that hid somewhere in the White House to the child he had loved so dearly it was enough for two lives, a thousand.

"It can't be real," he said. "That child—it is a treachery."

"Forgive me."

"I do. You only wanted the same thing I have wanted."

"I went further than that."

"You brought something into this house that has no right to it."

"Yes."

"I forgive you that too. Because I've come to suspect I have little right to be in this office myself."

"Why do you say that? You've committed no fraud."

"Not by intention. But I wasn't called to be here by purpose, Jeannie. Just like that boy who looks like our Bennie. I'm more puppet than president."

Jane's reflex was to defend her husband from this attack against himself. Yet she said nothing. Because Franklin was right, in a way she hadn't grasped before. She had been too occupied in aiding Sir, keeping

Sir a secret, waiting for Sir to give her what she ached for, that she'd failed to see how she had used Franklin the whole time. Her willing marionette. Just as she had been Sir's.

"You say you weren't called by purpose," she said. "Even if that's so, could you not find it now?"

"Oh, Jane. This again?"

She circled her hand over the bedsheets next to her, asking him to sit close. It was a struggle for him to slide along the few inches of the mattress' edge to her hip.

"For a moment, don't see me as the tricksome wife," she said.

"How should I see you?"

"As the one who knows you to be good."

Franklin almost yielded, if not to her argument than to her body, his head leaning closer to her shoulder in the yearning to be held, to rest. But his eyes found hers first and he saw in them the shards of the secret that still lived in her. He sat straight.

"Tell me this," he said. "The one you call Sir and the Fox girls called Splitfoot—what are his designs? To haunt us? To drive us to madness?"

"He's likely already succeeded on both counts."

"So it is only that?"

She removed the black shawl she wore and let it fall behind her. The simplest of gestures, yet they both saw it for what it was. A removal of armor.

"I'm not certain of his plans," she said. "But I believe he seeks to bring about destruction through us."

"By wrongful actions."

"By taking no actions at all. By plaguing you or whatever man is elected to replace you so that he can only see these rooms and the shadows that darken them, and not the people and truths outside the walls."

"He means to blind me to the world."

She remembered how Sir put it. *I can break the world by breaking the mind of the man with power over it.* Jane looked at her husband, gaunt and with a twitching blink she'd never noticed before, and saw how it was almost done. *You break his heart.*

"He means to turn you inward," she said. "To see only the self. And through you, he hopes the country will do the same. Twenty million souls suffering alone."

As had been the case on the occasions she'd been on her own too long, the speaking of her thought allowed her to see its meaning. Splitfoot could achieve little by himself. His power came through the division of man from neighbor, sister from brother, husband from wife. She had only to see what was left of her own family, her own marriage, for evidence.

"This matter we face—it's personal," Franklin said. "The nation doesn't see what's afflicted us here."

"But it *feels* it. Are we not the First Family? Or what's left of it."

"Are you saying he means to hurt many by hurting us?"

"Many were *already* hurting. Bringing you low is meant to let the wounds fester." Her voice quieted as it grew in intensity. "The newspapers confirm it. Every story tells a different version of the same condition. State against state. The rights of one race against another. The free and the enslaved. All of it as far from God's kingdom as he can drag it."

"But there's still further he can disassemble the union," Franklin said, and Jane understood what he referred to. The taking up of arms. The spread of bloodshed beyond Kansas and the western frontier. Civil war.

"Yes," she said.

Franklin looked down at his spotted hands laid unmoving on his lap. "How to divert him?"

"Do what you can. Call upon your goodness instead of compromise," she said. "That's how Sir can be confronted."

"Are you sure?"

"I'm sure that the time for evading choice is over."

Even in the candlelight they could hardly see each other. It drew them closer still. Jane pulled her dress from her shoulders, and Franklin put his hands on their pale corners, guiding his head to hers, his lips.

Both of them expected the other to pause, or speak, but neither did. There was enough warmth under the covers that let them undress without shivering. Their skin brought a new kind of heat.

Afterward, they lay on their backs, legs entwined. There was a quiet between them that was partly the calm that followed lovemaking, partly the strain to hear something in the darkness they felt was there.

When they finally heard it, their bodies went stiff. The heat drawn away from the points where they touched.

Something moved between the walls. Heavy and slow, yet never struggling to find its way. Every unremarkable thing it might be was eliminated from their minds. Mouse, squirrel, bird, bat.

It sounded less like a rodent than a snake, one of a length that could wrap itself around the entire room, its tail curling up into the ceiling, its head bumping and sliding under the boards beneath their bed.

"It's him," Jane whispered.

How did he know whom she meant? Because he was the boy's father, just as she was his mother. The two of them could recognize the sound of Bennie's step without seeing him.

They would have held each other closer if they didn't worry that the movement of their bodies would alert the thing in the walls to where they lay.

But of course it knew. It's why it came to this room rather than the hundred others in the house. Why it kept moving around them through the night, denying them sleep. Why at one point, minutes before the dawn when it could see that its prowling had left them as solitary and wrecked as they had been the evening before, it uttered a new sound.

From behind the plaster, muffled as a voice within a pine box, Bennie laughed.

29

The president's first order of the day to his secretary was to arrange a cabinet meeting to be held in the Blue Room that afternoon.

"Is there an emergency I'm not aware of, sir?" Webster asked, rising from his desk to summon messengers to descend on the Capitol offices and nearby apartments where the leadership of the Pierce administration would still be hunched over their breakfasts.

"Don't phrase it in those terms," Franklin said, rubbing his stubbled cheeks so hard it left scratch marks on his palms. "Tell them it's a conversation on policy. One that can't wait."

Webster gave him a look. It wasn't of the kind Franklin was expecting, the brow-raised show of doubt, or the fey curiosity that fell just short of disrespectful. This was concern. For Pierce's state of mind, yes, but also the state of the household, the nation, and most apparent, Webster himself.

"Are you feeling all right?" Franklin asked him as the man made his way for the door. "You look like you've been at sea."

"Fine, sir. It's only that I stayed late in my office yesterday and fell asleep in my chair."

"You slept here last night?"

"Didn't leave my chair."

"I see."

Webster looked down at his shoes, stricken. "It was— There were things that—"

"It can be a noisy place in the nighttime," Franklin said, sparing his secretary from saying something he clearly preferred not to. If Webster had heard even a fraction of the noises coming from within the mansion's walls that he and Jane had, Franklin pitied him.

"Yes, sir."

"Best if you slept in your own bed in future."

"I believe you're right, sir. Thank you."

It would otherwise be the moment for Webster to clip away to carry out his orders, but on this morning the secretary lingered.

"May I ask how *you* are, sir?" he asked.

"Would you prefer the truth or polite fabrication?"

"The truth, I think. There's enough of the latter in Washington to last anyone a dozen lifetimes."

Franklin sighed. A long breath that took longer to resolve than either of them expected.

"I'm not at all certain I'm fit for this position, Webster."

"None are, sir."

"No?"

"Polk. Jefferson. Washington himself. The nation has lifted them to the heights of deities, but in rooms like this, they were each of them only men, making decisions as best they could."

"It's the decision-making I'm never sure of."

"How could you be? Your choices won't be fairly judged until we are both long removed from this house."

"From this world, you mean."

"Yes. Possibly only then."

Franklin rose from his chair.

"I'd like to share something with you that you might find strange, but there's no other way to phrase it," he said. "I fear things may grow turbulent in the days to come. Not in the capital but here, in this house. Forgive me for not speaking of the threat directly, but I don't honestly know what shape it will take. I'm asking for your courage, Webster, but also your discretion. What you will see, what you may be called upon to do—it must stay with us. Do you understand?"

Webster looked shaken. Not by the mystery of Franklin's request, but his awareness of its meaning.

"I have lived easily and well until now, but also with the guilt of both," Webster said. "I welcome any test. Perhaps just as you do, sir?"

"How do you mean?"

"We're both driven by the memories of our fathers. And their fathers. A line of soldiers we wish to join."

"We're men in search of a battle. That it?"

"We're men in search of a chance to show we aren't afraid."

For the first time, Franklin saw the precise terms with which Webster cared for him. Prior to this he'd assumed his secretary was the sort of man who responded to authority with the desire to please, or perhaps to be transported on coattails. And there were moments when the thought occurred to Franklin that there was more to it in Webster's case, an intensity that came from attraction, the invitation to love he'd felt from a couple of friends in college, and later, even some married men in courthouses and Congress. But he saw now that his secretary was motivated by the opportunity to put aside the demons of self-doubt he carried. Webster was no unrequited lover, nor sycophant. He was a brother.

"Then let us be ready when the chance comes," Franklin said, and shook Webster's hand with a firmness that steadied them both.

★   ★   ★

Franklin arrived last. As he walked into the elliptical Blue Room with what he hoped was a purposeful countenance he saw how the faces of his government, secretary by secretary, fell before correcting themselves. His careful shaving and extra hair tonic hadn't worked. He looked worse than he already guessed he did.

"Welcome, and thank you for coming," he said, and the men, every one of them older than he, rose on stiff hips and gouty feet to shake the president's hand.

Pierce had forged a deliberately blended cabinet, each member selected to offset the baggage brought by the others. His picks included political rivals within the party (notably William Marcy, secretary of state, who ran for the leadership in Baltimore only to lose to an absent Pierce) along with those to be counted on for their faithfulness, all of whom were carefully pieced together according to geography, state by state, North versus South.

The idea was to avoid either side of the slavery question from being able to claim neglect. It had worked so far, up to a point. Aside from the predictable squawking from the extremes, Pierce was largely spared from criticism that he showed favoritism to either the Democratic Party's abolitionist or proslavery factions, the Know Nothings or doughfaces. But all this compromising was the cause of its own problem. The fundamental question of one's right to own slaves went undebated, beyond the government's position that some would have the right and others not, as determined by precedent within particular states and, in the case of new territories like Kansas and Nebraska, their own votes.

The issue, then, wasn't an issue. Except it was the *only* issue.

Over and over, in virtually every exchange of business or domestic policy, it hovered over the proceedings like a wraith, one that increased its demands to be seen the longer it was pretended not to exist.

That's how Franklin thought of it now and would continue to think of it for the rest of his life. A flesh-and-blood ghost. Like the dead child he'd let slip out of his room. The furnace keeper. The men who warmed themselves at the bottommost part of America's house.

"Well, Mr. President," Marcy began, assuming the role of chairman as was his habit, "we're all very curious to hear of the matter that brings us together in such haste."

"Won't you sit, gentlemen?" Franklin replied, acknowledging his secretary of state with a nod while ignoring his words. Each of them found the chair they'd risen from, letting Franklin take the one with its back to the windows. "I've called you here for an open discussion, one I've felt compelled to entertain with increasing urgency these last number of days."

They all sat forward at the same time.

In addition to Marcy, there was Kentuckian James Guthrie from the Treasury. Guthrie had the appearance of a man who'd survived an illness against the physician's predictions and had come out the other side with a glimpse of the afterlife that he found disappointing.

A fellow Southerner was Jefferson Davis of Mississippi, secretary of war. Davis's face was as puckered as a raisin, but without the promise of sweetness within. Yet he was noble in appearance compared to Caleb Cushing, attorney general from Massachusetts, a doughface in both the political and physical sense. Franklin noted how the absent members, away on travel or ill-disposed, happened to be those more friendly to abolition, relatively speaking.

"Be assured, sir, we relish open discussion," Marcy offered, once again overstepping his place, or at least this is how it sounded to Franklin's ear, sensitive as it was to condescension.

"As you know," Franklin carried on, "our policies are built on the foundation of westward expansion and the opportunities it will bring—"

"Has *brought*," Guthrie interjected. He liked to credit himself for cutting the national debt in half in record time whenever possible, preferably without mentioning the discovery of gold in California that paid for it.

"Indeed, we must acknowledge the opportunities it has brought to our pockets and to our global esteem. But it also brings conflict. And I now fear these troubles are bound only to get worse."

Davis rubbed his hands over the tops of his pants as if to dry them of sweat. "What conflicts and troubles are you speaking of?"

"We've got Free Soilers rioting in Kansas like medieval crusaders, and on the other side we've got Border Ruffians pouring in to tip the votes in slavery's favor. Arguably events occurring on the periphery. A flared temper here, a feud a thousand miles away. Yet I fear they won't remain so far off, nor will the resentments closer to home stay within our control."

He was saying too much, no matter how well he was saying it. This was Franklin's shortcoming, one he was aware of, but in moments of uncertainty—in all of the moments when the eyes of the meeting hall or churchyard or Congress fell on him—he reverted to the rag-and-polish of speechmaking instead of the hammer-and-nail of commands.

"Not following you, sir," Guthrie said, following well enough.

"If we can't do what's required to keep the peace, perhaps we should consider"—Franklin almost finished his sentence by saying *doing what is right*, but he hedged, again—"a change in course."

Marcy scowled. It was an effortless expression for him, as his skin was set in a mask of disapproval at all times.

"Just what do you mean by that?"

"A reconsideration. A hard look at how expansion without Washington's attention to its promulgation of slavery is a policy actively in support of it."

"We aren't in *support* of it," Davis said, as if the words were clumps of ash in his mouth. "We permit it. But we *are* in support of commerce, are we not?"

"In some parts of the country the two are bound together. Perhaps it is the time for us to separate the two."

"A fine thought!" Davis exclaimed, almost spitting on the floor before remembering his place. "As you may recall, sir, I'm a plantation owner myself. Cotton. Among my assets are, at last count, seventy-two Africans. How do you propose I *separate* my business from myself? Give it away?"

"I understand how you would see it in such terms," Franklin said. "I'm asking you to see if differently. As a matter of rights."

Davis was about to launch another rebuttal, but Guthrie raised an arthritic hand to ask for a turn of his own.

"With respect, Pierce, you sleep in this house and sit in that chair to serve a single purpose, and that is to hold up the principle of *states'* rights," the old dog growled. "Now you're saying—well, *what*? We're overnight abolitionists? They'll have *our* damned throats next!"

"Don't tell me what my purpose is," Franklin said. "We are all still free thinkers."

"Not *here* we're not. We've got a line to hold."

"What about the line between good and evil?"

"What about the Mason-Dixon Line! Can we keep our eyes on the map instead of scripture while in the White House? This is no church, Mr. President, despite your abrupt conversion."

"Gentlemen!"

Cushing stood, and the rest of the room looked to him. It prompted the attorney general to sit again, flustered, as if their eyes reminded him of his small stature, and that standing lent him no more authority than sitting.

"I ask that we let Mr. Pierce lay out his case," he said.

Only a few minutes earlier Franklin had entered the cornerless room tired but buoyed by the knowledge of what must be done. There was a shade in the president's house. One that would cast a lengthening darkness over the nation unless he could step outside his role for once, to act instead of being an actor. Now he surveyed the gray faces of the politicians in a circle in front of him and saw the depth of his error. Maybe there was another way, in another house, to vanquish the one Jane called Sir by shining a light into the corners where it dwelled. But this wasn't like other houses. And he wasn't its master, only a tenant. It would be easier to make a change in himself as a common man than as president.

"Rest assured, I'm not a mystic," Franklin continued, sitting straight. "But I have seen some things from the lookout of this office that, I believe, signal events to come. Conflicts greater than those we tell ourselves are presently being managed. Bloodletting of a kind that surpasses today's sporadic murders on the frontier. We need to pause and consider our path."

"Pause and consider."

Marcy repeated Franklin's words, and the effect was to make the sentiment sound even more ridiculous than in its first articulation.

"A modest request," Franklin said. "What is the wrong in it?"

"The wrong is that it goes against the very grain of this government," the secretary of state said. "Expansion is your *purpose*, sir. Slavery is a fact that we have inherited, not created. In any case, it is only a side cost to our main endeavor."

"What if we are wrong in weighing the matter in these terms?"

Marcy looked at every man around the room except for the president as if taking a silent vote. When he returned his eyes to Franklin it was with the satisfaction of a cat that held a mouse under its paw.

"And what other terms do you have in mind?"

"The moral," Franklin answered, holding his voice to a low register in an effort to maintain his authority. "Perhaps we could judge it as Christians."

"I didn't know you were such a churchgoer, Mr. President," Cushing asked with apparent earnestness.

"Unless you've joined a new congregation?" Davis suggested with equally apparent sarcasm. "Are you a Quaker now, sir?"

Franklin didn't answer. He was the only one to see it.

The secret door in the curved wall that he'd pushed open on his first day exploring the residence. Because of his position with his back to the windows, Franklin was alone in seeing it draw inward an inch.

"Can I suggest we avoid the personal insults and return to policy grounds for a moment?" Cushing said, interpreting the president's silence for contempt.

But Franklin wasn't listening. He was watching.

The door in the wall trembled, as if breathed upon from the other side, before it slid wider. The dark passage behind it revealing its depth like a curtain swept aside to show the night outside the glass.

"It's one thing to have your argument run aground," Guthrie said, "but it's quite another to ignore the navigation that steered it there, if I may say, sir."

Franklin slid his eyes past each member of his cabinet and saw, in this instant, the shallowness of their wisdom, the excuses they'd told their wives and children to explain their long absences from home, the lies they told themselves that none of it was ambition, only the compulsion to serve. When he stopped on the gilt Sheraton mirror on the opposite wall he saw all of the same things in his own face, along with something else. The wish to be anywhere but here.

"You must go," the president said.

None of them moved. Perhaps they suspected Pierce was expressing rare anger, and that someone—Cushing, most likely—would soothe his pique and they would return to their debate. Perhaps they wondered if there was something wrong with him, a failure of the heart or brain, and they were already calculating their new place in the line of succession.

"Go," Franklin said, a whisper this time, one meant only for himself.

The door pulled all the way inward. A rectangle of darkness cut away from the curved plaster the color of clear-skied dusk.

His dead son walked out from the wall.

The expression the boy wore was the same blankness it had shown when he turned to Jane before skipping down the stairs. But with each step he took, his face twitched something new into its composure: a smile, too wide at first, then fixed, shrunk to a mild grin. Slit eyes opened into curious ovals. The stiff steps lubricated into a skip-hop, as if he was pretending to ride a pony. It took only a second or two. The dead doll of a boy becoming the living Bennie.

One by one the heads of the cabinet members turned to look. Franklin hoped they would see only the open door—pulled ajar by a suck of wind from an opened window elsewhere, or perhaps some clerk's blundering attempt to spy on the proceedings—and not the boy. Because the boy wasn't there. He was buried in the ground of Concord, a place the assembled called "a lovely spot" the day he was covered with soil. What Franklin was looking at was a conjuring, and thus an affliction limited to him alone.

"And who are you?" Marcy said as the boy stepped into the room.

Franklin stood up as if to rush between Bennie and the still-seated men, but the child stopped him with a glance. Emptily playful, the tiny failures of its facial adjustments leaving it wearing a grotesque mask of "fun."

It brought a finger, white as a candlestick, to its lips.

Shhhhh.

"Is that—"

Cushing was the only one who recognized the boy in the moment. And with this recognition came its impossibility.

"Oh my . . . *Lord*," the attorney general said, though with a softness that could have been mistaken for a blessing.

The boy trotted directly over to Marcy. It made the old man uncomfortable to be chosen in this way, but he offered up an expression of benevolent interest, the one forged over years on the campaign trail.

Franklin was three steps away from clutching his hands onto the back of the boy's shirt when he crawled up onto Marcy's lap.

"Do you have children, Mr. Secretary?"

"Yes, I do."

The boy slid a hand around the back of Marcy's neck, pulling him closer.

"Do you like them?"

"Well," the secretary of state chuckled. "They're *mine*. I'm not sure that—"

"No," the boy said, and pushed the index finger of his free hand into the old man's mouth. "Do you *like* children?"

Franklin watched the implications clatter together in Marcy's mind. The suggestion behind the child's question, his too-close presence against his belly, the finger pushed past his lips. The wrongness.

Marcy heaved the boy off his legs. It took more effort than it should have, as if Bennie were twice the weight he appeared to be. Yet when the boy's body hit the floor it bounced and rolled about as if dropped from a great height.

Davis and Guthrie both gasped at once.

The boy stayed there, his legs tangled around each other in a way that wouldn't seem possible without one or both of them broken, but none of the men went to see if he was all right. They sensed that the child on the floor, still grinning, was unnatural in some way. It wasn't just the indecency of his question. It wasn't the way his body ought to be in pain yet showed not the least discomfort. It was the way they could feel how the child *knew* them. The secrets and shames so well covered they hardly thought of them day to day all pulled up like bile from their stomachs by the briefest connection with his vacant eyes.

"Get out," Franklin said.

The boy settled his stare on the president, and he felt it too. Exposure. The cowardice that lay behind his relief when his injuries kept him from the Mexican battlefields. The lustful imaginings for his substitute wife. The answered prayer he'd sent up for one son to die instead of the other.

Franklin was first to move. A stride toward the boy that almost resulted in his tumbling to the floor as well, his bad knee screeching at being bent the wrong way. He leaned to the other side, dragging the stiff leg behind him. It was far from the best moment to lay hands on the boy and pull him from the room, his cabinet a witness to whatever struggle might result. But this could be his only chance to capture the creature.

The boy untangled his legs. Jumped to his feet.

"Twenty million souls suffering alone," the boy said.

It didn't sound like him, because the words weren't his. They were Jane's. Precisely what she'd said to Franklin in their bed, clinging together.

This time, Franklin came at the boy and didn't stop. It prompted the child to retreat toward the secret door, still open, behind him. But he showed no fear at what Franklin might do if he grabbed him.

The boy looked back at them all when he reached the threshold.

"Won't you follow, gentlemen?"

Franklin found that his curiosity slowed him.

Follow the boy? To where? Being closest, and standing, allowed Franklin the best vantage to look past Bennie and down the passage. Except it didn't appear like a passage now, certainly not as it had when he'd opened the door previously. There was no light from the inner office he remembered it leading to, no detectable shape to the walls. It was as if the Blue Room had exposed a portal into the starless heavens, vacant and infinite.

"That's—" Davis said.

"Pierce's boy," Cushing said.

"Come," Bennie said.

The cabinet members sat in silence. Guthrie alone made a sound, something in his throat that began as a grunt of denial but dwindled to a whine.

The boy turned his back to the room and started deeper inside the wall. They didn't hear his footsteps because he wasn't walking, nor floating, but giving himself to the darkness. It reached out to him and he let it take him, detail by detail, color by color, until there was only the shining hair at the back of his head, the white hands.

Franklin went after him.

"Sir!"

A voice behind him. An urgent plea—Marcy's—for him to stop.

He pulled up when he reached the line between the Blue Room and the doorframe. Or was there something from the other side that nudged him back? An unfelt wind coming from the nothingness requiring his full commitment to let him through?

There was no time to take a second run at it.

As the president stood at the chasm's edge, the blue door swung into view from within. When it clicked shut his nose was so close to its surface he could smell the recently applied paint, the deep turquoise it had taken three coats to get just right so that Jane might see it as sky.

30

In Concord, just months earlier, when they were still a family, what Bennie loved most was to go on walks with his father through the woods that surrounded the town. Franklin had a naturally long stride and Bennie half ran to keep up. After a time the boy would have to stop for a break, winded from the effort.

"I'm sorry," Franklin remembered saying on what turned out to be their last walk together. "I forget my legs are longer than yours."

"That's true *today*. But one day mine will be longer."

"Oh?"

"Don't you see? I'm going to be tall."

And he did see it. The height waiting inside the child.

"You can't wait to be bigger than me," Franklin said.

"No, Papa. I can wait. I *like* to wait for things."

"Why's that?"

"Thinking of good things is even better than the good things when they come. Because once they do, they're gone."

Bennie had reeled at this, as if the wisdom he'd spoken had come from a future version of himself. The world around them took note of it—the breeze quieting, the sun holding the trees' shadows like charcoal on parchment. What struck Franklin even more than the truth of Bennie's sentiment was how it spoke to the very moment the two of them found themselves in. *That* was the good thing. A walk with his boy in an unremarkable New Hampshire forest. He would remember it as such even as the accomplishments he'd long dreamed of, including the presidency, were delivered to him.

Franklin had a glimpse of all this at the time. But what he couldn't have known then was how desperately he would cling to it later: the towering hickories and the root-ribbed trail and the boy reaching for his hand without embarrassment. What Franklin saw in Bennie was how much better his child already was than he would ever be. Bennie should be the senator, the candidate for anything. He was the natural leader, not his father, because it was his boy who held so firm to the clarity of his nature.

They walked on. The advance of the day—the movement of air, the arc of the sun—resumed. Yet through the almost overwhelming rush of love and the gratitude to Jane for giving him this child, Franklin was nagged by discomposure. They had made their way home before he saw where it came from.

Bennie wished to be like his father so much it shamed Franklin that he was not a better man. Did every father feel this way? It would explain so much. The ones who got into fights to appear stronger, the ones who lied to appear honest, the ones who gave up and ran away.

Bennie was gone now.

But Franklin wouldn't give up. For the memory of his one good thing, he wouldn't run away.

★　　★　　★

Franklin turned from the door in the wall of the Blue Room. The members of his cabinet were all standing, looking at him, waiting. For what? A reasonable explanation that would ease their minds, or a confession of necromancy, or denial that they'd even seen what they'd just seen. Mostly, they waited to be dismissed.

"That boy," Franklin started, reconsidered, started again. "That boy is not my son."

Each of the four men's mouths moved but their lips remained closed, as if they'd commenced sucking on lemon peels at the same time.

"But he—" Cushing began.

"He looks like our Bennie, but he's not," the president said.

"A visitor then?" Guthrie offered.

"Yes."

"One of Webster's?" Marcy said.

Franklin shook his head. "Just a visitor."

They had questions of course. As far as Franklin knew, they always would. But there can be a reluctance to speak of the astonishing in the moments after its occurrence, whether beautiful or terrible in its form. Even these men, politicians, professional talkers, were held speechless by it.

Franklin cleared his throat. "Thank you, gentlemen," he said.

One by one they filed out. He could hear their shoes tap over the tiles of the entrance hall, heard the main door open and close as they collected their overcoats and stepped outside.

Marcy was last. He lingered at the threshold, looking back with an imploring pout, the lower lip trembling.

Franklin knew what he was saying without the man saying it. Something had been exposed about Pierce, just as something had been exposed about Marcy, even if it couldn't be said precisely what it was in either case. The two men stood in silence in the way of gravediggers standing over the hole before filling it with earth.

"Sir," Marcy said, with a nod of the head, and left without closing the door.

31

He headed straight from the Blue Room to Jane's room. But he didn't have to go as far as that to find her.

"Jeannie?"

She was standing with her back to him, her ear to the door of Bennie's room. When she heard Franklin's voice she spun around and put her finger to her lips just as the dead boy had done after coming out from the wall downstairs.

Shhhhh.

He came closer. When she gestured for him to listen he did as she asked.

Voices. A pair of them. One deep, strangely flat. The other the higher pitch of a young boy. The former was doing most of the talking while the other answered with obedient replies.

Yes.

I will.

Yes, yes.

Franklin pulled away. Took Jane's hand in his. "Is it them?"

Jane nodded at the same time the voices from inside the Grief Room stopped. There was a shuffling as if one or both of them were approaching to listen through the wood just as Jane and Franklin had.

"Come with me," he said.

He led her downstairs. She attempted to ask where they were going but he refused to answer. They exited by the west door on the ground floor. When the staff stopped to watch them pass Franklin offered a brisk wave but made a point not to meet their eyes.

Once outside, the daylight struck them with a force that knocked all the questions out of them both. Jane slowed to feel it on her face but Franklin urged her on. She wondered if he was leading her away from the residence once and for all. An elopement.

She followed him to the orangery. They entered and carried on to the far end, Franklin asking the gardener he'd spoken with before if they could have the place to themselves for a time.

"Pleasure to have you both," the old man said, as if an innkeeper meeting expected guests.

When he was gone and it was only the two of them, instead of rushing into disclosures, Jane and Franklin sat on a bench in silence, breathing in the organic stew of lilies and sheep dung.

"Something's happened," Jane said first.

"Sit close. Let me say it in your ear."

He told her about the cabinet meeting. His failure to sway them to change the course of government, followed by the opening of the secret door. The boy that came out.

"What he said to you, about the twenty million souls," Jane said after mulling his account. "Are you sure you heard it correctly?"

"I'm certain."

"But that's what *I* said to *you*."

"Yes."

"Which means he was *there*. So close to our bed."

"That's why I brought you out here. So we may speak beyond reach of their ears."

"We ought to try again," she said. "Perhaps your men may yet be convinced."

"It's too late for that. They are here to carry out their instructions just as I am."

"Then defy them alone."

"To what end? A vote that's soundly defeated by Congress in a week? And they'd be seeking my resignation the week after that."

Jane smoothed her hands over the soil in a clay pot by her feet.

"You mustn't leave," she said.

"I thought you'd be grateful at the suggestion."

"I would have. Before. But I know now that if you were to go it would only leave Splitfoot here."

"And with new residents who have no knowledge of him. They would be devoured."

"You're right," she said. "On two counts."

"Two?"

Jane pushed her hands deeper into the dirt. The coolness felt good. She had the idea that she was planting herself. Soon, in this sun, she would start to grow.

"We can't singlehandedly alter the policy of the nation with a change of one man's conscience, even if it's the president's," Jane said. "We were wrong to think it was so, just as we were wrong to think a good deed would cast Splitfoot out of the house in any case. It might quiet him for a time, but he would stay on, wait for new opportunities to come."

"A new administration."

"A new family. There's always a child to steal, or some other crack in the spirit he can find a way in through."

Franklin raised his head high enough to look out at the mansion through the glass. He found the two windows of Bennie's room. The curtains of one were closed, the other half-open, but nobody was there.

"So there's nothing to be done," he said, crouching low again.

"Nothing on *this* side of heaven."

She pulled her hands from the soil. He watched the black crumbs fall from her fingers, exposing the skin beneath like roots.

"What do you mean?"

"We need to meet him not where *we* live," she said, "but where *he* lives."

"And where's that?"

"My father called it the otherness. Our world is on this side, his on the other. But now he's come to move between the two."

She placed her hands to the sides of his head. He smelled the perfume of her bath powder, combined with the lush rot of the potting soil. *Our world. His on the other.* When she removed her hands he brought his own fingers to his face, smearing the dirt she'd left on his skin. As he spoke, he looked down at the black lines of his palm as if the map of a land he'd never seen before.

"Look at us," he said with a laugh, loud and short as a sneeze. "Cowering in a hothouse, whispering about ghosts."

"He's not a ghost."

"No?" He considered it a moment. "No."

"But that may be to our advantage," she said. "I have a thought."

There was a creak somewhere ahead of them. They rose to find the gardener had returned. Franklin was about to ask him to leave again, but Jane started out before he could, thanking the gardener for the respite. The Pierces exited the way they'd come in, hands held this time.

"Keep your eyes down," Jane said as they made their way toward the mansion. Franklin realized she was trying to prevent him from looking up at the Grief Room's windows at the same time he looked up at them.

In one of the windows stood Franky. His child. The one at whose bedside Franklin had sat, had prayed to go instead of Bennie before having his prayer answered by Sir.

There was a boy in the other window as well. Younger than the other, just tall enough to peek his head over the sill. This one Franklin didn't recognize. But Jane did.

As her husband had paused to look up, she had too. It was John. The little brother she'd sat vigil by, witnessed the moment of his passing and in it, the possibility of bringing back the dead.

"Don't look at him," Jane said, seeing her husband's stare fixed on their lost son. "He's not real. Our boy is with God."

"He *knew*," Franklin said.

"It doesn't matter anymore. Come inside. Come—"

Franklin grabbed her arm. It wasn't meant to hurt her, but the grip made her wince.

"I wasn't a good enough father," he said, a gasp between each of his words.

"Nor I a mother."

"I have thought terrible things, Jeannie. Wished terrible things."

"And I have done them. But we must go inside now."

She led him toward the east door, his fingers still dug into her arm. *Don't look, don't look*, she said, over and over. Franklin kept his eyes lowered, whether from her beseeching or to hide his tears she couldn't tell.

Just before the second-floor windows of the Grief Room were angled out of view, Jane disobeyed her own command. She looked up and saw that someone stood there still. Neither Franky nor John this time. Her father. She had to squint to make out his face. Once she did, she saw that he was angry. A rage she'd never seen him show in life now directed down at her.

What broke her was the uncertainty whether he was real. While Jane could believe that her little brother and son were out of reach of demons, she wasn't sure the same was true for Jesse Appleton, given his transgressions.

Which would mean she would never know, after her own passing, if she would find the protections of God or not.

PART THREE

THE GRIEF ROOM

32

That night, Jane told him what she thought they must do. How they could pull Sir back into the darkness by visiting the darkness themselves.

She would write a letter to Kate Fox. Ask her to return to the mansion and conduct—what might it be called? Not one of her knock readings, nor a séance. Not an exorcism, certainly. Perhaps this: a cleansing. An opening of themselves of the same kind that had brought the false Bennie into the house, and also let Sir become fully realized. *Open the door for me. And I can open the door for you.* If Jane had been the necessary accomplice to opening the door to Splitfoot, then by the same means, she might bring him out and close it.

"But I will need help," she whispered.

She was keeping her voice low because they were lying together in bed. And though neither of them said it aloud, they were both aware they may be under surveillance by something in the dark of the room, or inside the walls, or hovering inches over them in the gloom.

"You mean the Fox girl," Franklin said.

"She has a gift for detecting these ways of passage. It may take some pleading—along with a healthy payment, I expect—but if she agrees, she will be our conduit."

"There is your 'we' again."

"It will require a circle. That's how she explained it to me on her first visit. The more people who open themselves to the one they wish to reach, the greater chance of connection."

"You have me in mind."

"You're the one he sought to influence from the beginning. I don't see the point of attempting it without you."

He kissed her.

Despite the strangeness of the conversation and the foreboding that had taken on a weight in the air of the house over the last hours, there was no denying they were together. Their bodies, their voices. He was grateful to have her close again. She felt it even more than he did. Jane was not only comforted by her husband's hand stroking her side, an up and down that made a whisper of its own—*I'm here, I'm here*— but she was unburdened. For the first time since the day she went down the cellar steps in the Bowdoin house, there was someone she'd shared the entirety of her secret with.

Her lips met his. Her mouth, arms. Opening—

Scrrrritch.

They didn't move. Something was crawling above them in the gap between the ceiling and the attic floor.

Momma? Papa?

The boy. The tone forlorn and wounded in a way the real Bennie never had cause to be.

"Don't be afraid," Franklin whispered. "He wants us to be afraid."

"He wants us to be alone."

I seeee you. . . .

Franklin slid away from Jane. Even under the bedcovers a cold air filled the space between them.

"Liar!"

He threw back the blankets and stood at the center of the room, shouting up into the chandelier that glinted wetly back at him.

"You are *not* our child! You are nothing!"

They both listened for the scratches but the air was still. It lent the sensation of being outside of time. Characters in someone else's dream.

The Fox girl—

THUMP

. . . the Fox girl—

THUMP . . .

Bennie half sang this in the way of a tune repeated by a child jumping skip rope. Where feet would meet the ground the boy thumped his fist down on the ceiling instead.

. . . the Fox girl—THUMP . . . the Fox girl—THUMP . . .

It would go on like this. They knew it without speaking it aloud. There would be this creature calling out to them from the boards and bricks, preventing them from rest, from clear thoughts. It would isolate them from each other as much as they had already been isolated from the country that lay outside the residence's walls.

"Come back," Jane said to her husband, not bothering to whisper anymore.

Franklin got under the covers, lying board-straight on his back. He listened to the undead laughter from above for what seemed like half the night before he wondered if she had meant for him to return to their bed, or for someone else who had left her to return from where they had gone.

★   ★   ★

It took almost a week of correspondence from Jane, the promise of three hundred dollars upon completion of the "cleansing," and a suite at the Willard, to convince Kate Fox to return to the White House. Franklin spent the time listening to counsel from his aides and congressmen on what to do about the Western problem, working long hours he experienced as a fight to stay awake while asking for more coffee from the steward. Because his cabinet insisted the meetings take place at the Capitol and not the White House (a demand the president was happy to accede to), Franklin was able to sneak away for naps in his office.

Once Jane had convinced the Fox girl to come, the two of them set to making arrangements that would have the best chance of success. Kate thought a big space more appropriate than a bedroom or salon, so that they could bring Splitfoot out into the open, deny him the corners and furnishings he could use to hide. It was also hoped that the vastness would simulate not a house but the country at large. Kate wanted to show how the mansion was special, too great a thing for any one imp to claim.

There was no chamber bigger than the East Room. Jane had the staff remove the few chairs and benches already there. She also asked for the mirrors to be covered in bedsheets, remembering the terrible visions they showed her when she entered the ballroom days before.

The other element Kate considered crucial was to make the circle as large as discretion would allow. *Representative of the nation,* as she put it in her final letter. *And, though he may be reluctant, the attendance of the president will be required.*

She was right to anticipate Franklin's hesitation. But it didn't arise from the weirdness of the proceedings, rather his worry that his participation become public knowledge. The balancing of confidentiality and the circle's size led to a guest list of those who could be trusted most: Webster, Hany, Kate Fox, Abby, Franklin, and Jane.

Kate Fox arrived on the afternoon of the day the ritual was proposed to take place. She made no mention of Maggie's absence, and Jane didn't ask, sensing a rift between the sisters. In any case, Jane was glad the elder Fox girl wasn't here. It was impossible to imagine Maggie bringing an equal intensity to the task. Kate spent her time in the East Room centering the round table she'd asked for, smoothing her hand over its top and repeatedly touching the six chairbacks as if engaged in some silent discourse between herself and the wood.

Jane was the only one to speak with her.

"I don't mean to disturb you," she said, halfway between the East Room's doors and where the girl stood, as if coming any closer might risk sharing a contagion. "I just wanted to declare my appreciation in person."

"I tried to pretend there was a choice in it. But I had to come."

"You felt obliged to the president."

"No. I felt obliged to you."

Kate smiled in a way that showed she was unused to smiling, and Jane saw in it how twisted the girl's life had been. A person more talked about than allowed to speak. A mystery, a story, a name. It was precisely the same way Kate Fox saw Jane.

"All the same, my thanks for—"

"I see us as friends, Mrs. Pierce," Kate announced. "As sisters. *Real* sisters. Though I doubt I will see you again after tonight."

Jane's instinct to provide comfort pulled at her to say something polite. *Of course we shall meet again, my dear.* But the girl deserved better than an empty lie.

"I see us as sisters too," Jane said before leaving. She'd meant to say *friends* but the truth came out instead.

★   ★   ★

The invitations that Franklin and Jane put to Webster, Hany, and Abby were combinations of apology and revelation. As it turned out, in all three cases, neither were required. This was because Webster, Hany, and Abby were devoted to the Pierces, perhaps the only ones in Washington who truly were. And because the three of them already had some idea of the White House's afflictions.

"I've been a witness to that which I haven't felt able to repeat to anyone, not even my wife," Webster said when the president asked him to stay late that evening to attend "a ceremony of a kind." "It can only be much worse for you. As you and Mrs. Pierce seem to be at the center of it."

"She is," Franklin said. "We are."

Webster turned quiet. The president thought it was his secretary considering his next words in the name of discretion, but once he began to speak it was clear his reluctance was the result of dread for himself. "Can you say what it is we're meant to combat, sir?"

"Jane and I have struggled to name it. Perhaps that's because we lack the expertise. Perhaps because it wishes not to be named."

"Because it's nature is evil?"

"I couldn't say what its nature is."

"Then what could you say about it?"

Franklin took his time, gave his secretary the benefit of his clearest thoughts. "It seeks chaos," he said. "It hates humankind. It is a spirit that has bodily reality. A malignancy we must remove."

Webster took in a breath so heaving and long Franklin wondered if the man would pop. "How should I prepare for tonight?" he asked finally, exhaling.

"Bring only your strength and your faith."

"Then I will summon all I possess of both," Webster said. "I believe this is the opportunity we spoke of earlier, sir. And I am ready for it."

Jane asked Hany to stay behind after bringing afternoon tea to the First Lady's chambers. She planned on telling her dresser only as much as necessary, as she struck Jane as a practical woman who would hear only the foolishness in what was being asked of her. Yet Hany's unreadable expression after Jane's initial statements—"I would ask your presence at a private event this evening"—prompted her to go on, explaining not only how she blamed herself for bringing Splitfoot here, but the dark bargain that saw Bennie return as a vacant shade, the trouble it would mean for all in the residence if they were permitted to stay.

The First Lady was exhausted when she finished. Only then did Hany move. The older woman came to sit next to Jane on the bed.

"I have children too," Hany said. "I've lost two of my own."

"So you know what it is to miss them."

"And I know what it is to blame God for taking them."

"It was wrong of me."

"Maybe. Or maybe God needs blaming now and again," Hany said, patting Jane's cheeks hard enough to waken her. "Right now we have to try to set things right, because the Lord doesn't seem inclined to do it on his own."

Jane put her arms around her. She hadn't planned to, but her gratitude, her need, overwhelmed her.

"I wish we had more time to share what we know of this place," Jane said into Hany's shoulder. "What we know as mothers."

"There'll be time on the other side for that."

"We live in different worlds, you and I. How I wish we shared only one."

"One day," Hany said as Jane released her. "Until then never mind the world. Let's do our best to share the same country."

Abby was approached last. There was no event on the president's calendar for that evening, so when Jane sent a messenger to ask her to come to the White House, Abby rushed there from her apartment straightaway, thinking her cousin had fallen ill once more.

"A sensible assumption." Jane grimly smiled once Abby had taken off her coat and found a chair in the Crimson Parlor where the First Lady was waiting for her. "It's strange, but I'm feeling as well in body as I have in some time. My trouble is of a different kind."

"The boy," Abby said. "The thing."

"You've seen him?"

"Glimpses. He always runs off, like he's playing a game. Hide-and-seek."

Jane sighed and her entire body trembled. "I suspect *we* will all soon be the ones hiding from *him*."

Abby got up and joined Jane on the settee. Their hands found each other in a sisterly reflex.

"He looks like Bennie," Abby said.

"But you know he's not?"

"Yes."

"Do you wish to know how he came here?"

"Not now. Perhaps when we have put this behind us. Because you didn't ask me to come so you could tell me a story, did you?"

"No."

"You asked me because you're in need of help."

Jane felt the tightening of the throat that usually preceded her tears, but none came.

"Thank you, cousin," she said.

"What is it you'd like me to do?"

Jane tried to think of a way to say it that might be simply under-stood. The problem was she didn't entirely understand it herself.

"Hold my hand as you're holding it now," she said, squeezing hard as Abby did the same. "Hold it and don't let go until we bring light back to this place."

*   *   *

Jane and Franklin ate dinner alone. Kate Fox chose to remain in her room at the Willard. Abby, Webster, and Hany would meet them in the East Room at nine o'clock, an hour chosen to ensure the darkness of night, as well as the absence of all but the minimal overnight staff.

"It seems they already knew," Franklin said after he and Jane had shared their conversations with Hany and Webster.

"Do you remember, as a child? When your mother or father would take you to visit some cousin or friend or colleague of theirs?" Jane said. "How some houses don't feel right the moment you enter them?"

"Yes."

"This is one of them. That's how they know."

They lingered in the dining room long after the bowls and loaf had been cleared. Jane spoke softly about their marriage. While the turning points of the story were familiar to Franklin, some of the details were new. The heat she felt the length of her spine the first time she saw him in the Amherst house. How sorry she was that he stayed with her over their intermittent courtship, particularly given there was likely a spell of some kind that led him to her.

"That was no spell," he said.

"How do you know?"

"Falling in love feels the same to all who succumb to it. It's a choice where there is no choice."

"My goodness, Frank. I believe that is the most frightening, most wonderful thing you've ever said."

"And you are the most frightening, wonderful thing to happen to me."

They looked at each other across the polished teak, the candlelight flickering their faces between old and young, dead and alive.

Jane laughed.

Outside, in the kitchen, the cook and the steward heard it and wondered what the gloomy president's wife could possibly have found so funny.

33

When they assembled at the East Room's double doors Kate Fox was already inside, standing behind the table within the candelabra's circle of yellow. Because its five candles were the only source of light in the enormous space, she looked like she was stranded on an island in an ocean of tar.

"You may have questions," she announced before anyone else could speak. "But I ask that you keep them to yourselves. I will explain all that need be known. My voice alone."

She gestured for them to come in. None of them moved at first. Some, like Abby, hesitated because of the apprehension at what was about to happen. Others, like Franklin, because the girl had a touch of the holy about her—a light that seemed not to reflect her but come from her—and he had always been bashful when entering a church.

Jane threaded through them and stepped into the black sea. It was only when she arrived on the shore of the island of candlelight and looked back at the others that they ventured after her, one by one.

Franklin was the last to enter, glancing back down the Cross Hall to ensure it was empty before closing the doors. He kept his eyes on Kate Fox. He was wrong, perhaps, in his initial detection of an angelic aura. She may have only been pretty. But even in this respect there wasn't a distracting abundance: narrow-faced to the point of malnourishment, teeth in need of brushing, eyes rimmed with the red of fever. She was appealing to him because he saw how alone she was in her suffering, and while he might never know its precise nature, he wished to stand with her against it. She reminded him of Jane.

"What we will do together is new to me," Kate Fox said as she motioned to where each of them ought to sit, Jane to her left, Hany to her right, Franklin, Webster, and Abby across from her. "But I'm confident that it's a simple matter: we join our wills to first summon, then cast out the being that besieges this house. We will take it back in the name of the president, his people."

Jane was only half listening. She fingered the locket at her throat, the one that contained clippings of her sons' hair, hoping to find strength from it, or protection. An odd dreaminess descended on her. She cast her eyes about the room, peering into the forty feet between herself and the windows, which felt ten times that. All was still, yet full of motion. It gave her the idea that something had shifted the instant she moved her head away. The curtains were pulled closed but the silk trim glinted back at her, as if pushed by a breeze from the other side.

"Jane?"

Franklin's voice brought her back.

"Join us," Kate Fox said.

Jane saw that all their hands were on the table's top except for hers. It required some effort to release her grip from the locket and link fingers with the Fox girl and Webster.

"Close your eyes," Kate said.

They did so in unison. The room so quiet Jane imagined she could hear their eyelids come together in a delicate click. After that there was only the contact of the hands that anchored her to the circle—Kate's worryingly hot, Webster's jellied and froggish.

"Push away the pictures in your mind," the Fox girl told them. "Each time you do, they will try to come back. And each time, return to the emptiness. Not *darkness*. Merely nothing. Push away, return. Push away. Return. Push—"

She cut herself off. All six of them held their breath.

It was as if they'd heard something, but the silence was the same. The dreaminess that first visited Jane had descended over all of them. It slowed them from realizing it wasn't an interruption of noise they strained to hear, but a change in the air.

The cold. A weight draped over their circle. And when they could hold their breath no longer it reached down their throats, cutting and hard as stone.

"What is—" Webster said, abandoning his query at the realization he had no word to finish it.

From above came a sound that Franklin thought he'd heard before, long ago. Something from his youth of hiking through the forests of

New Hampshire and Maine. Rain. Falling through the canopy of leaves with such force it was like a thousand galloping hooves.

Jane heard it as the clinking of glass against glass. She opened her eyes and looked up. Saw that she was right.

The two chandeliers that hung from the ceiling—one to the right of where she was sitting, the other to the left—were shaking. She could see the crystal cut in the shape of tears firing shards of reflected candlelight into the corners, polka-dotting the walls.

"Keep your eyes closed!" Kate Fox shouted.

Jane looked around the circle. All of their eyes were open except for Kate's and Franklin's. But only the girl knew what was causing the cold and the glass to shake without having to look.

The ceiling between the chandeliers, twenty feet directly over their heads, bulged outward. Not breaking. Bending. As if there was an over-flowing tub on the second floor that was flooding through the boards, pressing down, so that only a skin of paint held the water in. Yet they felt no drips fall through. And the ceiling only distended wider and lower. The plaster shaping itself round and tight as a pregnant belly.

"Don't be afraid," the Fox girl said. She sounded afraid.

Jane tried to close her eyes. She wished to add the force of her will to whatever defense they were expected to summon. That, and she didn't want to witness whatever was to be born from the ceiling overhead.

"Jesus help us," Hany said, her voice just audible over Webster's whimpering.

Now all but Franklin held their heads back, looking up. Their hands were still linked, they could feel it, not only from the pressure of those who sat next to them, but the tremor that ran through their fused arms. There was no way of knowing where their own body stopped and the others began.

The bulge in the ceiling split open.

Jane readied herself to be soaked—in what? Latrine water. Or afterbirth. Or blood. But nothing showered down. It allowed her to watch what came out without blinking.

A black oil swam out over the plaster like liquid shadow, clinging to the ceiling. Thick and glistening, aswirl in different shades of night, dusk purple, midnight slate, the crimson scar that precedes dawn. It felt to Jane like looking down on a pond after having poured ink into it.

She wanted to leave. Yet she knew, even if she tried, no part of her could move.

The oil contracted, reshaping itself. Definition and particulars added as if from the touches of a draughtsman's pen. Appendages grew out of it of roughly equal length, four of them, their ends twitching.

Legs, arms. Feet, hands.

A body.

Jane looked across the table at Franklin. His eyes remained closed, but his face was wrinkled tight from the effort of keeping them that way. Jane felt it the same as he did: the body on the ceiling *wanted* to be seen. By all of them. By Franklin most of all.

"You are not welcome here!"

Kate Fox declared this with such volume it startled the other five, their hands leaping from the table and thudding back but not unclasping. Jane struggled to understand the words. She knew what they meant, one by one, yet their collective meaning lay just beyond her grasp. It was the same sensation that came with being in the presence of Sir.

The body on the ceiling pushed out a new growth. A tube sprouting a ball at its end. Smooth skin, straight nose, eyes. A mouth that made Jane, even now, think *lovely*. A head.

Katie . . .

Once he was fully formed, Sir floated with his back to the ceiling, blinking down at them. The oil retreated into the hole it ushered from. Once it was gone, the hole was gone too, leaving the plaster dry. The long-limbed man gently undulating as if resting on waves.

Jane clenched her legs tight to the end of her seat to prevent herself from tumbling upward. The way that Bennie tumbled away from her when the train car flipped and the laws of gravity, of who should die first, were suspended.

After all I've done for you. Katie. Jeannie. Frank.

Sir was speaking without moving his lips. The voice came from every part of the room that expanded farther and farther until there were no walls, only the faint outline of the curtains, the sheet-covered mirrors.

"We stand for the people of this nation," Kate said.

Sir snickered. His body drifted down. Spiraling slow.

"We summon the power of millions," she said. "Black and white, man and woman!"

"Be silent, priestess."

This came from his mouth so that all of them could hear. He wasn't shouting. He didn't need to.

"We cite from no Bible, hold no holy water," Kate said. "It is the power of our union that enables us."

"Then you have nothing."

He spun, righting himself, so that he stood on the table. Or not quite stood—his feet, now in leather shoes so polished Jane could see the reflection of her stretch-faced self, hovered an inch over the wood. She had the idea that if she ventured a hand into the space between the table and shoes she would never be able to pull her fingers away.

Jane turned to the Fox girl. "Kate?"

She was there, but gone. Her eyes wide, staring up at Splitfoot in a kind of panicked awe. It took only a single assessment of what she'd brought against him—*you have nothing*—to leave her in silent agreement.

Jane tried to think of something she could say to prevent their failure, or stop something worse from happening. But it was another voice that spoke first.

"Be gone from this place!"

Franklin's eyes were open. Held to Sir's.

"I *live* here now," it said.

"It is the people's house! And it is the people's will that casts you from it!"

Sir laughed emptily. It carried on beyond the exhaustion of humor, so that it was just a tormenting noise. "Tell me," the floating man said finally. "Is it arrogance or ignorance that makes you believe such things?"

"It is the truth."

"The truth?"

Sir drifted around the candelabra on the table, the flames licking his pant legs without burning them. He lowered to stand on the floor behind Kate. She was shivering. He lingered there, relishing her dread. It allowed Jane to note how he wore a suit of fine cloth, dark navy, the shirt white. She had never seen attire like it, yet it struck her as a uniform of a kind, however free of medals or ribbons.

"None know the true inclinations of humankind better than I."

He started to walk in a circle behind their backs. Close enough to grasp them by the shoulder but far enough to easily step away if any of them attempted to spin around and grapple with him.

"There is little that unites you," he said. "Each of you pursues your own fortunes, pleasures, the highest walls against the strangers on the opposite side. When the walls couldn't be made long enough, tall enough, you invented borders. Nations. Which required ever more fictions. Rights. Votes."

The entity placed its hands on Franklin's shoulders. Jane saw the way it made him shudder at first and then, as Sir spoke, her husband fought the pain the hands were transferring into him. The whole time Franklin kept his eyes on her, anchoring himself.

"Since my brothers were cast out of God's house we search for new homes, new ways to make you open the door. Just as you did for me," Sir said, with a look Jane's way. "Which makes this place my home as much as yours."

"You must go," Franklin said, his voice thin as crumpled paper.

"I will not be cast out, not by witch nor priest nor people's will. Not by you."

One of the candles went out.

"I—"

The second flame snuffed dead.

"—will never—"

The third.

"—*GO!*"

All of them disappeared into darkness.

Someone screamed. Jane thought it was Kate Fox, followed by Hany a second later. And then, as far as she could tell, the six of them were screaming.

But she was the first to stop.

There was something around her feet, pulling her down. She looked under the table to find nothing there. It wasn't just the absence of hands or an animal that might have wrapped itself around her ankles, but the absence of carpet, of floor, of the foundation beneath it. There was nothing. Her feet hanging in space.

As the others noticed it, one by one, their voices quieted like turned taps.

Sir remained standing behind Franklin, hands on his shoulders. Jane saw that, judging from his expression, it wasn't physical suffering the entity was inflicting, but the agony that came with being made to see things you did not want to see.

"Look at what you've done—what you're doing now—in the name of union," Splitfoot said.

There was nothing to see but the oily black of the wall-less room, the curtained windows drifting away like unmanned ships. The table was

293

moving too, along with the chairs they sat on. Everything afloat, bobbing slower than if it were water beneath them, a series of sickening tosses and corrections.

"Look," Sir said.

Something reached up from out of the ocean of oil. Thin as a stick, with bulbed branches at the top. Another came up next to it. More of them closer, and more so far off they were bundled together like crosses stuck in the ground of a battlefield.

The one closest to Jane bumped against her leg. She looked down to see it wasn't a stick at all but a human arm.

Heads came up now too. The bodies of the nations here before. Shawnee, Apache, Cheyenne, Sioux. Men, women, and children. Some with painted faces, some naked. All of them grasping up at the nothingness.

"The people's will," the demon said.

The dead people made no sound. Yet their mouths were shaped into cries for help or calling for lost ones. Torments that had already happened, tied to the past, voiceless.

The bodies rose higher and higher, exposing their wounds, the holes and slits and sores where the bullets and bayonets and plagues had entered. Soon they would pull themselves from the oil and then—what would they do? Jane guessed they would descend upon the six of them at the table, still holding hands, and pull them down.

She tried to get Franklin to look at her. His line of sight was held on the dead closest to him, but in a frozen way that suggested he was seeing something other than their bodies or faces. Jane felt sure of it. Sir was letting him hear them.

"Franklin?"

He attempted to speak, acknowledge her with a nod. But once he'd managed the latter, he continued nodding—*yes, yes, yes, yes*—until he was trapped in a seizure from the neck up. Behind him, Sir lifted the weight of his hands away but did not release him completely. Ten filed nails remained resting atop Franklin's wool coat, now steaming with sweat.

From a great distance away, at the edge of the East Room's ocean, one of the window curtains pulled open.

Jane couldn't make out what moved them, or what came out before they slid together again. But it was coming toward them. A glint of silver-blue, long and narrowed to a tip, cast its own dull light as it swung about in the darkness. It made her think of the pendulum game, the silver ball lurching between the letters. It made her fight not to be sick.

Abby had resumed screaming. Jane could see that her cousin was looking away from the table toward the swinging silver-blue and she wondered what it was Abby could see that she couldn't.

"Not me! Not me! Not me!"

Jane read Abby's lips repeating the same thing. What did it mean? Her thoughts were as muffled as the sounds around her. Yet she could still see clearly, if whatever was there to be seen was close enough. As the boy now was.

He held a sword. Franklin recognized it. The one he'd been given on his return from the Mexican War.

Franklin had no experience as a soldier. And yet he was made colonel by President Polk and assigned leadership of the New Hampshire brigade. Every level of government endorsed Franklin's appointment, setting him up with a uniform that bore a row of medals before issuing him his rifle.

They'd reached the borders of a distant battle near Vera Cruz when the booms of artillery fire started up. The noise startled his horse. Franklin slammed into the saddle, fainted, fell. He was blinking himself back into consciousness when the horse brought its back hoof down on his knee.

He came home to be named a general and given an honorary sword.

The dead boy held it now.

It swung at Bennie's side as he walked on the surface of oil through the grasping dead. His eyes held on Abby's.

"*Don't!*"

Jane didn't know what she was asking the boy not to do, but felt it was about to happen, and that it would be something new, something it hadn't done—or hadn't been able to do—before this.

The boy brought the sword up high.

Franklin's spasming had spread to the rest of him, his chest jolting, arms flying bonelessly around him. He looked to Jane and she could see that this struggle was Franklin's own this time. An effort to free himself. To *do* something.

Bennie stood behind Abby. He was smiling in a way that had nothing to do with play, or happiness, or anything a smile can stand for.

"Momma!" the boy said to Abby. Wanting her to turn. To see him up close.

Franklin leaped from his chair. He'd stopped shaking, but hadn't stopped moving. He lunged to the side, his hands grabbing at Abby's arms as if pleading with her.

Their circle of hands was broken. It made things clearer, louder. It also made them go fast.

The boy brought the sword down at the same time Franklin heaved Abby against him, pulling them both away and tumbling into the chair where he'd sat.

The sword exploded into the table. Chips of oak flying up like sparks.

There was a confusion of new movement—Kate Fox running in the direction of the double doors, followed by Webster, then Hany—but Jane stayed focused on the boy, now working to wrench the sword from where it had bit deep into the wood.

She fought to catch up with what happened. It came to her just before Bennie pulled the sword free.

He'd been aiming for Abby, intending to cleave the blade into the side of her head. He'd chosen her, gone straight for her from where he'd been hiding behind the curtains from before they'd gathered at the East Room's single table, because he'd mistaken Abby for Jane.

Momma!

The boy raised the sword up over his head.

Franklin pushed Abby toward the doors. The others had already made it there, heaving them open. The gaslight from the Cross Hall tumbled into the room. It barely reached the table where Jane alone still sat. The light broke apart into airborne sand that settled over the dead people coming up through the floor, conjoining their thousands of bodies into one.

Jane expected Sir to be angered by the interruption. Instead, he stepped away from Franklin—his posture erect without being stiff, the physical eloquence of a dancer—and bent to whisper in Bennie's ear.

The boy lowered the sword level with his waist. He cast a vacant gaze over first Jane, then Franklin, before running after the others.

Franklin and Jane didn't move. They couldn't.

She watched the walls pull back into place, the floor drawn clear of the dead. It took only a moment, but when she tried to find Sir he wasn't where he'd been standing. There was only Franklin, hunched over, his breathing an irregular series of catches and sighs and snaps.

The screams came from outside the room. Echoing and amplifying as they traveled from their source at the far end of the Cross Hall. Abby.

It sounded to Jane like her own voice. The screeching panic that called herself out of a nightmare only to find she'd moved from a sleeping to a waking one.

34

He knew all of it was real.

What Franklin had seen when the man in the one-colored suit had descended from out of the ceiling and placed his hands on him—it wasn't a vision. It was more real than where he found himself now. The horror he would carry with him to his death was the certainty that what the demon showed him was a deeper reality than anything he would experience again in his life.

What had he seen? He would never attempt to describe it. The scale of it prevented him. And it was because he and almost everyone he'd ever known were complicit in it. Anguish. Theft. Atrocities. He saw how the human world, his nation, was born out of blood.

He was grateful to discover that it was too much to hold on to. It would return to his mind repeatedly to the last of his days, but never the whole of it, and with gaps of forgetting in between. Even now, as he looked across the table in the East Room at his wife, it had retreated from his mind in the way that a horn blown too close to the head can leave it empty but for the ringing.

"Who is that?"

He was asking about the screaming coming from the far end of the hall.

"It's after her," Jane said.

"The boy?"

"You saved her, Franklin. But it's after her now."

He saw the crevice in the tabletop from where the sword had come down and he understood.

"Stay with me," he said, but he needn't have. It was Jane who came around the table to help him from his chair. It was his First Lady guiding him as fast as they could move to the open doors.

★ ★ ★

There was nothing to be seen for the length of the Cross Hall except for a trail of blood spots, curving and random as rose petals dropped before a bride down the church aisle. It started outside the Green Room and carried on past the glowering portraits of dead presidents before turning right toward the Entrance Hall.

Someone was struck, Jane thought. *Someone is dying*. Even as she ran alongside Franklin, following the stains and, once, almost slipping when her bootheel found one, she hoped it wasn't Hany.

They came around the corner to be met by a scene requiring interpretation.

The front door of the White House was open. Webster stood a few feet outside under the portico, the top half of him leaning as if he intended to come back inside to lend aid, but his hips and legs were facing Pennsylvania Avenue, ready to sprint. Hany was at the threshold, her back against the frame and her arms held out straight, ensuring the door didn't close. And in the center of the Entrance Hall, lying on the marble tiles, was Abby. Her hand was cut. Not deep, from what Jane could tell, a three-inch slice across her knuckles where she likely tried to defend herself from a swing of Bennie's sword.

The boy stood over her, but had turned to face Franklin and Jane. The sword held absently over Abby's chest as if a weather vane, nudged by the wind.

"Watch me, Papa," he said.

Jane could see what was about to happen yet was fixed in place by the thing's command. *Watch me.* She could do nothing but what it asked. As she did, she saw something remarkable: Franklin rushing forward. His arms rolling in a headlong charge. He had found his battle, and no fall from a stallion or swollen knee or black magic spell would stop him.

The boy observed Franklin's approach as if awaiting instructions. By the time he swung around and brought the sword's tip even with his chest the two of them were already entangled, falling to the floor.

Someone was cut—Franklin—but Jane couldn't see exactly where. There was a fresh dappling of blood next to where the two of them fought. The spots were light, but she couldn't be sure if it was only the first spritz before the unstoppable letting.

Franklin grunted, one hand against the boy's shoulder, holding off his biting lunges, the other hand grasping for the sword. Bennie made no sound other than the snapping click of his teeth.

The boy's foot slipped in the blood. Only a brief loss of leverage, but it allowed Franklin to spin him onto his back. The impact released the sword from his grip and it clattered to the side. Franklin reached for it. This gave the boy the time to bring up his knee and thrust it into Franklin's stomach, throwing him off.

Franklin landed hard but kept scrabbling to the sword, grabbing the handle. Without hesitation he swung the weapon wide behind him, hoping to find the boy. But Bennie was already off. Sprinting away from the open door, past Jane, and into the Blue Room on the opposite side of the Cross Hall.

"Franklin!"

Her shout didn't slow him. He was up by the time she turned back to see if he was still alive. Her husband in pursuit of the boy, barreling across the hall with the sword tapping against his leg like a riding crop, urging himself on.

Jane went to Abby. The wound in her hand was shallow, though in need of sutures.

"My poor cousin," Jane said.

"Is it gone?"

"Yes."

"Not Bennie. The other."

"It remains. But not here. Not right now."

Abby rose to her feet and noticed her hand as if for the first time. "I should stay," she said, looking at Jane. "But this—"

"It requires a doctor's attention. Mr. Webster?" Jane said, and at the voicing of his name the president's secretary reentered the house with the reluctance of a cat being pulled into the rain. "Would you take Abby to have this tended to?"

"Of course, ma'am."

"I'm sure you know what Franklin would ask if he were here."

"Discretion," Webster said, offering Abby his arm to lean on. "You can be assured of it."

He started away with Abby a half step behind. Once outside they both accelerated their pace, so that by the time Jane lost sight of them in the night they were on the verge of breaking into a run.

Hany came inside from her place at the threshold and took Jane's hands in hers.

"What can I do?" she asked.

"I'm sorry you've done what you have already. It was wrong of me to ask it."

Jane embraced her. Neither of them saw it coming. The two women held on to each other like friends from their lives before, from childhood, if not earlier than that.

"You should go," Jane said when she pulled away.

"It's not right it's just the two of you here."

"It must be the two of us."

"President Pierce. He—"

"Go now. Please."

Hany nodded. She went to the door. When she closed it behind her Jane felt the house hold its breath.

Jane took in some of the cold air for herself. It steadied her. In fact, she found that she had no particular complaint of the body, no cough or headache or leaping in the stomach. Even in the eye of madness, she felt the most sane she'd been in weeks, perhaps years.

One more breath filled her with solid steel.

35

Jane entered the Blue Room prepared to witness some new and unthinkable scene, but the room was empty. Everything in its place except for a rectangular piece of the wall pushed in. The secret door Franklin had mentioned to her.

She went straight in.

A passage, narrow and dark. Ahead of her there was what she sensed to be another door that was shut. She felt her way along, sliding her back over the wall to her right. At what she figured to be halfway her hand fell into a gap. When she righted herself she waited for her eyes to find the dimensions of the new space she'd found in the darkness, and within seconds she was able to make out what was there. Another passage. Even narrower than the one she stood in.

The curvature of the Blue Room resulted in a space between its interior walls. A gap that, from the secret door's location, grew out wider than the spaces between the other walls in the mansion. This was the passage she had found. A space within what would normally never have been seen, let alone entered.

To go inside required her to advance sideways, squeezed front and behind.

Less than a body's length along her ankle bumped against something hard. She squinted. A set of uneven stairs rose up higher, curving along the Blue Room's wall where it widened until it disappeared in shadow.

She assembled what she saw and what it told her:

The stairs were made of irregular cuts of lumber and were constructed by the workers who'd been hammering and sawing throughout the residence so they could gain access to the vents and support beams from the inside. The entire White House had been built this way, with passages between the walls and crawl spaces between the floors to provide for maintenance to the latest systems of plumbing and heating.

There were probably other passages, other stairs like it elsewhere.

This was how the thing moved around. Where it lived.

The last conclusion she arrived at was that she must climb higher to find where the thing went. And she was about to when something shuffled down toward her from above.

Jane braced to meet it. She would not turn back. To get past her would mean going through her.

Whatever it was, it was bigger than she was. Descending from the wider space above to the bottleneck where she stood. Scratching over the wood frame on either side of it without slowing.

"Step back, Jeannie," it said.

She reversed to let Franklin descend. She could smell his sweat in the close quarters and recognized its sharp odor, the kind that came not from labor but violence, or sex, or panic.

"Gone," he said once they'd returned to the openness of the Blue Room.

"Where?"

"Between the floors and ceilings. I tried to follow, pulling myself along flat—I couldn't find him."

"We mustn't let him go."

"I know."

"He means to *hurt* us, not just—

"I know it."

She stepped closer to him. "He tried to kill Abby because he thought she was me."

He showed her his hands, the blood that was there. "I figured that. And I've seen what he can do."

"We must end it," she said. "Do you understand my meaning?"

"I understand. But I can't do it."

"He'll kill me if he has the chance. Or one of the staff. Or you."

"I *can't*, Jeannie," he said, and met her eyes for the first time since he emerged from the passage. "Could you?"

She hadn't realized the full implications of what she was asking him beyond ridding the house of its trouble. Now she heard it too, and thought on it. Could she put down something she knew to be a danger to the innocent? Kill it by her own hand?

It would be done in the name of necessity. It would right, at least in part, what she had done wrong. And it wouldn't be murder, not in God's eyes, as she and he both knew it wasn't human. The thing was Sir's child. Not Franklin's. Not hers.

These were facts. And they blew away like leaves when put against the idea of destroying anything that looked like Bennie, spoke like him, reminded her of him.

She shook her head. "Is there someone else who could—"

"Not with a task of this kind. There's nobody to be trusted with it. And there's nobody—nobody *else*—who can know."

"We can't let it run free."

"So we trap it."

"And if we manage that, we release it?"

"It will only come back. Or do harm to someone else. Or be recognized."

"We keep it here then."

He pressed his lips together. It was the expression he made when he was working to believe his own words. "As long as it remains hidden—as long as it can't reach out from where it dwells," he said, "we'll be safe."

"And the thing will be a secret."

"Between us."

"Only us."

★ ★ ★

She couldn't say whose idea it was. Both of them contributed to it, though there were very few spoken deliberations between them. What they did was the product of obligation, but it was carried out by way of the unspoken language of marriage.

They started in the Grief Room.

Franklin gathered some of the heavier tools and lumber left by the workmen around the state rooms and carried them up to the second floor, piling them outside in the hall. Jane helped with the things she could carry, the can of nails and crowbar and long saw. Once he judged they had all they needed she put her hand on the knob to open the door.

"Wait," he said, handing her a hammer. "I'll go in first. If it gets past me, use this to stop it."

It.

She'd forgotten about the general. They hadn't heard it marching about or knocking at the door as they had the first days they'd shut it inside Bennie's room, and her mind had shifted to other concerns since. Whatever was inside the toy's metal skin that had given it life may have perished by now. Or it might have been waiting for this very moment.

Franklin picked the crowbar up from the floor. Tested the weight of it. "Good?" he said.

She brought the hammer's head up next to her chin to show that she was.

He turned the knob and pushed the door inward.

The only illumination arrived from what fragments of moonlight found a way through the drawn curtains. It was still sufficient to flash off the soldier's red cheeks, its sword, before it rushed at Franklin from out of the corner.

Jane tried to anticipate the noise it would make. A shriek or chitter or wail. It didn't bother. It just came fast on its stiff knees, tottering and thrusting its blade, stubby but sharp as a hunting knife.

Franklin leaned back, raised his left leg. He did it sure and slow like something he knew he'd have only one chance at. When the general reached the spot on the floor his eyes were fixed to, Franklin kicked.

His boot met the soldier clean in the head. The general toppled backward, landing on its side. For a second its legs kept going, running without moving, before they went still. It rolled onto its front so that it could push itself back up with its hands. Movements that gave Franklin the time to step over to where it lay and smash the heel of his boot down on its back.

The little sword spun away. Jane thought Franklin would move for it as he had for Bennie's, but he just brought the boot down again. And again. Each time the general would push his top half up with his arms, Franklin would stomp its back, puckering the once smooth steel into blemish-scarred skin with his heel.

The soldier slowed. Franklin allowed himself a deep breath before starting at the back of its head with the crowbar. Once, twice. The impacts were sharper than his boot had been and on the first swing it cracked the steel. On the third it ruptured it.

Jane couldn't see anything inside of it from the distance and angle where she stood, though Franklin, standing right above the hole he'd made, paused as if he had. Revulsion, then pity, twisted his face. Jane thought he might be sick. He might cry.

He swung the crowbar down again. Kept at it, the force of it doubling each time. Blows to the back of its legs, its neck. He didn't give the soldier a chance to collect itself, though it tried. Somehow its pathetic attempts at a counterattack made it more frightening to Jane, the worry that it would never stop, relentless and immune to death.

The fatigue hit Franklin all at once, and the crowbar fell from his hand. The toy didn't move. Jane started for the general's sword herself, just in case, but Franklin spoke to her without turning.

"Help me with this," he said.

He reached into Bennie's crib and started to pull at the tightly fitted sheet. Jane did as she was asked. Together they yanked the sheet up and Franklin threw it over the soldier. He nudged it with the toe of his boot, and when the sheet remained in place, he gave it a harder kick. The tin of its body gave a squeak as it slid a few inches over the floor—or was it a voice from within?—but made no sign of returning to life.

"Stay here," Franklin said as he bundled the toy in the sheet and lifted it to his chest, slipping out of the room before she could ask where he was going.

Jane waited in her feeding chair, the hammer in her lap, listening for the approach of little feet, whether flesh or steel. The house was quiet in a way that pulled her deeper into it, numbing her in its silence.

Motherhood, she remembered, was full of silences like these. Protecting infants from having their sleep interrupted. Readying herself for the next task—the next feeding, changing, bathing—by gathering the strength to carry on through it. Labors she would do anything to have back, the quiet hours through which she thought of nothing but how best to satisfy her babies' demands.

Which made her think of Bennie.

Her mind had strayed from him for a longer stretch than she usually allowed and she chastised herself for slipping. She felt this was her failure as a mother: she had not constantly held her son's name in her mind, every second, waking or asleep.

This was how she let him sit behind her and not next to her on the train. How she let Franklin reach his body before she did.

No, Jeannie, he'd told her. *It's not for you.*

Not for her? It was *all* for her. The horror of losing her last child most of all. It was what she dreaded more than any torture, more than the end of the world. It was the moment she'd been waiting for.

All the boys will die. And all the women broken.

When Franklin finally appeared again, there were black smudges of soot on his forehead, the arms of his coat. The bundled sheet was gone.

"Is it—"

"The furnace," he said.

"Was it . . . *alive* when you put it in?"

Franklin gave a single shake of his head. She couldn't tell whether it was in negative response to her query, or his refusal to speak of any of it.

"It won't come back," he said.

Jane was less than sure of that, but she held to Franklin's assurance and did her best to mold it into certainty.

"Is there anyone downstairs?" she said.

"I told the sentry to leave us be. We have until dawn, I'd guess. After that even I can't hold back the country from demanding our attendance."

"How long?"

"Four hours. Five. Enough if we start now."

She got up from the chair and took up the hammer in both hands. "Show me what to do," she said.

$$\star \quad \star \quad \star$$

They built a cell. One that wouldn't be seen by anyone walking through the mansion's halls or visiting its rooms.

Franklin worked through half the night with Jane aiding him by bringing what he needed and nailing in the cut wood once he'd told her where it ought to go. Before that, he used the sledgehammer on the room's east wall. The plaster fell away in dusty chunks. With some hand-sawing, the wood framing was removed so that there was a hole big enough for an individual to enter. Once inside, there was a narrow passage between Bennie's room and the bathroom next to it.

Standing there between the walls, Jane turned her head one way and then the other, behind to the hallway's wall and forward to the building's exterior bricks. Then she looked up. The passage ascended into the black of the unfinished attic. She could sense its space, though there wasn't the light to see into it.

They nailed in some rough steps. It carried them up to a loft wider than any other chamber in the mansion, extending over the entirety of its perimeter, or seemed to, as far as their candlelight could reveal. Jane wondered what was in the corners they couldn't see. It didn't seem unoccupied somehow.

The ceiling beams were of a height that allowed for Franklin to stand if he stooped a little, which slowed the work but not as much as it would if he had to proceed on hands and knees.

He made two new walls with lengths of lumber. A crosshatched fence with gaps of a size a child's hand could push through, but no more. When he was done, he'd created a new room in the northwest, uppermost corner of the open space, out of sight of ventilation grills or trapdoors. A cell the same size as the Grief Room below it. The only way in or out was by the hole in the wall Franklin had made at the bottom of the improvised stairs.

"Should we put anything in here?" Jane asked, a candle held in each of her hands.

"Do you mean furniture?"

"Something it might find familiar."

"You're giving it memories it doesn't possess. Feelings it doesn't feel."

"You're right."

"My only question is how we bring it here."

"I think I know a way," she said. "When you're ready, I'll do it."

He sat on the cold floor littered with sawdust and mouse droppings. To Jane, he appeared spent but not beaten. The fear that had clung to him after the failed ritual in the East Room had been lifted, and there was only a man now, doing what he felt he must, not bothering to paint his actions with rhetoric or ceremony. She would never tell him this, but it was the most like what she considered a president ought to be as she had ever seen him.

"Ready," he said.

36

Jane sat on the attic floor, her back against the corner, the two candles by her feet. She wanted to think of Bennie. Her real son. She wanted to remind herself of something good before she did something bad.

What came to her was the memory of cookies. Jane was never much of a baker, but she and Bennie liked to make them together, a comical, losing battle against burning or over-egging the batter. In their failures there was never need for apology. In fact, the charred or flattened results tasted sweeter than if they'd found perfection.

"We're outside," Bennie had said to her once as she sat in a kitchen chair with him on her lap, the two of them speckled with crumbs, and she knew exactly what he meant. He wasn't imagining they were out-of-doors. He saw the two of them as she did: outside the rules of time.

For the other parts of their lives the clock ticked away, nudging them toward their futures and—most unthinkable—their eventual parting. But there were still hiding places that could be found. Eating terrible cookies of their own making. Lying in bed in the early mornings after Franklin was up and Bennie slipped into his father's spot, mother and son sharing their breaths, both pretending to be asleep. A song they sang together that looped back to the beginning every time they ran out of words.

She sang the same song now.

She'd sung it to the false Bennie too, only days ago. Humming it over the time she spent in the Grief Room, hoping for a sign of recognition from within it, for it to join her in the music.

It did. Once.

The being she knew to be a soulless replica sang along with her. No words, only the tune. The same melody Jane played on the piano in the Amherst house and that her grandmother forbade her to repeat, the music that seduced Franklin into proposing, at once lovely and off-putting, childish and perverse. Only now did Jane realize the composition was never really hers. It was Sir's. His voice humming in her head as she transposed it to the keys.

She sang it louder now.

The tune brittle at first but building as she went, casting it past the candles and into the skeleton of the house's structure, where it trembled to its deepest ends.

It's how she called for it. It's why it came.

She felt its footfalls in the room below, following her voice with the patient approach of a hunter. It found the hole in the wall and stepped through—she heard this too. It was coming for her, but it was important not to betray her terror, so she sang louder still, the music echoing the length of the dark attic and coming back at her, slightly altered, as it might in a cave.

It stumbled on one of the steps coming up and paused.

Jane sang on.

The light from the candles barely reached the place in the floor where the steps led up to, so that when the thing's head rose through, she saw it as something dead pushing its way up from its grave. The lace-collared neck, suspendered shoulders, followed by the arms. Her son's Sunday-best leather shoes.

It stood there watching her. She watched it back.

She noticed it held something in its hand. A chisel. One it picked up from the pile of tools outside the Grief Room. She realized it hadn't been drawn by the pleasure the song gave, or some deeply buried recollection from her real boy's past, but merely by the fact it told her where she was. It came for murder and nothing else.

"Such lovely music, Momma," it said, and took a step closer.

Jane sang. Her voice breaking. The song pulling it apart.

The candles flickered and she wondered if it was her exhalations whirling against the flames, but it was only the thing coming closer, pushing the air ahead of it in a frigid wave.

It held the chisel against its side. The look on its face an attempt at contentment, an expression meant to soothe her by appearing soothed itself, but it was too excited by what it was about to do to manage it. In its distortion it instead appeared wide-eyed, wanton.

Where was Franklin? Surely the thing was far enough away from the hole in the floor—close enough to her—for her husband to come out from his hiding place farther back in the attic and grapple the boy, take him down as they'd planned. Jane had been frightened before. Yet her singing had kept her level, connected her to a place of imagined safety outside of the mansion. Now, as her voice pulled the boy closer, she saw that the music had entrapped her more than him.

"Keep singing," it said.

She took a breath. Sang on.

As the boy took another step closer a second shadow materialized behind him. It moved so quietly she would never hear it, wouldn't know what it was, if she couldn't see the outline of its familiar shape.

Franklin stretched out his arms, ready to clutch around the boy and fall upon him. Jane sang louder to cover any creak of the floor that might reveal his approach. Yet even as this thought occurred to her the boy froze.

"Daddy," it said.

Without looking, the thing-that-wasn't-Bennie swung the chisel behind its back. Farther than its arm ought to extend and faster than a blink. The chisel met directly with Franklin's bad knee. Jane knew it because she heard the liquid pop of the skin splitting where it was stretched taut from swelling, followed by the screech of steel against bone.

Franklin howled. Shuddering and low. An utterance of a kind she had never heard from him. He crumpled to the floorboards, shrinking like a roll of parchment when the flames melt it to ash.

Once more without turning around, the boy took a step back and thrust the chisel down into Franklin's body.

"Oh! Oh, oh—"

But she would not let go. Not give her child's cuttings to the monster crushing her windpipe. Not yield. Because she saw, through a twinkling of lights that came with the denial of oxygen, that the thing's wish for her to die was made all the more urgent by the hair burning down. As if its desire to see itself in the curling strands was beyond its reach, would always be so, and now the hair and the creature were revealed to be the ghastly souvenirs they'd always been.

ME!

For Bennie, she would not let go. She would not pull her hand away.

As the pain in her hand intensified to a silent shrieking through her marrow, she also felt herself giving way, emptying out. Dying.

I am in agony. I am nothing.

She heard the contradiction in her thoughts but couldn't deny the truth of either. A moment on and all she was aware of was a gust of realizations that sounded above all else.

This is death.

I will not let go.

I have loved. I loved. I love.

The boy goggled down at her and appeared confused that she was still alive. It pushed all of its weight forward with its legs. Brought it down on her neck.

She felt herself cross a line. All of her filled with cold, hard and flowing like creek water under a crust of ice.

The last thing was the boy's screaming.

Its body crumpled forward. Head over chest, chest over hips, hips over knees. Folding on top of her.

She could tell she was breathing again because she could smell it. The boy's skin that bore a trace of soil after a rain. The hair sweetened with smoke from a fire of the kind built high to dispose of the dead.

The boy was rising again. There was blood falling from its jaw now, half-congealed wads of it building along the line of its chin before slapping to the floorboards. The eyes rolling about in its head until they found her.

"Momma?"

Jane squinted and found Franklin just behind the boy, crawling closer. He held something in his hand, dragging it along next to him. A hammer. The one she'd used to help nail up the enclosure of the cell, the steps to get up here, and left against the attic wall. The one he swings, for the second time, into the side of the boy's head.

A sharp crack of bone. Followed by a new veil of blood, thick as tar, falling on her chest.

The boy stared at her, baffled. But already a new rage boiled up behind its puzzlement, widening its pupils and thinning its lips.

Jane threw her unburned hand against its shoulder and it fell to the side like a toppled statue.

"It *hurts*, Momma," it said, but did not rise.

Franklin pulled himself next to her.

"Are you all right?"

"I believe so," she said, smoothing a hand down her front, though there was so much blood there she couldn't tell whether it was hers or the boy's. "What about you? Your knee? And where did the blade—"

"I'll be fine," he said, pressing the palm of his hand to his stomach.

Franklin found the chisel and tossed it through the cell's bars behind him before climbing over her and yanking the boy's arms straight back. She watched as he wrapped a length of jute rope around its wrists. It didn't fight for release. It just watched her, its cheek against the floor, not attempting to shape its face into anything but a vacancy she saw as hatred.

"Do the ankles," Franklin said.

Jane thought it would try to kick her but she crawled forward and wound the rope around the bottom of its legs as it lay still, breathing and wanting her to hear its breathing.

When she was finished Franklin gestured for her to get up, and then he did the same. He stooped next to her, watching the thing.

"I can't," Jane said.

"Nor can I," Franklin said.

They decided not to kill it without announcing so directly, the two of them wrestling down the stubborn memory of their lost child that the creature returned to their minds. A memory all the more vivid now for the crack in its skull the same as Bennie's when they found him on the train car ceiling.

"Come," Franklin said, starting for the steps down and collecting the hammer and chisel on his way.

She thought of touching the back of her hand to the thing's cheek. She thought of saying something to it. What? That she regretted what had brought it here and the role she'd played in it. That she hoped it wouldn't suffer too much, even if she knew it had no need for food or water or company. That she saw, even now, a reflection of the love she felt for her son and directed it at this fakery, an error she couldn't stop herself from making because it came from her sorrow, and her sorrow was endless.

None of it mattered. It would see none of it, feel none of it. It would sink its teeth into her skin sooner than search for a message in her touch.

When Franklin was finished nailing boards over the cell's one opening she remembered the locket. She saw it on the floor next to where she had sat. The boy saw it too.

"Jane?" Franklin said, and followed her line of sight to the locket.

"Should we—"

"We need to leave it behind," he said, and she heard him as meaning not only the locket and the creature that looked like Bennie, but the desire to retrieve the living things they were once attached to.

She bent down and blew out the candles.

"Come now," Franklin said.

He went down first with Jane following after. She knew it was a mistake but she looked back at the spot where they'd left the boy. Just like Sir's first appearance in the cellar of the Bowdoin house, all she could make out was an outline of darkness. A shadow that, if you weren't trying to see something in it, would appear as nothing at all.

"You will die barren," it whispered low so only she could hear.

She carried on downward, careful of her footing, hearing every last one of its words.

"Your children were weak. You were weak. We took the one you loved most and still you looked for a way to cheat God. Think on it or not, deny it or not. There will be no relief from it, ever."

She said nothing in reply to the things it said. In part because she knew it intended only to cause her the greatest pain it could. In part because everything it said was true.

37

They spent the rest of the night nailing boards over the hole in the Grief Room's wall and, when they were done with that, troweling plaster over it. It wasn't a pretty job. It didn't have to be. Later, they could instruct workmen to make it smooth, invisible. For now it just had to hold it inside.

Once they were finished they closed the door and told the staff who were starting their morning duties not to enter, and to avoid the western end of the second floor altogether. Only then did they summon a physician to tend to their wounds. Jane's hand slathered in a green-tea poultice before being bandaged. Franklin's side cleaned and stitched. Any who asked how they'd come upon their injuries were provided the same response. "It is a private matter, and all is well now," they said, hoping none would dare ask further, and they didn't.

Later that evening, when they were alone in their room, they shared their worry that the thing in the attic might cry out, or pound on the ceiling, or claw a hole through the roof. Noises that the rest of the house would be unable to dismiss as the squeaks of a bat or skittering of a squirrel.

Indeed the thing was clamorous over the first few days, though not with its voice. The sounds came from the feet that Jane's poor job tying together had allowed to be freed.

It walked.

The creature's containment limited its pacing to the ceiling over the room across from where the president and First Lady slept, the two of them sharing a room again. It left those who worked in the offices at the opposite end of the hall largely undisturbed. For long stretches the thing in the attic would sit in quiet—or lie down, or perhaps it stood, staring into the dark—before resuming its back-and-forth. It kept the Pierces from sleep. But they had mostly given up on sleep anyway.

As their time in office went on the sounds from the attic dwindled to rare knockings and random thuds. To hear its voice one had to enter the Grief Room, which only Jane ever did.

Why did she do it? Someone had to. To make sure the thing remained confined where it was. To check the plastered wall for cracks. But also to listen. This was what Jane had always done, whether in the name of self-punishment, or duty, or love: she endured.

She entered as quietly as possible but it always seemed to hear her. It didn't speak every time. But when it did, it would curse her, or remind her of the loneliness that would follow her the rest of her life. More frequently the thing would make sounds free of language. Laughter, weeping. A low wheezing of the kind that afflicted her brother John before he passed.

Jane visited the room less and less, even though she remained curious about the sounds. In time, she pretended it wasn't a child's voice at all up there, only the old house playing a trick with her mind. The wind against the windows. The sandy soil shifting beneath the foundation. Along with the explanation she came closest to actually believing: the sounds were bits of memory from her childhood echoing into the present, so that the voice wasn't a spirit's at all, but her own.

PART FOUR

HISTORY

38

The Pierce presidency lasted a single term. Even among historians, it's a legacy more overlooked than debated.

Franklin's attempts at placating North and South ended in dissatis-faction on both sides, the bloodshed in Kansas and elsewhere pooled at his feet. The Democrats overwhelmingly lost the House in the midterms. At the convention of 1856, just two years after being pleaded with to lend his name to the leadership race, Pierce failed to top a single ballot.

Never before or since has a presidential candidate for reelection not won his party's nomination.

★   ★   ★

He couldn't honestly say that the whiskey helped his performance over the last months of his term, but Franklin came to rely on it more and more nonetheless. His duties were tended to, letters and proclamations signed, speeches delivered, all through a fog of controlled drunkenness.

Like his father, he became an expert drinker. Not that he was able to hide the effects entirely, but for those few who knew the quantity he imbibed, there was a sad awe at how he could stand up straight let alone address Congress or raise a toast to the prime minister of Wherever.

It helped dull the apprehension that came with the banging in the walls, the specters of dead soldiers and slaves he would come around a corner to be confronted by. In place of horror, the whiskey brought him to a place of bleak amusement. He was a man surrounded by ghosts who came to see himself as a ghost.

★   ★   ★

On the Atlantic crossing of the trip they took upon their retirement Jane and Franklin agreed not to mention the things they had experienced in the White House for the time they traveled. It was a relief for them both.

They decided on their European destinations based on reports of the prettiest locales by season: Portugal and Spain in winter, France and Switzerland in the warmer months. All places Jane thought beautiful but taxing on her health. Franklin suggested recuperation in the Bahamas, which he didn't seriously think would make much improvement but was pleased when he was proven wrong. Jane, arriving weak as a puppy and pale as a plate, thrived in the Caribbean heat. Her complaints dwindled to misgivings about the food and the glorious flowers that could induce sneezing if sniffed too closely. She felt well enough, in fact, that she suggested they return to Concord, buy the farmland Franklin had long talked about. Be at home.

"We'll be two ancient fools out in the fields together, not a clue in our heads," he said.

"It's a lovely picture," Jane said, and it was, though she'd always regarded pictures as holding back as much as they revealed, because no matter how closely you looked, you could never know what the subjects were thinking.

★   ★   ★

Over the months the Pierces were abroad, three-quarters of a million men and boys died in civil war, their bodies buried in the fields where they fell. Given the suspected number of undiscovered graves, neither a precise accounting of the dead, nor their names, will ever be known.

★   ★   ★

Abraham Lincoln's beloved son Willie died a year after moving into the White House.

Pierce wrote the president a letter of condolence. Jane wrote an even longer one to the First Lady. What appealed to Mary Lincoln over their correspondence was how Jane did more than empathize with her grief: she seemed to be searching for practical remedies to it, not a salve to the pain but the solution to its cause.

Some of the newspapers reported that Mrs. Lincoln conducted séances in the residence and that even her husband secretly attended them. It was said that they were driven by grief, a harrowing need to speak with their departed child one last time.

Jane was inclined to believe the rumors.

★　　★　　★

A year after Jane's death, word reached Franklin that Nathaniel Hawthorne wasn't well. Despite his poor health, the author wished to go on a trip with his old friend Pierce.

Nate assured his family that it would do him good to be on the road for a time with his Bowdoin brother. What in fact motivated Hawthorne to travel alone with Franklin was to talk about something he'd kept to himself for years, namely the reason he hadn't produced any stories or novels of significance since his appointment to England—how he'd effectively stopped writing the day he visited his friend in the White House and opened the door to Bennie's room.

Franklin and Nate started out for Dixville Notch in the farthest corner of New Hampshire. Along the way they rediscovered the voices they used in the grubby Brunswick tavern of their college days. They ridiculed the pretensions of rivals, mocked the mustache of Poe and the "gimp's gait" of Lincoln, spat out the names of the critics lined up against them in the *Tribune* and the *Herald* as if comical inventions. More than anyone, they laughed at themselves. How they had always doubted their abilities even as they collected laurels and were ushered to seats of influence.

On their first night, Hawthorne pushed away the glass of whiskey Franklin poured for him and combed his beard with yellowed fingernails.

"I have pondered something for many years, and I wonder if you would allow me a question."

Hawthorne looked at him in a way that made Franklin worry he was going to be asked about what happened in the mansion. It prompted him to take a fortifying swallow from his glass.

"Of course," he said.

"Why Jane?"

Hawthorne's face contorted, and Franklin initially mistook it for a flare of pain. But the longer the expression rested there he saw it as genuine puzzlement.

"You had your choice," Nate continued. "The great Franklin Pierce! You had your pick. And it was Jane Appleton. Why *that* girl?"

"Because I could take better care of her than anyone else."

It came out too quickly, too hard. Yet now that he'd said it he heard it as the truth. He had disappointed his wife in many ways, and couldn't shield her from the unseen terrors that pursued her. But he had done as much as a husband could. He often worried he'd done more for her than for his country.

After two more days they stopped at Plymouth, where Hawthorne's health took a turn. Pierce suggested sending for a physician, but Nate waved off his concern.

"If I'm done with writing, I'm sure as hell done with doctors too," he said.

Later that night, Franklin heard the coughing and sighs from across the hall and wondered, before returning to sleep, if Hawthorne was dying. He reminded himself that both of them were: Franklin's end hurried on a current of grain whiskey and Nate's by lungs slowly filling like jugs in the rain. There was nothing to be done. They had already said their goodbyes to each other, indirectly, as men do.

In the morning Franklin rose to find Hawthorne lying faceup, and he knew the skin was cold before he crossed the hall and put his fingers to it, closing the lips and smoothing the brow to erase the expression of startled horror he'd been left with.

★　　★　　★

His last days were an unremarkable descent. Alcoholic, wifeless, childless. Ready.

Just as Jane had urged him to, Franklin ended his life a farmer, where that term applies to a man who purchased his acres too late in life to tend them. Still, he enjoyed the view from his bed. He would lie there and drink and chortle at the bitter humor that came with realizing all that could have been avoided by staying the boy who loved to walk in the woods, rather than the portrait who was chosen to hang in the long hallway of white. A man told that he looked the part so often he assumed he had no choice but to play it, following the duties that now seemed as empty as the lies shared over brothel pillows.

★　　★　　★

Jane's passing came six years before her husband's. She was fifty-seven. Still young among ladies of her class, though she judged she'd done well to endure as long as she had.

It was early in December, at her sister Mary's house in Andover, where she'd been taken after the diagnosis of consumption was confirmed. It was stated aloud among the family that Franklin obviously couldn't take care of the farm in Concord as well as Jane in such serious condition. What went unsaid, but was just as apparent, was that Jane would not recover.

Following the bowls of boiled lamb and potato that would prove to be their last meal together, they sat up in bed and talked. Because it wasn't their own home, because Jane's coughing was impossible to stop once started, and because they spoke of things that no one else should hear, they lay shoulder to shoulder. The resulting intimacy let them converse not as president and First Lady, nor as husband and wife, but with the frankness of lovers.

Bennie tumbling away the length of the overturned train car.

The true legacy bestowed on them by their fathers.

The horrors of the Washington residence.

Jane was the only one who spoke of Sir. For the first time, she described the experience as being "possessed by an intrusion of the spirit," and attempted to state outright what the intruder was. Give it a name of her own. None came.

As she pondered this, Franklin considered telling her of the presence he glimpsed standing over Franky. The same stranger who had revealed the unspeakable crimes to him in the East Room, and whose namelessness they struggled with now. But it was close to the end for her, and such a disclosure, coming so late, struck him as needless. So he turned his face so that his voice brought a small warmth to her cheek.

"Let's speak of something else, then," Franklin whispered.

"What?"

"The secret."

She hadn't thought of it exactly that way before—*the secret*—but it struck her as the right conception.

The two of them drew closer and shared what they had learned in their time in the mansion: that at the very heart of America there lives a darkness. Material and intelligent and alive. One that would outlive them both to sculpt the country in ways that, over time, might not be recognized as a darkness at all.

They were an old couple already half-forgotten by history and so with nothing of themselves to lose, yet neither Jane nor Franklin could capture the specific thing they were referring to. It could be spoken about, yet resisted any one identity. It had a shape but could never be drawn. As when seeing the form of something in a cloud, the very act of pointing skyward—*There!*—prompted it to shift into something else. The war. Their lost sons. The people sold and resold. The devil that hides in the White House. The dead rising up to claim the living even as they walked in sunlight.

AUTHOR'S NOTE

While *The Residence* is a work of fiction, it is sourced from a number of events known to the historical record. The Pierces' unlikely courtship, Franklin's preordained ascent to the presidency, the train accident, Jane's letters to her dead son asking him to return to her, and her subsequent insistence that he did, as well as her participation in spiritual readings and summonings in the White House—all of this is true.

Also true are the stories of apparitions that have appeared to guests, staff, and residents at the presidential mansion over the decades since the Pierces' term of service. President Truman wrote of hearing banging and scratches at his office door as he authorized the development of the atom bomb. Winston Churchill encountered a figure in his bedroom that disturbed him to such a degree he refused to ever spend another night there. Queen Wilhelmina of the Netherlands opened the door of her second-floor guest room to see something that caused her to collapse in shock.

AUTHOR'S NOTE

The forms these presences have taken vary from witness to witness, but one phantom that is uniform in its playful but unsettling appearances is a preadolescent child. A boy. One that, until 1911, when President Taft forbade any further mention of the entity, was referred to as the Thing.

ACKNOWLEDGMENTS

My gratitude to the following for lending their aid to me or to this book: Michael Braff, Laurie Grassi, Joe Monti, Sara Kitchen, Erica Ferguson, Kirby Kim, Jason Richman, Anne McDermid, Craig Davidson, Kevin Hanson, and my beloved family, Heidi, Maude, and Ford.